WICKED AS SIN

THE ACCIDENTAL EXORCIST

JENNIFER CHANCE

OLIVERHEBERBOOKS

CONTENT NOTE

This dark paranormal romance contains demonic possession and loss of bodily autonomy, body horror, complex consent dynamics, graphic violence, and explicit sexual content. Intended for mature readers (18+) who aren't afraid of the dark. Mostly.

ONE

E vil didn't need an engraved invitation to slip inside a home. It just needed an opening.

Unfortunately, so did I.

I stepped onto Mrs. Klein's front porch and wrongness settled over me like a wet blanket. The air was too still, too quiet. There were no birds or traffic sounds humming in the distance. Even the daylight seemed dimmer, as if what crouched inside this house was infecting everything around it.

I knocked on the door again, harder this time, and eyed the cracks spidering out from the tiny decorative windows that stair-stepped up the peeling red paint.

There'd been a lot of crashing around behind this door as I'd jogged up the concrete steps to 1865 Whippoorwill Lane, the kind I'd gotten used to whenever Mordechai worked. But the old man was supposed to *wait* for me.

He's holding you back. You don't need him anymore.

"Yeah, I fucking do," I muttered, used to my inner monologue getting mouthier right before an exorcism went down. But my shitty self-talk needed to take a break, for once. I had enough to deal with.

I lifted my hand to knock again when I heard the chain drawn back. Squaring my shoulders, I stepped away from the door.

A thin, worn-out face peered at me, watery eyes squinting, voice quavery. "Yes?"

I gave the woman who had to be Mrs. Klein my seriously capable smile, the one that clocked me at way past my actual age of twenty-five years. To be fair, though, they'd been a hard twenty-five years. "I'm Delia. Delia Thompson? I'm here to help Rabbi Mordechai. He should have told—"

"Oh, thank goodness."

The woman's hand trembled as she gripped the door. Noise started up again behind her, a loud BANG! that, once begun, didn't stop. BANG! BANG! BANG!

"The rabbi, he's coming today?" Mrs. Klein straightened a little, hope momentarily supplanting fear. Her frail body crackled with that hope. "He—I thought he was coming tomorrow."

"Really?" I slid a hand into my hoodie pocket to pull out my phone. It was, of course, dead. The damned thing couldn't hold a charge for half a minute anymore. "I'm sorry, I—"

The BANG! BANG! BANG!ing continued behind Mrs. Klein. Hope died in her eyes, replaced by something else. Dread. Despair.

I frowned at her. "Are you going to be okay until tomorrow?"

Her face shuttered, the resigned old-lady smile plastered on it once more, creasing powdery skin. "He's coming tomorrow," she said, almost like a mantra. "It will have to do."

She shut the door in my face.

If anything, the commotion on the other side seemed to get louder. I heard Mrs. Klein speak sharply, her shout almost a command, but not quite.

Good. I smirked. That was how you had to talk to them.

Approval ribboned through me on the heels of my judgy thoughts, as if I'd scored well on some demon-hunting exam. I gritted my teeth against the sinuous warmth of that approval, hating how my body responded to it. Because under that praise was something else, something slick and wrong, pulsing in time with the banging inside the house. A banging that didn't stop.

I pursed my lips and rocked back on my heels to scan the shuddering house. It *was* today I was supposed to meet Mordechai here—wasn't it?

It was definitely today.

I'd skipped my Thursday psych class at UIC for this. Mrs. Klein had called Mordechai about her sister ten days ago, hearing about the unorthodox exorcist the usual way—a cousin of a friend of a brother. He hadn't been formally ordained in years, but people still called him Rabbi Mordechai, and he rarely corrected them. Ex-rabbi, former consultant to the Catholic Church, and quiet neighborhood legend, Mordechai operated well outside any official order now. He didn't even need to advertise.

BANG! BANG! BANG!

The afflicted found him.

I stepped off the porch, glancing at the neat little yards on either side of the Klein residence, taking it all in and knowing I was seeing more than I should—feeling more. I'd always had a knack for noticing the dumbest things, picking up on people's emotions no matter how hard they tried to hide them. Fear was copper and ash. Lies were bitter, like burnt coffee. Love—the few times I'd encountered it—was either thick and sticky or light like rain.

Most of the time, I said nothing, because the kind of things I noticed weren't the kind of things anyone wanted to hear about. I also didn't generally like to advertise that I was a freak.

But here on Whippoorwill Lane, the cracked paint and weeds didn't just stink of neglect. The houses on this block all carried the same faint odor of injury, hunching over the chopped-off lane. It was a street full of old people, or the grown-up children of people who'd gotten old when they weren't paying attention. The kind of street no one expected to find themselves living on, at least not on purpose. And certainly not for very long.

BANG! BANG! BANG! Bang-Bang-Bang-Bang-BANG!

I glanced back at the house. *Stupid bitch.*

Well, if she wanted to wait for Mordechai, she could enjoy another 24 hours of suck.

I stalked away, timing the cadence of my walk to the crashing going on behind me. Mrs. Klein screeched out another sharp word.

Only this time it ended on a scream.

"Iris!"

I heard the old woman's fear, shocked and high, sounding not only panicked but terrified. Then steps were running through the house as another voice's laughter surged forth on the trailing edge of her cries.

I pictured the frail Mrs. Klein I'd seen in the doorway, racketing around her tiny little home, about to break a bone or shatter a hip. Her fear pierced through my sneering dismissal, and before my brain could conjure anything else, I ran back up the steps and did my own banging, pounding once more on the front door.

The moment my fist hit the thin wood there was silence inside, like children caught acting out at bedtime. Then came the swift shuffle of feet approaching, the equally fast swipe of the chain being drawn away.

"Oh." Mrs. Klein took me in, once more glancing behind me. Her face fell.

Nope. Still no rabbi.

"Can I come in, Mrs. Klein?" I asked in a rush. "I might be able to—do something. About Iris."

Mrs. Klein didn't even hesitate as she opened the door. At that point, she probably would have taken help from the Easter Bunny.

I stepped inside with my shoulders back, my chin high, acting like I knew what I was doing.

Of course you know. You've known for a long time.

Heat prickled along my spine as my inner voice whispered its support, leaving me unsteady, unsettled...needful. I shoved those feelings away and looked around Mrs. Klein's living room. The afghan-covered couch pressed against one wall, glaring at the dead eye of a silent TV. The gleaming grandfather clock hugged another corner, slightly off center, as if hoping to escape unnoticed when no one was looking. The whole place crouched with an air of expectation, and I exhaled slowly, steadying my nerves.

I could do this.

Once again, the softest brush of sensation slipped along my neck, a prickling of awareness, a murmuring of a thousand voices and none at all. I barely kept from letting my eyes drift closed, wanting to lean into that dark invitation, to slip away on its lies, to immerse myself in—

"You can help her? Today—without the rabbi here?"

Mrs. Klein's desperate plea sliced through my warm haze, and I jerked my gaze back to her. She stood wringing her hands in the center of the living room, but she was alone.

"Where's your sister?" I asked abruptly.

She flinched, and even I tensed a little at the sound of my voice. It sounded too clipped, almost angry.

"In her room." She waved vaguely toward the back of the house, and I nodded, working up a reassuring smile. I was doing this all wrong, dammit. I needed to slow down. Mordechai always treated the family of the afflicted as if they needed as much help as the victim. The more wounded the family, the more ceremonial he got. "To each according to his needs," he'd always say.

Mrs. Klein seemed pretty traumatized, but I couldn't brandish an ancient shofar or suddenly whip up ten holy men and all their whispering chants. So I did the best I could. Blowing out a calming breath, I set my pack on the ground and pulled out the small metal mezuzah case I'd tucked carefully inside, offering it to her. She took it almost sheepishly, a thin stain of color warming the ash away from her cheeks as she stared down at it.

"We had one years ago, but we just—it got stolen, I think. Or fell off. But there seemed no reason to..." She sighed. "I never expected anything like this."

"It's okay." I folded my hands over gossamer-light fingers, absorbing her tremors while she held the small cylindrical case. "Rabbi Mordechai created this himself to bless your home. When you're ready, after I leave, put it up, okay? It'll make you feel better."

She began to nod, then a new sound issued forth from the back of the house. Not the BANG! BANG! of something big anymore, but a low rhythmic thump, like a piece of furniture thudding against a wall.

Mrs. Klein clearly knew what it was because her face tightened into an anxious mask, and she turned away from me. With almost exaggerated care, she set the mezuzah on a small, doily-covered table. Then, with quick, shooshing steps, she led me toward the back of the house. I didn't miss the fact that my inner voice and all its brash confidence had now gone silent, just when I needed it most.

Thump. The house shuddered again with the force of whatever was being shoved against the wall.

I swallowed. Unlike Mordechai, I had no more scrolls, no jewelry bearing a Hamsa hand to add to my gift of the mezuzah. But the ex-rabbi had taught me long ago that true exorcists didn't really *need* their vials of holy water, their beads or symbols. Such tools and totems had been created over the centuries to represent the essence of God, so that everyone could tell themselves it was God who had the power. God, and not the exorcist.

Thump.

Still, as far as an actual vanquishing of evil went, those tools weren't truly required, Mordechai had always said. All you needed was words, faith...and an exorcist too stubborn to fail.

Thump.

Mrs. Klein started crying as she shuffled closer to the door at the end of the hallway. I huffed a shallow breath, suddenly wanting to cry too.

I couldn't fail this test. Not even a little. Once challenged, a demon either fled—or it killed. There was no other option.

Thump.

Demons were only instruments of trial, Mordechai always said. When they trespassed into God's sons or daughters—pressing against the souls of the weak and forcing a choice between fear and faith—an exorcist merely had to send them on their way. And we could, he insisted. We always could.

Thump.

We could.

I walked down the dark, narrow hallway toward whatever was waiting in the back of Mrs. Klein's house and dearly hoped that he was right.

CHAPTER

TWO

As usual with diabolical possession, I smelled the afflicted long before I saw them.

The afflicted *stank*.

Not like sweat or unwashed bodies. Worse. Decay and burning sulfur and something sweet underneath, fruit rotting in summer heat. My stomach rolled, and I had to breathe through my mouth as I finally stepped into the tiny back bedroom.

Mrs. Klein's sister's name was Iris, but there was nothing flower-like about the creature who stood against the far corner. Her forehead was split open, apparently from where she'd been banging it into the wall. Blood streamed down her face in a thick, smudged line, the same color as the smears on the faded wallpaper behind her. She huffed in low, short breaths, clearly aware I was there, though she wouldn't look directly at me. Her hair was lank, the color of dirty snow, and her thin housedress was stained with food, sweat, and grime.

My gaze swiveled back to Mrs. Klein, as neat and carefully pressed as an old sheet, smelling of desperation and stale tea, and my question must have been obvious.

"She hasn't let me near her in days." Mrs. Klein's smile was tremulous, apologetic. "It gets better. She'll wake up." She fluttered her hand. "She'll wake up from this, and she'll be fine. Or at least, she always used to wake up, come out of it. This time..." Her words trailed off.

"How long has it been this bad?"

The smile slipped a little. "Since I spoke with Rabbi Mordechai. Since he told me he would come."

I nodded, a sliver of apprehension worming through me at what I was going to attempt alone. Still, I couldn't back down now. Didn't want to back down, I realized.

It was more than time.

Relief knifed through me. "Yeah, well. Don't leave me hanging here," I muttered, so softly Mrs. Klein couldn't hear me, Iris couldn't hear me. I could hardly hear myself...but someone could.

A soft, curling sigh drifted up within me, and I realized I'd never—not once—asked the voice within me for actual help before. I'd cursed it, tried to drown it out, damned it, begged it to leave. But I'd never asked it for assistance. Maybe that wasn't allowed?

Too late now. And I needed all the help I could get.

I took a step toward Iris, and the woman seemed to snap to awareness, pressing herself against the wall.

"Aggie, get her away from me!"

Mrs. Klein jolted at her words, visibly shaken. "Iris?" she asked, and by the eagerness in her voice, I could tell that the sister probably hadn't said anything intelligible in the past few days.

"Get her away, now. *Please.*" Iris lifted quavering fingers to smooth her hair back against her skull, as if that was all she needed to do to set herself to rights. "I'm okay, Aggie, I just had a spell. You know how my spells are." Iris's face tried to work its way into a smile, despite the line of blood trailing down her cheek.

"Iris, there's nothing to worry about." Mrs. Klein shifted forward, then faltered, her eyes flicking to me, as if checking for my approval before she continued toward her sister.

Instantly, I sensed the danger. "Mrs. Klein—"

"I said get her *away!*" Iris's fingers had clamped onto her own head, twisting into her hair, pulling it out by the roots. Mrs. Klein stopped, paralyzed. New blood welled against her sister's brow. "Now. Make her go *now*. She'll hurt me."

"She won't, Iris," Mrs. Klein tried again, her words desperate. "She's trying to help."

I began with the first psalm, the one Mordechai always started with, the one that flowed like a cool mist from his lips but sounded harsh and jangly coming from mine. "Whoever dwells in the shelter of the Most High, will rest in the shadow of El Shaddai—"

"Make her *go-o-o-o*." Iris's cry stretched out too long this time, and her fear was palpable, a living thing.

I didn't stop my recitation. If anything, my words gained strength as I spoke them, even as my stomach twisted and rolled. "...Surely he will save you from the fowler's snare and from the deadly pestilence..."

"How can *you do* this to me?" Iris clenched her hands into fists and banged the wall behind her. Surprise, rage, indignation, and horror all played over her face, its thin skin stretched to the point of translucence over bulging veins. Her mouth gaped, displaying worn-down teeth and a pale, twisting tongue, trying to work up enough saliva to spit at me. The first bug crawled out from her cracked lips.

I took another step toward the old woman. As Mrs. Klein half-sobbed, Iris screamed something I couldn't understand, then jerked against the wall as if I'd shoved her. I tracked her movements, seeing and smelling and tasting her truth like I always did, even when I didn't want to. Beneath the spit and thrashing, I caught a flicker of what Iris once had been—a happy woman, a contented wife, comfortable and neat...and not alone.

"*No*," the creature in front of me wailed now, spewing more bugs—fat ground beetles, earwigs, even a couple glossy roaches. Her eyes rolled back in her head so fast, I almost didn't catch her glance as it raked across my face.

Almost. But not quite.

Got you.

I might have laughed if my stomach weren't heaving. Fear churned through me at what would come next, but I'd *done* it. I'd seen the thing inside Iris. And it'd seen me too.

You're so good at this, the voice whispered.

"*Focus*," I thought back, but my pulse quickened anyway as the ghost of a laugh slipped through me, and for a second—just a second—I rode that pleasure, savoring it as I stared into Iris's eyes.

"I see you," I hissed.

The old woman spasmed, her stasis cracking with another slam of her head against the wall. Her scream became a howl of anguish. Then she tried to climb *into* the wall, scrabbling at its surface as her sister gasped. Apparently, this was a new experience for Mrs. Klein.

Not for me.

I stalked toward the creature hiding within Iris, certainty locking into place with each step.

The temperature dropped. Not gradually, but all at once, like someone had opened a freezer door. My breath misted in the suddenly frigid air. Behind me, Mrs. Klein whimpered.

The lightbulb overhead flickered. Once. Twice. In the stuttering light, I saw something jitter in Iris's shadow. Something with too many angles, that didn't match her movements.

"I see you," I hissed."

Anger licked and rattled through me, my inner voice howling with full-blown rage.

How dare you try to get away—how dare you? You know why I'm here. You all know, have always known. All of you know.

Iris's gnarled fingers clawed at the faded wallpaper already shredded to tatters. The place suddenly reeked like an outhouse, the stench overwhelming. Mrs. Klein staggered back, retreating to the doorway of the room. She gagged for air and retched loudly, desperate not to leave her sister but unable to come any closer.

I smiled, leaning forward into the rotted stench of Iris's breath.

"Bring it, you bastard," I muttered.

It was showtime.

THREE

"Foul one," I murmured, my blood thundering in my ears. "Why do you plague this daughter of Abraham?" I'd heard these words so many times I knew exactly what to say—just not, apparently, how to say it.

Because unlike Mordechai's gently reproving recitation of recognition and rebuke, my question was spoken almost like a sneer, heavy with both disgust and a hint of glee. It sounded awful, even to me. No wonder the rabbi never let me speak when he conducted his solemn ceremony. No wonder he seemed angry every time I tried.

Still, I continued, mockery slicing sharp. Words Mordechai would never say, but that I couldn't help but speak. "How far you've fallen, to choose such weary chattel as this? She's *disgusting*; you should do better."

Behind me, Mrs. Klein gasped, but in that moment I loathed the wretched old woman cowering in front of me far more than the demon infesting her. *Iris*. Poor, pitiful *Iris*. She was weak and frail and pointless. Revulsion shuddered through me at her smell and at the sticky fluids that bubbled out of her, her rheumy eyes and swollen knuckles—

I shook myself, hard. What was my *deal*?

But I couldn't stop. I wouldn't stop. I would pry this weak and stupid human open and get at the creature inside her if it was the last thing I did.

"What is your *name*?" I growled, trying to keep my voice low, trying to focus on the demon, only the demon, and not the woman it inhabited.

Iris, of course, heard me plainly. Or whatever was inside her did.

She froze like a rabbit against that stained wallpaper. Her heart thudded so hard beneath her thin ribs that I could hear it plainly, but I drowned out that sound with my own twisting, sneering abuse.

"Do you know what I'll *do* to you for making me wait?" I hissed. "I'll stretch you wide, rip you apart, turn your moments into lifetimes of agony—and you'll thank me for it before the end."

The old woman shuddered, and her breath became a shallow, guttural huffing as I continued, never letting up. Her fingers dug into the wall, her sobs rasped out. But she didn't speak. Seconds lengthened and warped, taking on a life of their own. My words blurred into snarls I couldn't even understand anymore—until, at last, something inside Iris shattered, pushing the darkness within her over the edge.

With excruciating slowness, she turned her head around to face me even though her chest was still pressed tight to the wall. The eye-popping display of flexibility was one I'd never gotten used to, no matter how many contorted bodies I'd seen.

Iris's eyes were wild now, the pupils huge and black. Her face remolded, unnaturally smooth as her skin stretched over the harsh edges of her bones and sank into the hollows of her cheeks. In that moment, it was as if she had lost fifty years—or gained five hundred.

She screamed something at me then, a howl of rage that burst apart like rats flying out of a hole. A name—the demon's name. It scraped across my mind like something half-remembered, forbidden. A name I knew, somewhere deep inside me. A name I recognized.

"Mammon," she gasped.

Mammon. Of course.

Thick pleasure swelled up, and I reached out to the wall blindly, steadying myself as I leaned against it, my knees suddenly unreliable. But the moment passed as Iris turned the rest of the way to face me. Clarity returned, and slowly, steadily, I advanced against the stench, even as snot rained from her nostrils and vomit spilled from her mouth—vomit that was half bile, half blood—and—

I finally reached the woman and put my hands on her shoulders, shaking her hard enough that her gaze snapped back to mine, her eyes liquid as the demon stood naked and writhing within the withered husk of her body.

Gripping a shoulder that was little more than a stick and ball, I moved my other hand up to Iris's forehead and plastered it there, ignoring the sweat, the sticky fluid oozing down her chin.

"Leave this daughter of Abraham, Mammon," I snapped. Not as Mordechai's typical gentle suggestion, but as an order. A command. "Leave her and do not return. Else, I will hunt you without ceasing, and you shall *never* know a moment's rest."

Iris seized, vibrating violently in my grasp, and a chill ran through me. This shouldn't be working this fast. Mordechai never connected so harshly, so quickly...

But I can.

Iris's body slammed against the wall hard enough that I heard something crack like dusty crockery. She lifted her left arm, and it seemed to swell with putrid sickness, turning purple with the weight of rot and fever. Then her wrist bulged, and her hand snapped to the right at an awkward angle, the sound of a bone breaking as she screamed, her fingers splaying wide.

A cold wave rushed through and past me, leaving my skin icy. I didn't feel afraid, though. For a moment, I felt *glorious*. The moment Mammon left Iris, an electric pleasure coursed through me—not just satisfaction, but something deeper, more intimate. A spinning *whump* of power that stretched out in all directions. I had battled evil, and I had won, and nothing—*nothing*—could stop me anymore.

Nothing could stop...*us*.

The thought came clear and strong, and for once, I didn't fight it. We *had* won. Together.

Magnificent, the voice whispered, and there was something almost reverent in it. Something that made my skin prickle with awareness. *You were* magnificent, *Delia*.

My name in that voice did something to me I didn't want to examine too closely. Made me feel seen in a way that was both thrilling and deeply, deeply wrong.

Then my brain came back online, and I remembered where I was.

A bone-shaking wave of panic flashed through me, icy nausea freezing all my thoughts, the disorientation so over-whelming that I jerked with real surprise as Iris fell forward into my arms.

Blood and vomit stained her chin, the front of her dress, the floor, even me. I staggered backward, hugging her awkwardly.

She looked, for the first time, like any old lady who'd lost her balance, as light and insubstantial as dried leaves. Her left hand bled, and her wrist looked dislocated. I reached down and popped it into place again, shocked at my calm efficiency. How did I—?

It didn't matter. Iris swung her gaze to meet mine, eyes wide and confused. The old woman appeared unharmed.

The stench and the bugs were completely gone.

Mrs. Klein rushed up. I couldn't understand her words as she gathered her sister close, helping Iris to the bed. Her grief billowed out from her in waves, like stiff laundry in a hot breeze, but she'd been happy, too, once. Satisfied.

I had to get out of this room.

I stumbled into the hallway, aiming for the front door. Desperate for the ringing in my brain to stop, I lurched down the too-long hallway, not seeming to gain any ground until—finally—I reached the doily-covered living room. I shivered, unfathomably cold, and glanced at the grandfather clock.

Then blinked.

Only thirty minutes had passed?

Impossible.

Mordechai's exorcisms typically lasted hours, sometimes days. I was used to that. Did I really think I had been able to, ah, *expel* a demon alone in just a few minutes?

Behind me, Mrs. Klein called out something, and I jumped. I was doing this all wrong! Mordechai would have stayed back in that room to comfort the sisters. He would've helped them understand what had happened. He would've prayed with them, spoken more psalms, and blessed their house, then left with words of reassurance. Hope. Forgiveness, if that was what they needed, which many seemed to. Words, words, and more words would flow from him to fill all the empty spaces completely, clearing away the darkness, making everything fresh and new. And safe. Above all, safe.

Nothing is ever safe.

As I blinked around Mrs. Klein's living room, clarity hit me like a thunderclap.

What was I even *doing* here?

Panic surged, clawing up my throat. Today was Thursday, not Friday. I wasn't supposed to meet Mordechai until tomorrow. Tomorrow!

I knew the truth, of course, knew it as much as I knew that my shirt was flecked with vomit and blood, my hands wet with another woman's tears.

I'd come here by myself intentionally. Deliberately.

I had *known* Mordechai wouldn't be here. Yet still I'd come. I'd done the one thing he'd instructed me never, ever to do. I'd confronted darkness without him.

What had I been thinking?

Somehow, I made it to the other side of the living room. I stumbled into the front door, then stepped back, jerking my glance to the side as I tracked a sudden movement there. A decorative mirror hung on the wall, and my gaze raked across it for barely a second.

Only a second.

But a second was all I'd ever needed.

My breath stopped as something else looked back at me from the glass. Not my reflection—though that was there too, pale and shaken. But behind it. Through it. Like there was another face superimposed over mine...

A face of knife-twisting beauty.

Dark eyes gleamed beneath a lush fall of hair that seemed to move with a life of its own, catching light that shouldn't exist in the dim hallway. Winged brows arched in something between amusement and assessment. A smirk both brutal and sly curved lips that promised torment...

And rapture.

And death.

The face was masculine—distinctly, devastatingly so—but not quite human. Too perfect. Too sharp. Like an artist had sculpted the ideal of male beauty and then added just enough wrongness to make it dangerous.

As I stared, the eyes narrowed. They weren't cruel, exactly. But they weren't kind, either. They were interested. Curious. As if I were a puzzle it had been working on for a very long time, and it had finally figured out the solution.

Hello, Delia, it whispered, and I felt the words slide across my skin. *You were so very good today.*

My mouth went dry. Not from fear, but from something that felt disturbingly like recognition.

As if I'd been waiting my whole life to be seen by those eyes.

"No," I whispered.

The thing in the mirror smiled.

Yes.

Heat curled through me, thick and full. I should be terrified, some tiny part of my brain realized. I should run. This face in the mirror, this voice, was a mirage of lies and bullshit and I knew—*knew!*—I was out of my league.

Instead, I found myself leaning closer to the glass, and finally a spindly strength welled up from somewhere even deeper than the voice that plagued me. Words flickered within me; old words, my words.

"As wax melts before the fire," I whispered thickly. "So the wicked perish at the presence of God."

The ebony eyes went flat. Quick as a heartbeat, the monster's beautiful, sculpted lips twisted into a sickening snarl. Fury cracked his face, revealing a boiling scramble of worms and viscera beneath the now-puckering skin. As I stared, unable to breathe—to move—to think, a violent spew of bone-splintering rage ripped through me, shattering the heat and leaving only spine-freezing terror behind.

"No!" I gasped, wheeling away from the mirror as if it were going to explode off the wall at me. I spun and slammed my back against the front door, my eyes going wide as I took in Mrs. Klein standing in the center of the room, her powder-white fingers clutching something that looked almost familiar…

I swiped my hand awkwardly at my hoodie pocket, but there was no phone there, of course. My phone was in Mrs. Klein's hand. I'd dropped it—where? Probably in the hallway.

"Your phone, dear," she said, her lips trembling as she tried to form a smile. She stared at me, and I stared back, neither of us able to make any more words come, and nothing but the soft, wracking sobs of Iris in the back filling the air between us.

I'd failed this poor woman, I realized. Here I'd done everything I could to save her sister, and the result wasn't joy, or gratitude, or even relief.

It was fear.

Mrs. Klein was afraid of me.

And…she probably should be.

I blew out a long breath and took my phone from her, careful not to look anywhere but at her, then at the front door. I shoved the phone in my pocket and left.

CHAPTER

FOUR

My palms were still sweating as I walked up Mordechai's driveway, never mind that I'd avoided mirrors for a full day after I'd left Mrs. Klein's, until I forced myself to stare into the one in my bathroom this morning.

Nothing had stared back at me, lurking in my eyes. Nothing spoke to me. Not even when I'd screwed up the nerve to ask it to.

"Hey," I'd managed, my voice dry as chalk. I'd gotten nothing but silence back.

I was just me, alone. Same as always.

I mean, sure, I'd seen...something. In the mirror. Or I thought I had. But it could have been stress, or an adrenaline crash after the exorcism. My overactive imagination combined with Mrs. Klein's decorative mirror and bad lighting.

That made sense. That was rational.

The alternative—that there was a presence in there with me, something with a face and a voice and intentions of its own...No. I wasn't going there. Not yet. Maybe not ever.

Because if I admitted that what I'd seen was real, I'd have to admit what it meant. And I wasn't ready for that.

I may be going crazy, but at least I wasn't possessed.

Even stranger, I'd had no nightmares. I'd woken up this morning freaked out at what might be covering the walls, but they were white. Pristine. The usual post-exorcism pornographic slurs scrawled in garish craft paint decrying me as a whore and a slut, a useless cunt with shit for brains...were nowhere in evidence. Everything I'd come to expect—the bumps in the night, cold hands on my throat, needles pricking my skin, screams howling in my ears—had taken the night off, apparently.

Why?

Was it because I was stronger? More confident in myself? Because I'd shown Iris's demon who was boss?

I had no clue.

Now, however, the huffing was back; short bursts of hyperventilation that I couldn't seem to calm. I forced myself to stop, to focus, to huddle beneath a tree until I could breathe normally again.

Finally, I hitched my bag higher on my shoulder and peered into the shadows at the little stone house with moss growing on the roof. Mordechai's home. I'd never been inside it, but it looked pretty nice.

The rabbi's backyard office, however, was a dump.

Books, documents, files on back jobs, notebooks, and a lifetime of office supplies were crammed into a room the size of a mousetrap, and I doubted the place had been aired out in decades. It was as much Mordechai as his shawl and rumpled pants.

But something felt different today.

I couldn't put my finger on it at first, but the air seemed too cold, even for Mordechai. And there was a smell...faint, barely there, but it reminded me of Mrs. Klein's house. Of Iris's room.

Brimstone and rot.

I glanced around, but everything looked normal. The same cluttered shelves, the same stacks of papers. Nothing moved.

Still, the wrongness clung to me, and inside, something stirred.

Not quite a voice, not quite a feeling. But...awareness. Like I wasn't alone in noticing.

Like something else was paying attention too.

The door to his office was shut, and I checked my newly charged phone. It was five o'clock. Nobody should be in there but him. Half the time when I knocked, Mordechai didn't hear me anyway, so I opened the door and let myself in.

As usual, the wave of chilled, air-conditioned air made me smile. Most old people couldn't stay warm enough... Mordechai preferred to live in a refrigerator. I could hear him mumbling to himself in his back office, and I opened my mouth to call out, then shut it again.

Why bother announcing myself?

Just go in. See what he's doing.

The idea struck me so quickly that I didn't stop to analyze it —it sounded like my thoughts, my own inner voice, not like some dark, nebulous entity potentially lurking inside me. A perfectly reasonable thought from a perfectly reasonable woman, who'd conducted a perfectly reasonable exorcism all by herself yesterday. Nothing to look at here.

I didn't even try to be stealthy. I threw down my backpack in the corner of the reception room with a loud clatter, strode the ten steps it took to get to the back office, then stuck my head in.

Mordechai was bent over a pile of file folders lying on his small meeting table, papers everywhere, along with photographs of a giant old house that screamed money and a whole lot of it. Some of the pictures were in black and white, others in color. All of them looked creepy as shit, but that was probably because Mordechai was looking at them. He didn't care about anything that *wasn't* creepy as shit.

He was also so into whatever he was reading that he clearly had no idea I was even there. "Hey," I finally said. This time, there was a reaction.

"Delia!" The rabbi jerked back. His hands spasmed on his papers, sending the farthest ones flying.

"Oh, jeez, I'm sorry." I moved forward and didn't miss the way Mordechai pulled everything he could back toward his body, almost like he was trying to hide contraband. I tried not to be hurt as I dropped down on one knee, gathering up the glossy wisps of paper. One of them featured a twenty-something frat boy with dark curly hair and a nice jawline.

My brows shot up. Who was *this*? Even in faded black-and-white photos, the guy's eyes seemed exhausted, somehow— the kind of eyes that had seen too much and would never be able to see ordinary things the same way again. Granted, I picked up odd, totally random insights from photos, the same as I did people, but this guy's energy seemed to leap out of the photo and snatch at me, pleading for me to come, to see, to help. He wanted me—*needed* me—and something hard and angry lurched deep in my gut at that thought, making me gasp.

I coughed to cover the punch of pain, flipping the photo around casually to Mordechai. "Well, at least he's cute," I managed. The pain twisted deeper, possessive and furious. Something inside me didn't like that observation. The sheer rage of its reaction startled me into response.

"*Get a grip,*" I thought at it. "*And not on my guts.*"

Instantly, the sensation eased, and I blinked. Since when

could I negotiate with my inner voice? How had that become a thing?

"Give that to me." Mordechai plucked the photo out of my hand. Feeling abashed at his rebuke, though I had no reason to be, I gathered up the rest of the pictures, scanning them rapidly before dropping them into his open file folder. Quite a few of them featured a house. The same house as before, big and made of stone, with at least twenty windows on the front, an over-large door, and a flat roof, which made it seem oddly fortress-like.

There were also pictures of a field full of horses, a lake with a gazebo, and a much smaller house set back into the trees. Silver-spoon hottie guy showed up again, too, this picture in color, not fifties-era black and white, so it could be he was still cute and not a million years old, tottering around his sad lonely castle.

"Sorry," I tried again, my hand dropping to my belly to rub away a renewed spasm. "I didn't mean to surprise you."

Mordechai didn't respond to that, simply took the folder and set it with the others, most of them still open, while I turned and looked at his shelves to give him a moment to figure out how to yell at me.

I'd memorized these bookcases a long time ago. They were filled with files, dating back fifty years. Back to when he'd been an official rabbi, and before that, a consultant to the Vatican. I suddenly wondered: Who had Mordechai been as a young man? What kind of kid actually grows up to become—

"Why did you go?"

His words pulled me back around. The rabbi had composed himself. Now he studied me from his customary position, rocked back in his ratty old green suede upholstered office chair, his hands clasped together on his belly. He usually wore long jackets and woven scarves when we visited peoples' houses. But, like the scrolls, the horn, and the ornamental cases, I knew those clothes were a prop. Something he used to strike equal parts fear and reassurance into both the possessed and the possessor.

Today, however, Mordechai wore his more usual office attire: ragged-edged khakis and a button-down plaid shirt, with a thick green cardigan over top that sort of made him blend in with his chair. His curly gray hair hung a little past cool and well into eccentric, and his face was clean-shaven. That meant he'd gone to see the Klein sisters, I knew. Rabbi Mordechai didn't shave unless he had to see people. Real people, not me.

But he was waiting for a response, so I sat in my customary armchair, too, fatigue all of a sudden weighing me down.

"I don't know." I shrugged, surprised at my own honesty. "At first, I thought for sure that we were supposed to meet yesterday. Like, it was completely locked in my head that yesterday was the Klein's appointment. My phone was dead, you hadn't texted me anything else that I knew of, so I just—went."

"You frightened Mrs. Klein." As usual with Mordechai, there was no judgment, no censure in his words. Somehow, that made me feel even worse, and I squirmed a little in my chair.

"I didn't mean to." I leaned forward, and something flickered in Mordechai's gray eyes. Interest? Curiosity? Surely, he wanted to hear my side of the story too. "Is that what she said? That I scared her? Honestly, I just wanted to help. I was standing right there on her porch and there was all this noise inside the house, and *she* looked so scared, and I thought if I could go inside and see what was going on, that maybe I'd be able to—"

"You shouldn't have gone in without me."

Mordechai's voice had turned slightly harsher, and I sat

back again, nervous now. "Well, I was already there. I thought you were inside."

His eyebrows were the kind that seemed to be constantly sprouting new hairs, most of them dead white. And now those brows drew up in a bushy question mark. "You knew I wasn't inside."

"Not at first, I didn't. I came up the steps and there was all this noise, and it stopped when I banged on the door, and then she answered, and—"

"And she told you I wasn't there."

"That's not the *point*." Anger seared through me. How could he not see this? "The point is that even though you weren't already inside, she was clearly in trouble, or her sister was, and I could help. I *wanted* to help. I wanted to ease her pain, her sister's pain. I don't see why that's so wrong. And it's not like I could stop once I got started. You know that better than anyone."

Mordechai's hands had shifted a little higher on his belly as I spoke, but they were still clasped together. He wasn't a fat man, but he seemed spongier now than when I'd first met him. A little more stooped and tired. He should be welcoming the assistance I was giving him, not constantly putting me off.

Instead, he simply looked at me, and after a moment or two, I felt a sudden easing of my own stress. All the anxiety, pain, and hard-sharp angles were softening like he was soft, rounding under the cadence of his words.

"So, then, tell me, Delia," he murmured. "How was your first experience confronting evil all alone?"

CHAPTER

FIVE

The question seemed curiously weighted, and I tensed, searching for a trap. But Rabbi Mordechai never set out to trap me. That wasn't his way. He taught by drawing me out, reminding me of what I'd forgotten.

"It was fine." That was nowhere near accurate. I tried again. "I mean, it was kind of fast, if you want to know the truth. Easy, even. I saw the creature, got its name. Mammon. Thirty minutes, start to finish."

Mordechai was quiet for a long moment. Too long. When I looked up, I caught him staring at me with an expression I couldn't read. Not fear, exactly. Not pity.

Definitely curiosity.

"What?" I asked, suddenly defensive.

"Your eyes," he said softly.

"What about them?"

He didn't answer right away. Instead, he reached into his desk drawer and pulled out a small hand mirror, offering it to me.

I didn't want to take it. But I did.

My reflection looked normal. Same pale face, same tired expression. Same empty definitely-not-possessed hazel eyes—

Except.

For just a second—the barest flash—I could have sworn they looked darker. Larger. Like the pupils had swallowed the iris whole.

I blinked. Nope, normal again.

"I don't see anything," I said, handing the mirror back too quickly.

Mordechai took it, still watching me with that unreadable expression. "No," he said quietly. "I don't suppose you would."

Setting aside the mirror, Mordechai raised his hand, his mouth moving with words I couldn't quite make out. Then I realized he was giving me a blessing. A blessing! I didn't need it, didn't want it, but still...

The image seemed to loosen in my mind, and I breathed easier.

"Darkness knows your weaknesses, Delia," he said, matter-of-factly. "Your past and every hidden thought. First, it will try to frighten you. Then it will try to seduce you. And when you confront it directly, it will trick you, make you see that which isn't there, and expose you to all who might tear you down."

Seduce me? Of all Mordechai's words, those were the ones that caught me, pulled at me, like fingers twining through my hair, tugging my head back, my chin up, exposing my mouth and my neck to hot, hungry—

The air conditioner chose that moment to kick on, and I nearly jumped out of my chair. I drew my arms into my body, hunching over, wishing I had a sweater. "It doesn't do that to you."

"Doesn't it?" Mordechai looked old again, but his eyes were serious. "You aren't wearing the Hamsa hand amulet I got you, Delia. You should, now more than ever."

I shifted uneasily. "You said I didn't need that stuff."

He didn't look away. "You may not, but it is protection, and protection is grace. As agonizing as evil's attack on your flesh may be, Delia, the attack on your mind is far worse. There is always pain. Always. But bodily pain fades. Wounds heal. A torn spirit is far harder to repair. You *cannot* let that happen. It's why you should never confront evil alone and unprotected."

"But I *helped* her!" The anger burst out of me unexpectedly, fueled by a wave of indignation. "It left. I got rid of it."

"*You* didn't, though, yes?" Mordechai lifted a weathered hand again. "It's not by your strength but by the Almighty's power. And by His hand you are a witness to an act of grace, over and over again."

Something slithered inside me then—fear, apprehension, resentment, outright pain. I stiffened in my chair, unreasonably angry. "Whatever, Mordechai. Don't act like either one of you is doing me any favors."

His smile was gentle. "I know I'm not. You're the one helping me."

And just like that, the anger bled away.

"Oh. Well, fine." I nodded again at the papers on his desk, desperate for a change of subject. "So, what's that about? It looks like a lot more information than you usually get."

He didn't glance at the files, though I was doing my level best to read everything upside down. There were letters and what looked like copied pages from a journal. The letter was new. The copied pages looked old, though. Tattered, even. A sudden thought struck me. "Is this some sort of cold case? Like an unsolved mystery you've been asked to consult on or something?"

I tried hard not to watch the paranormal reality TV shows about ghost hunters or demon chasers, but suddenly everything on the rabbi's desk made sense. Of course, someone from a TV station or whatever had come to him with a case that had some sensationalistic angle. Of course, they'd asked for his help. People tracked Mordechai down all the time, even though he didn't exactly advertise. He only went to temple on rare occasions, and he'd taken me, like, twice. I'd fallen asleep both times, but he'd kept trying for a while after that. I couldn't remember when he'd stopped suggesting I go.

I scooted the chair a little bit closer to him. "That's it, isn't it? A cold case. And who's the guy? Is he still a college kid or has he grown up now?"

Mordechai was watching me with interest now, but I couldn't read his face. Nothing new there. "He's twenty-seven, so hardly a kid. Only a little older than you."

"Ah—right." My stomach tightened again, but Mordechai kept going.

"He's the one who contacted me. Why have you singled him out from the others?"

"What others—" I frowned and looked down at the pictures again. The buildings, the horses. And there *were* other people in the photos too, I realized. People I had totally missed during my first glance through, somehow. They stood in front of the house, then back at the fence watching the horses. Even in the picture with the guy, they ranged around him in a stilted family portrait—Grandma, Mom and Dad, a much older sister or a young aunt holding a little boy, and the guy who looked super young, no matter what Mordechai said. All of them smiled at the camera.

"Oh." I struggled to come up with an excuse. "Well, I noticed him more is all, I guess. Who are these people?"

Mordechai tilted his head, and once again, I had the feeling he was looking not at me, but past me. Like he wasn't seeing me at all, but imagining this poor family and their problems. That tracked, I supposed. Because if nothing else, these people clearly had problems. That fact shimmered off the pages in front of Mordechai like a living thing.

After a second, though, the rabbi shrugged. "I don't have enough information yet."

I looked at the pile of paperwork. "You're kidding me."

"I'm not." His glance was keen on my face again. "And I believe you need to reflect on the significance of what you've done with the Kleins, so that you understand your strength and your weaknesses before we move any further."

"What I've *done*?" Just like that, the anger was back. "You mean expelled a demon out of an old woman so she didn't puke bugs anymore? And that's supposed to be wrong? And yes, I know, I *get* it. I shouldn't have gone in there alone. But you weren't *there*, Mordechai. You weren't *supposed* to be there."

Even as I said the words, fear coalesced inside me, hardening into a lump. Somewhere far away, I heard a cruel, satisfied chuckle.

"I *was* supposed to be there." Mordechai shook his head, his smile still gentle. "Isn't that what you meant to say?"

I stood up abruptly, swinging away, unable to meet his gaze anymore. "I gotta get to work."

CHAPTER

SIX

My reprieve from night terrors didn't last.

That night, I woke on a half-choked scream, delirious on fumes and wielding a paintbrush like a switchblade in my pitch-dark room.

My hand swept across the wall both in broad, sweeping strokes and short, jagged strikes, the paintbrush moving with a confident precision I'd never possessed. Up, across, down, over. Disgorging some twisted vision from deep inside me. Willing it into being. Giving it life.

I tried to speak, but my mouth wouldn't open.

I tried to stop. Couldn't.

I was a prisoner in my own skin, trapped behind my eyes, watching my traitorous hand paint something so fucked up I couldn't fully see it, didn't want to see it, was desperate not to—

Shhh.

My inner voice was louder than it had ever been—not in my head but in all of me, weaving through every nerve and muscle. It swelled and pushed like a living thing, guiding my body with the casual ease of someone who'd been doing it for years.

Maybe it had been.

"What are you?" I tried to ask, my voice strangled in my own throat. It heard me, though. It answered, anyway.

Almost done. Along with the murmur, satisfaction bled through me like warmth through thin cloth. *It's more than time.*

My hand dipped into the paint can at my feet—when had I opened that? How long had I been standing here?—and came up again, dripping black. The brush moved with aching tenderness across the wall, adding shadows to whatever I...it...was creating.

Making it more real. Making it something I couldn't ignore anymore.

I tried to scream. Nothing came out.

Terror crashed through me in waves, but underneath it, I felt a different sensation: Focus. Concentration. An artist's absorption in his work.

The scent of embers and chocolate wove around me, heat and want. It smelled almost like...

Longing?

My hand jerked away from the wall, moved to my face. I felt the brush stroke across my cheek—a slide of thick paint marking me. The liquid dripped down my jaw, my throat, sinuous fingers slowly exploring unfamiliar territory. And I sensed the moment the pressure of those fingers shifted, hardened...held.

Mine.

The word ripped through me like a violation, the pressure expanding so abruptly it felt like my skull would explode, my bones shatter, my blood spray out against this wall of filth and horror—

Then everything went black.

.   .   .

THE NEXT MORNING, I awoke in utter darkness, the smell of craft paint nearly choking me. But I didn't look at what I'd done to my bedroom walls.

I never looked right away.

Instead, I locked my bedroom door, crept downstairs with my blanket, and made coffee with shaking hands.

The next few days passed in a blur. Work, couch, library. Couch, library, work. I avoided my bedroom, but my housemate, Steve, was out of town, so there was no one to judge me for being unwilling to face four walls of hideous epithets in the light of day. And there were no more dreams, no more murmurs, no more whispers in the dark. Of course, the silence was worse. At least when the thing inside me talked, I knew where I stood.

Finally, on Monday, I found myself thinking more about those walls as I wiped down the plexiglass shield protecting the food we served at Kershman's Deli from the gross people who ordered it.

I'd deal with the walls tonight, probably, after work. I was ready, I thought. I was chill, again, easy. I could handle it.

Working in the deli had certainly helped dull the edge, anyway.

For one thing, customers at Kershman's Deli only had a limited number of items they could request: sandwiches, salads, or salads on sandwiches.

For another, they usually didn't give you much attitude, because their eyes weren't on you, they were on the various items you were putting on their sandwich. You didn't touch their food ever, thanks to the plastic gloves, and you didn't touch *them* either, thanks to the thick barrier between your hands and theirs.

Which was why I generally liked my job at Kershman's Deli. At least until 1 p.m. rolled around every weekday, Monday through Friday, and Claire Bickwell from the pharmacy down the street showed up in line—this time behind some guy I'd never seen before.

I didn't know Claire Bickwell, not really. She had bouncy blonde hair, a cupid's bow pink smile, and she was small boned and slender. Delicate. She looked to be about thirty or so, but her energy skewed younger. She tried to chat whenever she came in, like everyone was her friend. And so, of course, I should be too.

I didn't like her. If she wasn't alone, she was almost always with the same guy, but that guy was an absolute jerk. He smelled like someone else almost from the beginning, I finally realized. Not like her.

There was no way I would have told her that, though. I mean, who said things like that? Who could scent betrayal the way some people picked out floral notes in wine?

Still, Claire had asked a question about her boyfriend, I thought. The last time she was here. A question that had unexpectedly come along with the order of an avocado turkey sandwich and green tea. A question I'd responded to, possibly quick and harsh, probably quick and harsh. But still true. I tried hard to be truthful. The truth was always simpler, cleaner. More powerful.

Now Claire was back and ordering something different. With a new guy who smelled like her.

"What would you like on your turkey avocado?" Polite and cheerful, I remained ever the helpful counter girl. Claire made meaningful eyes at me, then at the guy in front of her. She didn't introduce us. I didn't care.

After a second, she gave up. "Everything but peppers and onions, like always. No salt, but please add the vinaigrette. And *thank you*," she said, emphasizing the words as I busied myself with her preparations. I looked up again, then passed along the sandwich to the cashier.

"No problem."

"No, I mean, *thank you.*" Again with the eyes. I looked at the guy who wasn't her old boyfriend but could be her new boyfriend, then back at her. Had I told her something about the previous guy? Aired my olfactory suspicions out loud?

I grimaced. If I had, I wouldn't necessarily remember. I said what I knew to be true when people asked me. It'd been a problem of mine since way back. That didn't make me some kind of hero.

"Anything else?" I asked, not trying to soften the edge in my voice, and she blinked, a blush climbing up her cheeks. Claire was only a little older than me, but unlike me, she hadn't been working her way through college one class at a time. She'd graduated on schedule and was a pharmacist, working shit hours at a fancy Oak Park pharmacy in pursuit of earning an eventual fortune by dispensing pills to supplicants at her plexiglass shield. She'd always seemed nice, and I'd never wanted to talk to her.

"Yes," she said, surprising me. She had a card out—a business card, cheap white stock with blue and black printed letters. She flashed the back of it to show me the cell number she'd written there, then handed it over the counter.

"I can't handle not speaking up when I see an issue, and I see one," she said. "You're too pale, Delia. It's Delia, right? Too tired. I can help you get better sleep. Call me."

I stared at her, and she stared back, with all the imperiousness of a woman who wore a white coat most of the day.

"No," I said.

But this was Claire Bickwell, her shiny nameplate pin said so, and I could see her story in her eyes. Small upper-middle-class family, loving parents, teachers who were too easily impressed. Shitty taste in boyfriends, even the new one, who seemed vaguely uncomfortable as he glanced between us, a frown marring his too soft lips.

Oh, honey. I fought the snicker. *If you think Claire makes you uncomfortable now...*

"Yes," Claire countered over my counter, and she flicked the card toward me, a neat little frisbee spin. I couldn't help myself —I ducked. Not really even ducked, just got out of the way of the spinning little card, harmless and stupid, but still a threat, still a—

I stopped. Claire's eyes were wide now, and so was Skye's, the teenage cashier beside me. "What?" I snapped. "I don't want your card."

"I can cash you out," Skye squeaked.

"Thank you," Claire Bickwell said with her lips pursed into their little bow, unruffled, unworried. She swung her perfect blonde hair and faced forward, the fluorescent lights catching the little gold cross on its delicate chain at her throat, and I turned to the next person. Nevertheless, I felt uneasy until she and her newest arm candy had paid for their subs and left the building.

They wouldn't eat at the little metal tables in front of the shop. That would be way too down-market for Claire. She'd probably invited her new guy over specifically on her lunch break from the pharmacy so she could give me the meaningful eyeball. Now that she'd done so, she'd go back to her perfect, plastic life with her perfect, plastic boyfriend, crisply pressed in khakis and a light blue button-down the color of his eyes. Probably sold insurance and owned a Prius he couldn't afford. They'd be insanely happy together. I didn't care.

The shuffle and thrum of customers continued, soothing and easy. After the lunch rush was done, the mid-shift cleaning began, and I lost myself in the bright aluminum and sparkling plexiglass and lumbering rumble of the six refrigerated units.

Then something moved close to me—too close. But it was a quiet, gentle intrusion, apologetic and uncertain. Skye, with her white-white, freckle-covered skin, her natural red hair, and her large, sea-glass green eyes. Those eyes were as big as saucers now, and she held something in her hand.

Claire Bickwell's card. "Do you do yoga?" she asked, a little breathlessly.

I barked out a laugh. Out of all the things that could have come out of the mouth of Skye Drury—the mostly ignored single daughter of a single mother, the below-average student, above-average worker who chewed on the inside of her mouth whenever she had to work the infernal cash machine, so nervous about getting it right that she had a mat of scar tissue no one would ever see—*that* was not what I expected. "Do I what?"

"Do yoga. You, like, bent to avoid that woman's card. All the way around. It was so fast that I probably wouldn't normally have seen it, but I did, and...well, it was awesome. You should take the card. She's a *pharmacist.*"

I blinked at her, confused by her words but more upset about the card. Everything inside me recoiled at the stupid fucking card, but that pissed me off too. It was paper! Paper and ink and the faint stench of hand sanitizer and Chapstick. Nothing else.

I took the card, and Skye's lips parted in a smile, her sigh a gusty exhale of relief and pickles. She turned away.

The other benefit of working in a place where there was no grill was that while you still stunk when you got off work, you didn't stink-stink. And you left your apron behind, so you pretty much could shed the reek of the place by the time you walked all the way home. Assuming, of course, that you walked, which

I generally did, no matter how late it got. Public transportation grated on me, especially at night. Too many people packed in too tight a space.

Mordechai might have gotten me a pay-as-you-go scholarship and this deli job to boot, but he wouldn't co-sign on a car loan for me until I finished college. Zealot.

Worse, I was beginning to wonder if he was blowing me off permanently, my mood sliding between hurt and outrage and back to hurt again. He'd told me he'd call me after we'd had our little pow-wow at his office on Friday, which had ended after another half-hour of him warning me about the dangers of the dark side. Like I didn't know that already.

He didn't know half the shit I was dealing with.

I thought about what waited for me at home and forced myself to keep walking even as my stomach churned. Streetlight to streetlight, shadow to shadow. And with every shadow, I half-expected to see those eyes again—either the half-visible ones I'd caught in Mrs. Klein's mirror, or the college boy's from the photograph. Both seemed to watch me now, as if waiting for me to choose which darkness I wanted most.

But it was the mirror eyes—and what had happened after I'd seen them—that lingered in my mind. Thank God Mrs. Klein hadn't told Mordechai about me freaking out right in front of her, or I'd probably still be in the man's ice-box office, getting lectured.

He didn't need to know.

For once, I agreed with the stupid voice in my head. I'd stopped telling Mordechai my every waking thought after I'd graduated high school, when things had started to turn a little weird. Mom had finally succeeded in drowning herself in her bottle. I'd stayed in the house we'd always rented, with the help of a guy who sublet Mom's bedroom, and pretended to grieve. It hadn't been all that hard, and I'd been motivated. I didn't want to do anything that would make Mordechai stop asking me to help him.

But now, despite all that effort, he was the one acting weird, shutting me out. He'd told me he would call me, and he hadn't. Granted, it was only Monday night, but still. He should have called.

I wiped my hands on my jeans, hating the feel of them slick with sweat despite the night's damp coolness. He couldn't shut me out now. Not when there were people I could help. He'd see —they'd all see. I was managing everything just fine.

I turned up the walkway to the shared duplex I now rented with my housemate—Deadbeat Steve—who should be back in residence by now.

The name I'd given him made me smile, because it wasn't really deserved. Steve wasn't a bad guy. He didn't pay his rent on time, but he eventually did pay it—or left enough cash lying around that I could find the money when I needed it. He went to the same school I did, though full-time, and his parents sent him money, probably hoping if they did, he would stay away. But most importantly, he was a drunk, and I knew drunks.

My mom had been a labor and delivery nurse who could handle crash C-sections and screaming heroin-addicted mommies bitching about having to have their labia piercings removed prior to going into surgery. She had also been a drunk, right up until she'd wrapped the family car around a telephone pole the summer of my senior year. Her vehicle had been totaled. So had she. No more car, no more Mom.

I hadn't been surprised. Despite the show I put on, I hadn't been especially sad, either, which bothered me more. I'd mostly been happy that she'd had the decency to wait until I'd turned eighteen to check out, so I didn't have to deal with Child Welfare.

I hadn't talked to Mordechai about it until after her memory had curled up and withered a little, because I knew what he wanted to see. Tears. Loneliness. Fear.

I hadn't felt any of that. I'd mainly wanted to get the place repainted, top to bottom—instead of just constantly repainting my room.

Fresh paint meant control.

The Soos, the family on the other side of my duplex, had lasted in the dumpy little house for almost ten years, despite my ongoing thievery of their craft paint. Probably because they couldn't speak English, so they'd never had to have a conversation with Mom, or now Steve, sober or otherwise. They also hadn't spoken much to me, come to think of it.

I let myself into our side of the house. "Steve?" I called out, my voice unnervingly loud.

There was no response.

SEVEN

Calm down. He's here.

I released the breath I didn't realize I was holding. Steve almost certainly was here. The place smelled like Apple Air-Wicks and had an inhabited feeling. He was probably just passed out somewhere I couldn't easily see.

Still, I crept slowly through the house until I reached the living room, relieved to see it was almost as tidy as I'd left it. I was also relieved to find Steve there, his body large and boneless on the old couch, my mom's afghan reaching all the way up to his chin. The purple fringe draped along his smoothly shaven jawline, and his dark, flawless skin, glowing faintly blue in the reflection from the TV, made him almost look like royalty, though his slackly open mouth and the line of drool glistening at the corner ruined that effect. Still, he looked peaceful, I thought. Happy, kind of.

It was nice.

The kitchen had dishes out on the counter, so I stopped there, taking the five minutes needed to quietly clear every surface and load the dishwasher. Each dish I put away made me feel better, but I knew I was stalling. Still, the routine of cleaning things and tucking them into their proper place in every room I passed, had its purpose. It reminded me that I had some control over my surroundings. Control over Steve, even, who seemed more childlike when he woke to a clean space, and whose breathy snores I could now hear in quiet counterpoint to the sound of running water, clinking plates. Control over myself.

But eventually everything was cleaned and put away. I couldn't run the vacuum, because that definitely would wake up Steve. I had other stuff I needed to handle, anyway. Now that Steve was back onsite, it was time.

I jogged up the stairs lightly, gaining speed as I went. The duplex had two bedrooms and one bath, and Steve's bedroom door stood open. His room was spotless, the bed untouched, and I withstood the urge to go in and mess something up ever so slightly, just so it looked lived-in. Steve had occupation issues when it came to bedrooms. I had no idea what'd happened to him in one, but it'd been bad.

That was why he didn't sleep in Mom's old room. I was pretty sure.

It didn't bother me that he'd moved to the couch after the first week. He said he preferred it, so, okay. We didn't talk about it. Things had been strange with me at night for several months now, so I was glad for the space. Besides, Steve drank hard, partied hard—was almost certainly into some sketchy stuff, but he'd never smelled wrong to me. So far as I could tell, he had two hobbies: playing the newest and loudest online video games with an ever-rotating circle of friends, and collecting the drink coasters of the clubs, bars, and breweries he frequented, probably comforting reminders of drinks gone by, only to leave them scattered around the apartment. The coasters were attached to wildly disparate drinking establishments with names like Whiskey Run, Soul Crypt, Hoppies Brewhouse, and The Descent—but if having them around made him happy, I didn't mind picking them up on the daily.

Still, I could sense there was a fragility to Steve, like something was breaking down his defenses, stripping away his control. Booze and whatever else he was doing could take a lot out of a person, I supposed, so a first-floor couch made sense as a place for him to crash.

I reached my own room and held my breath as I unlocked the door. Steve never really poked around in here, so far as I knew, but having the locks changed out ensured me that he never would. I slipped inside, then shut the door behind me with a quick, decisive click. I locked it once more from the inside and threw the deadbolt for good measure.

Only then did I turn on the light.

Jesus. What I saw on the walls around me was way worse than usual.

Worse and different.

The sheets I'd strung up against the walls had been ripped to the side—some of them actually ripped for real, but most of them simply yanked down and shoved out of the way. The stark white walls were now crisscrossed with black and red paint, all of it dried, thank God, but still stinking to high heaven. The cans themselves were sealed shut, standing in a mini tower by my bed.

I grimaced as I glanced at them. Even after all these years, I still felt bad about the cans.

The first time I'd woken up to graffiti-covered walls, I'd had no idea where the paint had come from. I'd searched everywhere, finally making it out to the back deck where Mom and I had never hung out, no matter what the weather was. There, all lined up along the bottom of the banister separating us from the Soos next door, were fifteen cans of paint, identical in brand to the now-empty ones in my bedroom.

Since that first night, I'd spent probably five bucks a week replacing cans of the Soos' craft paint. Clearly, I'd have to buy a few more.

I blew out a long sigh. As usual, I'd left the fans going all day with the windows open, never mind the drain on electricity. Nevertheless, seeing the words again in the harsh fluorescent light ramped up my anxiety. Worse, this time, I hadn't stopped at words.

Along with the foul litany I'd transcribed onto two of the walls, Iris's demon had made its presence known on the third. In the center of the graffiti-thon, I'd painted a huge, disgusting depiction of a fat, half-human, half-goat creature with a giant penis and snakes for fingers. It was rolling around in a pit filled with what might be money, except my artwork was never the best when I worked in the middle of the night.

"Goddamned freak," I muttered.

Nothing on those three walls was all that unexpected, of course. Curse words, threats, attacks—even horribly grotesque artwork—that, I understood. I had faced down evil, and as soon as my febrile little mind unkinked enough to give it an opening, evil had wanted to claw back.

But the fourth wall...

Grimacing, I turned and forced myself to look at it.

Here, I'd painted a masterpiece.

The figure stretched across nearly the entire wall, rendered in sweeping strokes of black and deep crimson that seemed to shimmer even in the harsh light. It was a man—or something that had once been a man—caught in a moment of exquisite anguish. His head was thrown back, dark hair flowing like liquid shadow, arms spread wide as if embracing the void itself.

But it was his face that stole my breath: beautiful beyond reason, with sharp cheekbones and full lips parted in what could have been ecstasy or agony. His eyes were open wide, fixed on some dark truth I could only guess at, but they stared up with infinite longing, ancient and desperate...and utterly alone. Massive wings unfurled behind him, not the leathery appendages of nightmares, but something magnificent and terrible, feathers that caught light like oil on water.

He was falling—or maybe rising—through a landscape of stars and shadows, his expression one of such profound isolation that my chest tightened with unexpected sympathy.

I'd painted this. Or something inside me had.

But what?

My subconscious? My hidden artistic talent surfacing during a fugue state?

Or something worse?

Unbidden, Mordechai's words flowed back to me. *First, it will try to frighten you. Then it will try to seduce you.*

My heart thudded with something that wasn't quite fear... then anger erupted inside me, a punch of fiery pain.

My eyes widened, and I drew in a deep breath, steadying myself. "Is that what you're trying to do?" I gritted out as I stared at the wall, my voice sounding scratchy and broken to my own ears. "You lying sack of split-personality bullshit, is this some new game you're playing, to get me to fucking *want* you creeping around inside me?"

But there was no response. There'd been no response all weekend to my half-formed questions, my stunted blurts. It was as if Mordechai had dropped a caul of protection over me to keep me from doing something idiotic until I shook off the effects of my first solo exorcism, and...well, now I was finally understanding that he was right.

I was being played by my own sick fantasies.

Worse…I didn't know if I minded it so much.

Without moving, without breathing, I stared at the image on the wall for a long while, knowing what I needed to do but not wanting to do it yet. I stared until I had burned the demon's portrait into my very bones. I stared until I could make fun of myself for staring. This wasn't real, I knew. This was bullshit.

Evil was, ever and always, evil.

And through it all, no murmur of argument surfaced from the depths, which was the clearest indication of all that I had made it through; I had passed the test. My inner voice was taking a dirt nap.

I blew out a long breath.

First things first.

Calmly, I walked to my bed, fishing between the mattresses for the notebook I kept tucked there. Sitting on my bed like some sort of deranged tween with her secret diary, I opened the notebook to a fresh page and began to write.

Ignoring the pitch and roll of my stomach, I wrote out the *Lord's Prayer* three times. Then the *Memorare*. Neither of those was part of the rabbi's canon of prayers, but I figured I should at least give a nod to all the earnest training I'd received at St. Catherine's High School and All Souls Elementary before that. Mom had trusted in Jesus almost as much as she had the bottle, and Mordechai had helped with tuition to those schools, too, I was pretty sure. Although we didn't talk about that, either.

The prayers finished, I wrote out my baptismal vows, vows which I assumed had been made on my behalf when I'd been a baby, but were just as true now, dammit. Once again, not really copasetic with Rabbi Mordechai's current spin on the Almighty, but two thousand years of Jesus-believers couldn't be completely wrong.

With every line, I felt more in control. Not better, really. The words hurt too much for that. But sharper. Focused. I murmured the words aloud as I wrote them.

"I reject Satan, and all his works, and all his empty promises.

I believe in God, the Father Almighty, creator of heaven and earth..."

As I wrote, I paid attention to my body. Was I writing the words correctly? *Yes.* Was I emitting any sort of foul smells or fluids? *No.* Other than the nausea, did I have any physical complaints? *No.*

Was there anything lurking behind my eyeballs, trying to talk to me?

I waited. *No.*

I. Was not. Possessed.

I was just me.

Fucked up, sure. Given to seriously dark and twisted thoughts that sometimes seemed like they took on a life of their own, oh yeah. But me.

Slowly, gradually, relief washed through me. I wasn't corrupted. I wasn't evil. I wasn't harboring something dark and sinister inside me against my will.

I was suffering from bad dreams, anxiety, disgusting thoughts and daydreams, and even a fucked-up kind of literary somnambulism brought on by my part-time job as a ninja warrior demon slayer, that was all. Everyone had to have a way to let off steam. Nighttime auto-writing seemed to be mine.

Ready at last, I set aside the notebook, then worked methodically to clean my room, pulling out new bedsheets to hang on the walls, bundling away the ones too ripped to hide much of anything. I'd sew them up later. I couldn't cover this mess with fabric alone, though. Instead, I pulled out an industrial-sized tub of KILZ, then the smaller cans of plain white paint I kept under my bed. I painted over the walls as quickly as

I could, trying not to pass out in the process. By the time the walls were a uniform white again, I was reeling despite the fans. I stumbled to the door and pulled it open.

And jerked back just as quickly.

"Steve!"

"Yo...fuckkkk, what the hell." Still wrapped in Mom's afghan, he blearily peered past me at the now stark white room, blinking at the smell. His heavily fringed dark eyes swiveled around, not quite tracking. "You could kill yourself in here with all these fumes."

"Sorry. I didn't want to stink up the whole house." I slipped out and shut the door firmly behind me, hearing the lock snick closed. I had the keys in my pocket, and now that I was out of the room, I could smell the booze on him more easily. "How are you feeling?"

"I'm good, man." He let me lead him back downstairs. "I'm off tonight. I got a job, I told you that, yeah?"

"You did," I lied. That explained the shaving, anyway. Despite my nickname for him, Deadbeat Steve really did try to put the function into functional alcoholic. I had to give him credit for that. And between his work at various shit customer service and barback jobs and my hours at the deli, we survived, no matter how many cans of paint I had to buy. "You working tomorrow?"

"I think so." He wandered back into the living room, and I saw the new bottle on the coffee table. Where he got it, I had no idea. Booze seemed to show up in Steve's world the way paint cans did in mine. But I'd learned not to take a bottle away from him, the same way as I had with my mom. They both would drink it 'til it was gone, then eat everything in the house they could keep down. Then they'd go back to work.

I'd always wanted Mom to just be okay for a few more weeks, a month, a year—it was my ongoing mantra. All the way up until senior year, when she'd saved me the trouble of wondering how much longer she would last.

I did miss her, I realized suddenly, in the haze of the paint fumes. I'd needed her, and she had left me.

You know, Steve has a car. That could be helpful.

I blinked at the unexpected thought. Who gave a shit about Steve's car?

My housemate yawned now, rubbing his eyes. "Your buddy Mordechai called me on my cell earlier. Said your phone was dead."

I took it out and checked it. He was right. *Fuck.* "When?"

"Six?" He waved his hand. "Something like that. Where's the remote?"

I left him to the television and retreated to the kitchen, still a little light-headed. My hands shaking for no good reason, I dialed Mordechai's number. It was late, after ten o'clock, but he still picked up on the second ring.

"Delia, you're okay."

"I'm sorry, my phone keeps dying—"

"Your phone..." Mordechai's voice trailed off, as if my words had caused him to remember something. He sighed heavily. "Yes. Of course. We should meet tomorrow if you're not working."

I perked up immediately. "I'm not. I'm off tomorrow." When he didn't say anything right away, I pushed for more information. "Did you get another call? Or is this about those photographs I saw?" I didn't really care, as long as it was something new, different. Anything to get me out of this house. Anything to keep me from coating my walls with disgusting pictures and curses, and now something beautiful and terrible and infinitely worse.

"Tomorrow night—seven o'clock is probably best. They close at nightfall, but we'll be out by then."

"Sure, no problem. Where?" "Close at nightfall" sounded promising, but the rabbi had been walking the streets of this neighborhood for far too long. He sometimes got his past screwed up with his present.

"Holy Angels Cemetery. Wear your amulet, if you would."

Everything inside me froze into a clutch of—what? Fear, maybe. Excitement. Anticipation. But Holy Angels was on the other side of forever, easily a two-hour walk. "You want me to meet you there?" I asked. "Or are you getting a cab or something and want me to come with?"

"What? No, no." Mordechai seemed distracted, like he'd forgotten he was talking to me on the phone. "Seven o'clock will be fine. It's time. It's long past time, really." He blew out a hard breath. "You'll come?"

"Of course, I—"

"Good. I...that's good."

"Mordechai, are you all right? Is this about the photos, and —um, those letters?"

"I'll see you at seven, Delia." He sighed again. "I'll continue to pray over you, too, to keep you safe—"

"Oh, Rabbi Mordechai, you don't have to do that," I murmured in a rush, suddenly ashamed. But he continued as if he didn't hear me.

"—until you can keep yourself safe. 'He will save you from the fowler's snare, and from the deadly pestilence. He will cover you with...'"

In a flash, shame morphed into anger, then indignation. *I don't need your stupid psalms, old man.* Maybe I didn't want to be safe. Maybe I wanted to lean in, not away. To see, to taste, to *know.*

A dark, curling lick of pleasure slithered along my belly, slipping up my spine. It was everything wrong and everything right and everything I wanted and feared—

I blinked hard, shaking myself back to the moment.

Only, I kept shaking. Trembling, really. Cold sweat dripped off my eyelashes. My face felt clammy, wrong.

"Mordechai," I blurted, before I could change my mind. "I, um, I drew something you should know about, I think. Something on my—"

The line went dead.

CHAPTER
EIGHT

The walk to the Holy Angels Cemetery felt longer than it should have. It was six, and the heat of the day was finally beginning to wane. Still, it seemed unusually cold when I slipped into the shadows and weirdly hot every time I came out from the shade and into the full sun. For a Tuesday night, it was a fairly quiet evening. Very few sirens, the traffic fading to a dull hush.

The whole day had seemed wrapped in a cocoon like that. Even Claire had been a relief when she bounced into the deli where I'd picked up a shift at the last minute and treated me like her new bestie. There hadn't been a lot of customers, and she'd seemed brighter than usual. Chummier. She'd offered me another card, but I told her I still had the first. That'd wound her even tighter. She asked a bunch of questions, but I couldn't remember her words so much. Just that she kept talking and talking, raindrops on aluminum siding, clattering, chattering on.

Nosy bitch.

But I didn't mind Claire so much. Not today. Mordechai had a new problem for us to solve. It was a big one, too, if he wasn't going to tell me about it in his office. The little jobs came to him. He went to the big ones, like the Kleins.

And the Kleins had been fun, in their way.

A little too fun?

Was that possible?

I made it to the cemetery a few minutes before seven and admired the old brick wall surrounding it, with the large arched gates that looked like something out of a movie. They didn't build cemeteries like this anymore, which was too bad. You needed a cemetery with a sense of grandeur sometimes.

This one was so old that it actually had a section devoted to people of Jewish descent, and I followed the signs to that section now, the odd chill coming over me again as I slipped in and out of the shade. The deeper I got into the cemetery, the older the markers became, some elaborate, some simple, but all of them steeped in an ancient solitude I felt I was breaking.

I finally came to an open space where I found Mordechai. He was in his long jacket and dark suit, his head covered by his flat-brimmed hat tonight instead of his more usual kippah. He looked like the respectable rabbi I suppose he'd been at some point, but not an outwardly flashy one. He wasn't expecting to see anyone besides me tonight, clearly, not looking like that. I fought the disappointment that curled through me. I really needed to *help* someone. It was almost like a fix that I'd been deprived of too long.

"Delia." Mordechai's voice floated over the open space, and once again, a shiver of fear and something darker lanced through me. I found myself narrowing my eyes at him, instantly distrustful. Why had he brought me to this place if we weren't going to perform an exorcism or even meet with a victim? Why had he wasted three hours of my life just to have a conversation with me?

I halted summarily, raising my voice, though the place was quiet. He had no problem hearing me, I was sure.

"Why here?" I asked. My voice didn't sound quite like my own, and I frowned, hoping he wouldn't notice. And what did it matter where we met? Mordechai had been my friend for going on fifteen years. If he wanted me to meet him in a Jewish cemetery there had to be a good reason.

Mordechai didn't respond, but he did wave me over. He was studying a cemetery marker, and I relaxed a little. Okay, so maybe there was a reason for coming here after all. Could someone have been buried here who was haunting a living person? That would explain it.

Despite my growing freakout, I forced myself to move closer to the rabbi at the far end of the courtyard. Tension mounted inside me with every step, but I didn't stop until I stood next to Mordechai, squinting down at the marker. It was blank.

"Who's buried here?"

"No one, yet," Mordechai said. His hands were clasped in front of him, and he had the demeanor of a man praying. "It was placed in this cemetery years ago but was not needed so quickly. I visit it to remind myself that sometimes, the Creator has different plans for us than we might expect."

"Okay." I could sense there was a reason for all of this, though it wasn't clear to me. And I was growing more nervous, not less, now that I was in Mordechai's presence. "Does your newest call have something to do with this cemetery? Is that why you brought me here?"

"No." Mordechai seemed to shake off whatever he saw on the smooth surface of the gravestone. "I brought you here because it seemed the best place to warn you about what is to come." He gestured. "Walk with me."

I fought my irritation and impatience but fell into step with him. Mordechai thought better when he walked—he'd told me that often enough. Movement centered him, made him feel more in control. How he could *not* be in control in the middle of a freaking Jewish cemetery, I had no idea. These were his people. If he wanted to walk, though, we'd walk.

He didn't talk right away. I was used to that, too. I tried to keep my attention from wandering in and out and through the headstones, but I couldn't resist for long. My gaze chased the shadows and the vines that curved over the ground, vines that seemed to gain hold on some of the older stones, pulling at the rock, grinding it to dust. A sort of curious fascination took hold of me as I marked their progress; nature destroying the edifices of man, time pulling things down, apart. It felt right. It felt good.

I didn't understand why I was shivering.

The strangest part was the silence inside me—no whisper, no taunt, nothing at all. That quiet felt sharper than the wind in the trees, and I hated how much I noticed it.

"You're not wearing your—"

"I'm not, no," I snapped, cutting Mordechai off. I'd hoped he wouldn't ask, but of course he had. I forced my voice into a quieter, gentler tone. "I keep losing it. I'm sorry."

Mordechai didn't question my lie, just sighed a little. That sigh felt like a knife between my ribs, but I couldn't find the damned thing! It wasn't my fault!

"The Hinderer takes many forms in this world, all of them part of God's plan." Mordechai's words were so faint, they almost seemed to be spoken inside my head. I shook myself back to attention, but he hadn't actually asked a question, so no reply seemed appropriate. "He finds ways to whisper into the ears of the faithful, to worm his way into their hearts. To take root in the innocent and profane the sacred. To play upon the prideful and trap them with their own hubris."

"Is this what happened in that old house in the photos?" I

was desperate to focus on that house, that case. Any case. Mordechai now seemed impossibly old to me, and old in a way that marked him as feeble. I didn't want to think of him as feeble. He needed to be strong. Strong enough to take on the job that involved a strange old house that clearly was far away from here, and strong enough to take me with him. Strong enough to take me anywhere that wasn't here.

"The affliction visited upon that house has many layers. From what the son has told me, it has lasted for at least seven years but is now manifesting in more...obvious ways."

I felt my brows lift, though I struggled mightily to keep my voice steady. "What do you mean, layers?"

"Infestation. Oppression. Obsession." Mordechai ticked the words off, a somber litany of evil incarnations sent to plague the righteous, each of them a progressively worse form of demonic work, but not *the* worst. Infestation was the least intrusive, but perhaps the best known: the haunted house. Oppression and obsession preyed upon the minds of actual people. They saw things, heard things, that shouldn't be there... and they grew more and more isolated, confused, depressed. Damaged. But these weren't the terms that made my own heart thump in my chest. Those levels of affliction the rabbi could handle with a phone call sometimes, a visit to the office, or a well-intended prayer. The big house with the flat roof and the strange family didn't just have a ghost in the attic.

"And possession, finally," Mordechai said, sounding mournful. "Possession is the most dangerous of all the Hinderer's work. We cannot always see it for what it is."

"How many demons are there?" This was important to me, for some reason. Mrs. Klein's sister had only one demon inside her, but that wasn't always the case. Still, the most I'd ever heard of was—

"The son couldn't say. At least six separate creatures have

made their presence known, but he has heard the refrains of many more, the voices of a multitude, in fact."

"*Six.*" I didn't even bother hiding the excitement shimmering inside me now. We'd never taken on six before. I suspected that somewhere, in all those binders on his shelves, Mordechai had confronted multiple demons, but six—six surely was a lot. Six was a television series.

Six would be a fucking joy.

We were back to where we'd started in front of the empty gravestone, and I refocused on Mordechai. Once again, I was struck by his age, his fragility. He wasn't a small man, but he seemed more bent-over than he ever had, more unsure. "Mordechai?"

I reached out a hand, but he straightened then, eyeing me with a sudden fierceness. "Everything that is good and right has its time in the eyes of the Almighty, Delia. Everything on this earth has been granted by Him, its beginning and its end."

I frowned. "Okay, but—"

"You came to me as a gift from the heavens, a gift I sorely needed during a time of great trial. A gift, but a test as well. It was a test I didn't pass that first day. Or any day since."

That didn't sound good. "Um, what are you talking about?"

Mordechai looked beyond me then, into the shadows. "It's no longer a battle I can put off fighting, I fear. Perhaps no longer a battle I can fight at all." He sighed, his lips twisting with a hint of bitterness. "I had prayed for more time to prepare you. I just —I needed more time."

"We'll have lots of time." I really didn't want him to devolve into one of his muttering rambles.

Suddenly, though, the strangeness of our location struck me anew. "Why did you bring me all this way if you just wanted to talk about the guy and his photographs? We could have done that back at your office." I looked around. "Wait, is someone buried here who's important to that case? Are there members of the family in this cemetery?"

Still, that didn't make sense. The house had looked old, fancy, and most importantly, far away from any city. Why would a family who lived on some sort of palatial estate have a cemetery plot in the middle of Holy Angels? A curious excitement had taken hold of me as another thought occurred. "Or did someone they hurt get buried here? Is that why we're here, to discover why they're being infested in the first place?"

"There isn't always an easy explanation," Mordechai said. His words sounded too far away though, like he seemed far away, as I searched the names on the worn-out headstones, a thousand thoughts whispering to me at once. "Evil can find its way into even the most righteous of hearts and most sacred of places. And sometimes...it has help."

"Yeah, yeah." I frowned back at him, startled to find him staring at me. "Then why? You had to bring me here for a reason."

He nodded. His gaze not leaving mine, he reached into the pocket of his long jacket and pulled out a carved spiral, one I recognized immediately. "Your shofar," I said. The weirdest riffle of panic sliced through me—panic and anger, too. Mordechai was playing games with me. He'd dragged me two hours out of my way to play *games* with me? "You're going to blow that here? I thought you didn't even believe in it."

Mordechai's smile was grim as he lifted the horn to his lips. "I'm not playing it for my ears."

He blew a single, light, clear note.

The sound pierced the twilight air—loud, raw, accusatory. A call to judgment, I thought fleetingly. A call to fight.

For one heartbeat, the cemetery held its breath.

Then it screamed back.

CHAPTER

NINE

The sound came from everywhere and nowhere—from the ground beneath my feet, from the trees overhead, from inside my own skull. A howling that rattled my bones and made my teeth ache, rage and agony and hunger all twisted together into something that shouldn't exist in the natural world.

I clapped my hands over my ears, but it didn't help. The sound wasn't outside me.

It was inside.

And it was *furious* with outrage.

Pressure closed around my lungs, crushing inward, making it impossible to breathe. The temperature dropped so fast that frost formed on the grass at my feet, spreading outward in crystalline fingers.

Mordechai remained in the center of the small courtyard, shofar still raised to his lips, and his eyes were on me, bright with fire. Not metaphorical bolts of strength or power, but *actual* flames, golden and terrible, burning away everything false to leave only truth behind.

Shadows peeled away from the gravestones like living

things—twisting and ripping up from the earth. They lunged at Mordechai with too many angles and edges, converging on him, swallowing him whole.

"Go, Delia!" His voice came out wrong—so wrong—layered and harmonized, like a dozen voices speaking in unison. The flames in his eyes blazed brighter. "Run! Get as far away as you can—go *now!*"

I didn't think. I didn't question.

I fled.

Arms churning, mouth agape and gasping for air, I stumbled out of the cemetery almost wildly, sure the cops were on their way. There was so much screaming! So much fire, pain, and fury!

I ran the whole way back from Holy Angels cemetery, my mind blanked with terror. Smoke clogged my nose, and explosions jarred my ears, a terrible, racking pain clutching my throat like a vise. I fell down more than once, the last time on the sidewalk leading up to my house. One of the Soos saw me through the window, but no one came outside. Just as well. I gagged and retched on my own front steps, reeking so strongly of burning sulfur I kept checking myself for scorch marks.

Eventually, I dragged myself inside and shut the door.

Steve was asleep on the couch again, dead to the world, but messy, human, and real.

Real.

Everything got quiet after that. No voices shouted anywhere. No people, no smoke. I tiptoed through the house, dumped my smoky clothes in the laundry, then retreated to my freshly sterilized room. I opened the door, the smell of the dried white paint calming and familiar, then dragged myself toward my bed.

. . .

I passed out before I reached it.

The TV came on downstairs, blaring at top volume.

"What the fuck?!"

Steve's protest was so freaked out that I practically vibrated off the floor of my bedroom, jerking upright and half-stumbling against the bed. I bolted for my bedroom door and yanked it open. "Steve?"

"What the *fuck*!"

I clattered down the stairs, my steps in time to Steve's staccato fury as he crashed around the living room, apparently looking for the remote. He found it and stabbed at it as I bolted into the room, but I caught enough of what was on screen that I screeched "Back on!" as it winked out of sight.

"Fucking so *loud*, man," Steve groused, but he turned the TV back on, scrolling the sound all the way down as I stared in disbelief.

On the screen was an outdated picture of Rabbi Mordechai, grinning self-consciously at the camera, juxtaposed over a live feed of Holy Angels Cemetery—only it was now cordoned off with police tape.

Steve stooped his long, lean body forward, squinting. "Hey, isn't that—"

"Shut it."

Together we stood and watched the smoothly perfect news anchor of the local TV station explain that Rabbi Mordechai Schneider had been discovered at the Holy Angels Cemetery after a loud commotion had drawn the attention of neighboring residents. Nine-one-one had been called, and he'd been rushed to the nearest hospital, only to be pronounced dead at the—

I didn't realize I'd backed up until I smacked against the wall of the living room, the sheer solidity of it the only thing that told me this wasn't a dream. "Dead?" I rasped through parched lips, a swollen tongue. "But—how? Who?"

Steve shook his head, then swung his face toward me. I stared at him, shocked by the empathy, the real emotion in his deep brown eyes. Something skittering and nervous curled in my belly. He looked—weirdly sober. "Shit, Delia. I'm so sorry."

He might have tried to step toward me, I didn't know. I stiffened up against the wall, wanting more than anything to crawl inside it like Mrs. Klein's sister had done. To get away, just get away.

How could Mordechai be dead?

Steve said something else, but my feet were moving now, and I didn't hear his words, didn't hear the TV. I stumbled out of the house and onto our little stoop, my mind balking and stuttering like a car that was slowly running out of gas and hadn't realized it yet. I stepped down the few steps of our rental and onto the sidewalk. It was still warm out, but dark now, of course. It would be dark at eleven o'clock. It was supposed to be dark. Just like it was supposed to be warm, and it was supposed to be Tuesday, and the only thing that wasn't right was—

"You all right?"

I jolted, shocked to see I wasn't alone on the sidewalk. The short, dark-eyed Mrs. Soo stood in front of me. She was old, but I couldn't tell how old, her burnished skin and bright eyes making her seem almost timeless as she stared up at me, with a soft, sad smile and softer, sadder eyes. She wore a thin white T-shirt and blue pants, and she put a frail hand on my arm.

"You all right?" she said again, in that confused way of someone trying out a language they weren't too sure about.

I stared at her fingers on my sleeve, tiny, gnarled fingers that suddenly seemed wrong to be touching me. Like anything that could touch me would be destroyed, defiled.

"I'm fine," I said roughly, and shook her off, stepping

around her like she had some sort of disease. Or I did. "I'm sorry. Thank you. I'm fine. I have to go."

Then I was walking, moving faster now. Down the street and through the alley and into one of the forlorn city parks with its tiny jungle gym and swing sets on patchwork pieces of concrete. A place I used to be afraid to come to at night, scared of everything that was out there in the shadows. Now I just stared at the swing, then up at the stars.

It was like I was the only person in the universe, now forever and completely alone.

"What happened, Mordechai?" I whispered.

His house, I thought suddenly. His pretty little house and his messy, terrible office. Would I even be able to see it again? How would I know where to go—where to see him? How could he possibly be dead, and what did I do now? I didn't know if he had family, not real family. I mean, he had a brother, nephews and nieces, and even grandnieces and grandnephews in Missouri. All their pictures were on his office fridge, slowly shifting over the years as toddlers turned into messy-haired kids, and the messy-haired kids turned into gangly, awkward teenagers. He had people who still knew him at the Rockdale Temple too.

The temple. I would go there. Of course, I would go there. I would go there, and they would tell me what I could do, where I could see him. How I should act. How I should be. They would tell me.

The hole in my heart didn't shrink with that decision, however. It didn't go away.

I shoved my hands into my hoodie pockets, chilled despite the warm night. My breathing wasn't right, too shallow, too quick, like I wasn't bleeding enough oxygen from the air. But I had to try and remember. Slowly, I shuffled over to the ancient slide, and sat down on its surface, everything still and silent around me. The night held its breath even as I fought to fill my lungs. Fought and failed.

What happened to Mordechai?

I frowned fiercely, trying to recall, and my headache came back with a raging force. Not enough caffeine today, I thought. Not enough water. Too many fumes.

Remember!

Pain lanced through me as I hunched over on the edge of the small slide. My nails cut into my palms, but it was no use—nothing came back to me. The police said there'd been no indication of foul play, according to the TV reporter. So he hadn't been shot, hadn't committed some sort of spontaneous suicide. He'd simply been a rabbi with a shofar in the middle of a Jewish cemetery, dead as a flipping doornail.

Had he even died right away? Or had he been still gasping for breath, still reaching for me, only I was nowhere to be found? Instead, I'd been running through the night, running so hard and so fast I could still feel the jarring strikes of my feet against the pavement. Had he even reached for me? Had I known he was dying?

Dying!

How could he possibly be dead?

A new fear slid through me. What if they were secretly looking for Mordechai's killer right now? What if the killer was me? What if I had somehow managed to kill Mordechai without touching him, or even remembering it?

How could he be dead?

"Pull it together," I hissed to myself, looking up suddenly to see if anyone was there, anyone who was listening to me. I had to remember more of what had happened tonight in case the cops intended to talk to me. Though why would they talk to me? I hadn't done anything wrong.

I stared into the dark shadows of the playground, hearing

the echo of children who'd run and laughed here, seeing them in flashes and spurts, their energy still radiating off the monkey bars and slide. I wasn't afraid of anything waiting for me in the dark, I realized grimly. But I was still more afraid than I wanted to be.

What had I done?

And then after all that silence, after all those empty hours without a sound—a whisper from deep inside me finally spoke, flowing through me like poisoned silk.

Nothing, beautiful Delia, it whispered. *Nothing.*

My lips twisted. It was right. I'd done nothing.

And Mordechai was dead.

TEN

J ewish funerals took place within twenty-four hours of death, so I couldn't wallow for long, no matter how much I wanted to.

Mordechai's funeral sucked.

Everyone said the right words, but all I heard was the silence where he should have been. The prayers, the platitudes, the murmured condolences—they slid off me like rain on concrete. I kept my arms wrapped tightly around myself, gripping my elbows as if I could hold in everything that was threatening to spill out.

I knew what I wanted to do next—the only thing I wanted —though I hated myself for it. I wanted to read Mordechai's newest case file. The one that discussed the big house with the flat roof. There were six incidents of possession in that file. Six. A family that seemed to haunt its own photographs. What had happened there to make demons feel so welcome?

And why did it matter to me?

Mordechai had been the exorcist, not me. He was the one God worked through. I was a stunt double at best, a fraud at worst, sneering at victims like Iris even as I tried to save them.

The memory of my own voice in Mrs. Klein's house still made my stomach turn. But that file, this case that wasn't even my case, was all that I could hold onto, with Mordechai gone. It was the only thing that gave structure and form to the world.

It was all I had left.

The street to Mordechai's place was already crowded when I turned down it. Cars lined the driveway under the heavy trees. Sad faces going in, sad faces coming out. I didn't want to see any of them. I didn't want another ceremony where I didn't belong.

Head down, lost in my thoughts, I swung around the corner and collided with someone—a tall man in a long black coat. Not an old man, I thought. Not a boy. Too close. Usually, I was more careful.

"Sorry," I muttered.

"No, no, my fault," he said easily.

I looked up, and up a little more—and froze. For the first time in days, the thing inside me went silent as the world snapped into razor-sharp focus. A face from a grainy photograph stood in front of me, suddenly real.

"It's you," I whispered.

I was super subtle like that.

"Sorry?" the guy asked with a mild smile, sounding exactly like I expected he would. His voice was high and clear, as open as his expression, and hinted at education and wisdom and more than a little weariness, despite his hope.

I...he was kind of cute, actually.

With that traitorous thought, something inside me woke up. Something with claws and teeth and rage, sending bolts of jagged pain punching through my lungs, my stomach, burning bile climbing up my throat. *What the fuck is this?*

My mouth twitched despite the pain. The voice inside me was asking what this was...not who.

Because we both recognized the boy-man from Mordechai's case file.

The pain finally escalated strong enough to make me gasp, and I lurched away from the guy and hurried up the driveway, now forced to act like I was actually going inside to sit shiva.

What was he doing here though?

I'd called in advance to find out if attending Mordechai's funeral was even allowed for someone who wasn't Jewish, and some kind-voiced person had assured me that, of course it was, had even explained how to show my respects in full without looking like a complete moron. But I'd never intended to do any of it. All those clumps of dirt raining down on Mordechai's casket had been more than enough. I suppressed a full-body shiver.

"Hey, I'm sorry," the guy piped up behind me, startled and hopeful. Too loud. Too hopeful. "Are you Delia Thompson?"

My traitorous feet stopped moving, rooting me to the ground as the guy came back up to me. This time, I looked at him with nothing but clinical interest, and the pain winked out.

He wasn't a college kid anymore, Mordechai was right. He was a straight-up adult—hell, maybe he *was* older than me. Or maybe grief had aged him beyond his calendar years—

Who gives a fuck? Answer the question.

"Oh," I said, trying for a smile as I shoved down my still-fuming inner voice. "That's who I am, yes. I—I don't think we've met?"

"Gosh, no. I'm sorry."

Gosh?

The guy held out a hand, and despite his sophisticated haircut, expensive clothes, and intelligent eyes, he seemed adorably awkward. His eyes were blue—startlingly blue, like open skies and cool waters and...and something I didn't think I'd ever find my way back to again.

My gut tightened sharply with a warning jab of irritation, so I forced my focus down to his hand, anything but his eyes. The hand was long and sturdy and tanned, with slender fingers. A good hand. A strong hand. Warming mine on this suddenly far colder day. His hand was too warm, actually, too steady.

And there it was again—that flicker of story I shouldn't know, shouldn't want to know, waiting under his skin.

"I'm Maxwell Graham," he said as we shook. "Max, really."

I blinked up at him and pulled my hand away. From the way he'd said it, clearly, Maxwell here had thought I would recognize his name, but I didn't. I didn't know anything about him or his disappearing family in the giant house with the flat roof and the horses all around.

"Um," I said, going for innocent. "Were you a friend of Mordechai's?"

"What? Oh." Max blushed, and finally, I did allow myself to focus on his face. He was as cute as he'd been in Mordechai's photos—tall and lean, his angular features cut with sharp cheekbones and softened by a slightly full mouth.

That mouth tightened as he spoke again. "Sorry, no. I— well, I've been trying to meet with him. I looked him up on the internet, found him, I mean, from articles he'd written. Stories about him."

I nodded. I wasn't really into the whole body of work about Mordechai available online. He'd always been super careful not to mention me, and besides that, he'd been around for a lot longer than my decade and change with him. Any of his articles I'd found online I'd already read in his office at one point or another.

"We talked once, on the phone, after I contacted him," Max continued. "He seemed interested. I sent an entire package..." He looked at me expectantly. "Anyway, I hadn't heard from him, and then I read online yesterday that he *died*."

He sure did.

"Yes!" I said quickly, startled by the smugness of the voice inside my head. "Yes, that caught us all by surprise."

Max glanced sharply at me. "They're sitting shiva or whatever in there. I've never felt more lost in my life."

That made me smile, despite everything. "It can be a little overwhelming. They're very nice to people who aren't Jewish, though, or at least they have been to me." Suddenly, that anomaly struck me. "You're not Jewish?"

His smile was self-deprecating. "Like I said, I've never felt more lost."

"But then—why a rabbi?" It really was none of my business, but curiosity shot through me. "Catholics kind of corner the market on, ah, Mordechai's specialty. And he wasn't even a rabbi anymore."

"Yeah, well. Let's just say good help is hard to find." Max's words were light, but there was no mistaking the pain in his eyes. Pain and fatigue.

I recognized it, of course, the curious mix of defeat, bewilderment, fear, and horror, tempered with the faintest twist of hope.

Hope was always the most pathetic.

And it wasn't surprising that Max hadn't found anyone to help him in the Catholic church. Demon possession was seriously old-school stuff, and not many of the current crop of Roman Catholic priests thought enough of it anymore to go through the training to become exorcists. They also had *so* many rules. Mordechai hated rules even more than he hated demons, I sometimes thought. He didn't care who he helped. It was just what he did.

I cleared my throat. "I'm sorry he didn't get back to you in time. He was a good man."

"He was." Max stared at me hard, seemed to come to some

decision. "So, I was given your name by one of the ladies inside. She *whispered* it."

I grimaced. "Whispered?"

He nodded, studying me with his clear light eyes, like I was some mystery he was supposed to solve.

My stomach clenched again. *Good luck with that.*

"I was standing there, not sure of whether I should sit or stand," he continued. "She came up to me and asked me how I knew the rabbi. I said I'd contacted him for help—nothing more than that—and she patted my hand and smiled, and told me to find, well, you."

"She's got the wrong idea. Sorry." I turned away as Max reached out for me, his hand connecting with my arm. Once again, a jolt of awareness moved through me at the touch of his fingers, half dangerous, half reassuring. I didn't know this Max or his electrical current, but a part of me definitely wanted to find out more about him. The other part, the darker, twisting part, wanted him to disappear into a hole. And the two kept changing sides.

"No, I'm the one who should apologize," he said quickly. "I don't mean to be rude, but my family's in pretty desperate straits. Based on everything I read, I was convinced that Rabbi Mordechai could help."

I sighed. "He probably could have helped. He was really good at...what he did."

Max ducked his head, clearly grateful for my discretion, but I could sense his deep, overwhelming need as well. His need for someone—*anyone*—to believe him. How many times had Mordechai lectured me on this, on how the affliction of possession affected not only the individual possessed, but everyone around him or her? That just as much care and grace was needed for the supporters as for the sufferer?

I sighed, trying to channel my inner Mordechai. "There are

other people who do that work," I said gently. "I'm sure if you go to Rockdale Temple and ask, they can help."

"No." His mouth tightened, and his expression turned sour. "I'm tired of the search. Really tired. Half the 'experts' I've contacted think I'm making it up somehow. And I'm convinced half of them are stringers for *Paranormal Investigators*. We're not a sideshow, we're people. Good people. And what's happening to us is real." He looked at me fiercely, as if I was going to disagree with him. When I didn't, he glanced away. "I—I don't want to search anymore."

I bit my lip, nodded. "I totally get that."

"But you can *help*." Maxwell turned back, newly urgent. "That lady said you helped Rabbi Mordechai. That he'd chosen you or whatever to be his assistant, and that you actually went to her house on your own, and you *helped*. Can you come out and, I don't know—take a look? At the...at what's going on?"

"No," I said firmly, never mind the thrill that leapt within me. "No, really. I just helped Mordechai out on occasion. I didn't do anything, not really." I shoved down my own objections to my false modesty. Now was not the time for me to show off. This guy needed help. Serious, authenticated, *consecrated* help.

"But that woman and her sister—"

"That was a mistake. I shouldn't have done that."

Max didn't seem to be listening to me anymore, though. The hope was burning stronger in his eyes, and I knew I'd been the one to fan it. "Look—I just need someone to come out. To look at it. If you can tell me the right words to say, I can at least have a leg to stand on when I go find whoever Mordechai's replacement is going to be."

He scowled up at the rabbi's tidy house. He probably had no idea about the office in the back, all of Mordechai's binders. A lifetime's work in a clapboard shack with a rickety air conditioner and threadbare chairs. "Assuming he's going to get a replacement, that is. I'm going to have to start over."

He looked back at me, panic rabbiting behind his eyes. "Do you know how hard it is to try to *explain* this to people? To tell them what's going on?"

"Look, I'm sorry." I made my words as gentle as I could, but the more I saw Max's hope, his desperation, the more nervous I got. "I'm not your girl. I can't help you with this."

"Ten thousand dollars."

The words were so unexpected, so bald and unvarnished in the soft morning air, that I could only blink at him. "What?"

"Ten thousand dollars." He said it flatly, dismissively. "Just to come out and take a look at the house. Give your unprofessional, unauthorized opinion, but maybe write up something official-looking that I can take to a new...to someone who can help. That's all I'm asking for."

I couldn't keep from staring. Ten grand. Rent for months. Gas. Food other than ramen and frozen peas, for at least a little while. The weight of it dragged on me harder than Max's stare. "You'd pay me ten thousand dollars—"

"Yes. I've got the money, don't think I don't. I already explained that to Mordechai."

"He didn't take money for his work."

"Well, he should have."

Take the job.

The voice had stopped clawing at me, punching in fury. Maybe it had realized that Max wasn't the enemy—he was a guy with demons to exorcise.

Take the job, it hissed again.

I shoved the inner voice down as deep as I could push it while Max's smile veered a little more toward confidence. "Think about it, okay?" he pressed. "I'll be in town for another day or so anyway, trying to figure out what the hell to do. I don't even know where to go at this point, who to talk to. Call me." He handed me a slip of paper—an actual honest-to-God business card—that had his name and telephone number imprinted in gleaming raised letters.

I stared at it, dumbfounded. What was up with all the business cards this week? "You have your own card?" I managed.

"I also have ten thousand dollars. So please. Call me."

CHAPTER

ELEVEN

It was Saturday, a few minutes after seven. Mordechai's key felt wrong in my hand—too light for what I was about to do. But I didn't have a choice anymore.

I needed answers.

Do you?

The return of the voice in my head made my hands sweat, my heart jerk against my ribs. I buried my fear under the wall of scripture Mordechai had constantly been chanting, pulling a few of my favorites together in the mantra that had become my constant companion.

"You—are not—sovereign," I gritted out beneath my breath as I hurried toward Mordechai's backyard office. Saying the words aloud gave them form and strength, and the pain that raked through me felt like vindication, not abuse. It was proof I was pissing off the thing inside me. Proof I could win.

The main house looked empty. No mourners roamed around, and there probably wouldn't be many people here today, given the rules for shiva on a Saturday. So there was no one to hear my desperate, fiercely muttered rebuke.

"You are not many. You are not God. You are a slithering, disgusting parasite. The Lord is One."

The thing inside me hissed and writhed, retreating as I stalked up to Mordechai's backyard office, but I knew mere words wouldn't keep it at bay forever. I unlocked the door and slipped inside, then paused, savoring all the familiar scents, the memories. Tomato soup, basil, crackers. Warm shawls and the faint hum of the air conditioner—Mordechai. The room felt like he'd just stepped out, and I sagged a little, grief washing through me.

The last few days had been hell. The pressure inside me had changed—expanded, as if Mordechai's passing had allowed it to grow bigger, fuller, more intrusive—poking into parts of my brain and body that before had been strictly off limits.

For the most part, I fought it successfully, punching it back with loud, delirious music I played through headphones borrowed from Steve, drowning it with prayers that scraped against my throat with every word.

But sometimes, when I wasn't paying attention, it would find something new to entertain it. My hand would drift over my skin without me consciously directing it. My nerves would prickle in a long, intimate shiver down my spine. I'd huff short, panicked breaths for no reason, catching the attention of anyone around me. And my eyes were darker, deeper and more crazed looking, every time I caught sight of them in a passing mirror.

I couldn't run away from it, I knew. I'd spent over half my life with a fucking *exorcist*. Whatever this thing was, however it had gotten inside me, it couldn't have been there long— Mordechai would have seen it. He'd noticed something was wrong only days before he died. Which meant I was still me. Mostly me. I could fight this using the same tools he had.

I could get this thing out of me.

I blew out a long, shaky breath, going immediately to Mordechai's desk and snagging his copy of the Sefer Tehillim. The slim book of psalms made my skin itch, and I grimaced against the spurt of pain as I shoved it in my backpack. Touching holy things was starting to seriously suck. The book felt heavier than it should, like it was resisting me. Or I was resisting it, which seemed worse. This sort of reaction was only going to get more intense, I suspected. I didn't have much time.

I scanned the room a second time, because I wasn't just here for my own personal demon. If I wanted to take on Max's job and score his ten grand, I needed a lot more details on his case than I had glimpsed during Mordechai's hasty re-filing job. I needed everything I could get.

Unfortunately, the Graham file wasn't on Mordechai's desk. It wasn't in the usual paper stacks, either. I finally found it in the front of the file cabinet, like he'd meant to put it away and couldn't quite do it. Why file it at all if Max was coming back?

I spread everything on the table, poring over each page. Money showed in the photos—hair, clothes, posture, horses. Nobody looked possessed, though. They looked rich. I mean, the grandma was a little rough around the edges, but that was how ancient grandmas looked: startled by mortality, frozen in mid-wtf face. A teen girl vanished from later photos. Max showed up off and on, earnest and more competent-looking the older he got. No grandpa, though. There was never a grandpa. Unless he was behind the camera?

Mordechai's "notes" were his usual chaos, of course: under-lines, circles, symbols. Unfortunately, there was no accompanying Rosetta Stone, which I seriously could have used. Still, it was a fair amount of information. There was a lot I could use here. I copied Max's letter and a few photos, lingering over the flat-roof house and the smiling older couple with windburned cheeks. Staff, I decided. Not family.

"Desperate straits," I murmured, remembering Max's phrasing. Who talked like that? Rich people. Also, this house was rocking six separate demons, according to Mordechai. What did you do to roll out a welcome mat for six?

The copier thunked to life. Several hasty pages later, I tucked my new copies in my back pocket and started shoving the original sheets back into the drawer...then saw another file folder directly three tabs back.

DELIA THOMPSON.

My name. Mordechai's block letters. Stark and official.

With hands that were shaking for no good reason, I pulled the folder out. It was newer than the ones behind it, its crisp edges folded short and squat, like it was meant to hold a crapload more documents than normal.

Only there wasn't a single scrap of paper in it.

"What the—"

The exterior door to Mordechai's office rattled loudly, making me jump. I shoved the empty folder under a paper stack, slid the drawer shut, and shot around the desk as the door opened.

We both froze.

Because, for one thing, I was technically trespassing. And for the second, the woman in front of me was a cop.

"Are you Delia Thompson?" she asked, smiling. Not a sneaky smile, or even a stern one. Just steady. Five-eight, compact, tight bun, scuffed shoes. TV-ready uniform, real-world eyes.

"Yes, I am. I have a key," I said hastily. "I'm a friend of—was a friend of—wait. How do you know who I am?"

"Rabbi Mordechai's nephew mentioned you. He didn't know you had a key, though." She smiled, smelling faintly of paperwork and deli wraps. "I'm Officer Hernandez, and I'm following up on the rabbi's passing."

"Why?" I blurted, hating how sharp it came out. "What happened to him? The news said it was a heart attack."

"May I come in?" she asked, never mind that this wasn't my place.

I stepped aside, surrendering the entryway into Mordechai's inner domain. "I mean, of course. Sure."

She took off her hat—a trick to relax people they'd probably taught her in cop school—and palmed it by the brim. She instantly seemed less imposing, so I guess it worked.

"You spent a fair amount of time with him, right?" she asked. "His nephew said you were close."

I lifted my brows. What exactly did the nephew know about me? Had he read the mystery file? "I did, yes. We were friends."

I realized belatedly how weird that might seem, so I dumped more revelations over the first, to muddy up the mix. "Mordechai first knew my mom, and he helped me get into All Souls. Now, well, I'm...working through college one class at a time. It's kind of slow going."

Her glance said: obviously. I flushed a little but didn't say anything more.

"Were you with him the night he died?"

The urgency to lie to her was almost unbearable. No one had seen me. We'd been in a freaking cemetery. At night. Alone. How weird was that going to look? Probably pretty damned weird.

Tell her the truth. See where this goes.

I pursed my lips, questioning the value of listening to a demonic entity on this topic, then launched in. "I was. But earlier. I'd left the cemetery before he—before he got sick. Or died. Or—God." I shook my head, tears somehow springing up out of nowhere that I refused to let fall. "I should have been there, but he told me to leave, so I left."

"Anyone see you?"

"No." Suddenly, all my years of watching cop shows caught up to me. Did I need a lawyer? "Sorry. I know that's probably not helpful. He was alone when I left," I said again. "Praying. The way he did."

"Had he injured himself earlier in the day?"

"What?" The sudden question threw me, and I frowned at her. "Oh. No. Not that I could see anyway."

Hernandez's brows lifted. "He hadn't cut his face? Hurt his hands?"

"No! No. I told you, he was fine." My voice rose a little. "There wasn't a mark on him."

Officer Hernandez didn't say anything for a second, and I leaned forward. "What happened to him, really?" I fixed her with a stare, my need to know so great it practically boiled out of me. "How was he hurt?"

Something in my face either convinced Hernandez I was telling the truth, or she simply wanted to play me a little bit longer. "There was a wound on his forehead that, due to the blood loss, seems to have occurred slightly before his death," she said. "And his fingers were blistered. Like he'd burned them."

I frowned at her. A wisp of the rabbi's cracked hands flickered in my memory, though I couldn't swear it was real. "Burned them how?"

"You didn't notice anything wrong with his hands?" she asked again.

I shook my head. I tried to remember Mordechai that night. It had only been five days ago, but it felt like a decade had passed. He'd been praying, his hands folded. When we'd walked, his hands had been folded as well.

"He generally walked with them clasped. That's just what he did. But if he'd burned them, they would have been wrapped up or something, right? Protected. There was nothing like that."

"How was he otherwise?"

"He was fine, I told you that. We met, we talked, we walked around the cemetery for a little bit, and then he told me to leave."

"Why did he tell you to leave?"

"Um, maybe because he was tired of talking to me?" I felt an uncanny urge to laugh. Something tugged loose within me, knowledge about her I didn't want. She'd lost someone once too, I thought. She didn't feel sorry for me, exactly, but she did feel sad. Wandering around the office, she asked a few more questions—easier ones now. What we did when we met, what else we'd talked about, if he'd ever taken me anywhere. She seemed pretty much willing to believe my answers. I spoke more about going to All Souls, how Mordechai had helped get me a scholarship to UIC, and that seemed to reassure her. As if God was looking out for me somehow, and I wasn't simply the victim of some weird old man. Or, worse, that the weird old man wasn't my victim.

"Well, thank you," she said eventually, turning to me. She put on her hat again and held out her hand. I shook it automatically, and I didn't miss it when her gaze fell to my wrists, my fingers.

I held up both of them for her inspection. "You're welcome to look me over. I honestly didn't hurt him. I'll take a lie detector test or whatever—"

Hernandez only smiled. "No, no, nothing like that. It's just —there was a word dug into the ground. Part of a word anyway."

My stomach clenched. "What word?"

Hernandez consulted her notes. "We could only make out some of the letters. P-A-L-E...something. The rest was scuffed away."

The thing inside me froze—then retreated completely,

leaving me wobbly with newfound freedom. "Pale?" I asked quickly. "Like the color?" The phrase 'Behold a pale horse?' shot through my mind, a snippet from Revelations. That was strictly Christian territory, not Jewish, but Mordechai wasn't one to give a shit about that. Had he been trying to send me a message?

My demon remained silent, but Hernandez only shrugged.

"Could be. Or part of a longer word. Palestine? Paleontology?" She waved off those ideas, giving me a wry smile. "We'll probably never know. Either way, there were no indications that Rabbi Mordechai had written it—no dirt on his hands, just blisters."

"Oh." I frowned, deflated. For the life of me, I couldn't remember another biblical reference to pale. Why had Mordechai used his last bit of strength to write it?

"But your nails are all clipped—the dirt would have been gone, but something dug that deep would have broken at least a few nails, unless you had them professionally manicured."

I snorted. "I'm not really the manicure type."

"No, I can see that." Hernandez looked at me as if she were measuring each of my words, trying to find the balance of bullshit in them. "You said you two met when you were ten years old?"

"Yeah." I offered my best "My how the time flies" grimace but didn't trust myself to say anything more.

She didn't give me much of a chance, anyway, moving straight into her next question. "You went with him on his visits to, ah, exorcise demons?"

So she did know about that. "Sometimes." I nodded, resisting the urge to cross my arms over my chest. I read somewhere that when you did that, it looked like you were trying to hide something. I didn't want to tuck my hands in my pockets either, because surely that also meant something bad. Instead, I gestured to the sitting room where she stood, looking once again too big for the space. "Sometimes people just came here, and he helped them."

"And you were present for those as well. I did a little research about exorcisms. You working as his assistant seems… unusual."

"Not for him," I told her truthfully. "I mean, I stayed out of the way, of course, but yeah. It was like a doctor's appointment, but not really a private thing unless people wanted it to be. Sometimes it was better to have more people around."

"Fair enough." She looked again at all the shelves. "I was kind of curious to see if he fell in here."

I frowned at her. "Fell? Oh. The mark on his head." I studied the casually cluttered room. "Possibly?"

"Possibly," she agreed. She blew out a long breath, rocking back on her feet. "Sure looks like there's a lot of Jewish demons out there."

I refocused on her. "Oh—there are a lot of demons, sure. But they aren't, like they don't…" I frowned, trying to explain. "It wasn't only Jewish people who came to Mordechai, that's not who he was." Now I did shove my hands in my pockets, grief creeping up on me unexpectedly. "He helped anyone who showed up at his door."

"Including you?"

I looked up at her sharply, something else curling inside me now, next to the grief. Surrounding it. Something that felt a lot like anger, though I couldn't let this woman see it. She didn't know me; she shouldn't judge me. But I didn't say any of that. After all, I'd already told her about the rabbi. About how he'd been a good role model, gotten me into school. How he'd always been there. Until suddenly, he wasn't.

He's not coming back. Ever.

My heart shriveled at the parasite's unexpected return.

"Especially me," I said.

"Well, I appreciate your time." She fished in her pocket, pulled out a card. "Please don't hesitate to reach out to me, if you think of anything I should know. It's not an official investigation, but—it's bugging me. His injuries."

"I appreciate it," I said, holding up the card. "If you learn anything, please call me. I don't have a card, but..."

She pulled out a cop-standard notebook and wrote down my number. When she got to the door, she looked back. "You said you have a key?"

"Mordechai gave it to me," I said. "After he fell asleep with a candle burning."

Her mouth tilted. "I'll keep that our little secret, then. Just lock up when you leave."

She stepped out into the morning and was gone.

CHAPTER

TWELVE

On the way home, I stopped at the library. I had a junky old laptop that was one of Mordechai's hand-me-downs, but half the time it didn't work, and the other half it was too slow. The community public library was on the way to my house from Mordechai's, so it worked out. It wasn't like Steve was going to miss me. I suspected he'd already left the duplex again, destined for another couch.

I settled into the workstation, glad I was one of only a few patrons in the computer room. I cleaned the keyboard with one of the hand wipes at the corner of the table and pulled out the copies I'd pocketed from Mordechai's office.

Officer Hernandez hadn't objected when I offered to leave her to her review of the rabbi's files, silently praying she wouldn't find my file but thinking even if she did, it was empty—and possibly had always been that way. Could be I was just that boring.

Could be.

She asked if Mordechai's nephew knew I was there, and I

honestly told her I didn't think he knew I existed. She didn't seem surprised, just smiled a little sadly. I think she'd started to like me, or at least was willing to believe I hadn't somehow caused the rabbi's death. Either way, I marked that as a reasonable step forward in our relationship. I hoped she didn't search too hard, though. If the nephew found her in there, would he let her see the files? Wasn't there some sort of rabbi confidentiality thing in play?

The pages of Max's letter felt solid and reassuring beneath my fingers as I smoothed them out on the table. I scanned his neat, close-cropped handwriting. *Handwriting.* That startled me. He'd written an honest-to-God letter, not a text, not an email. Who did that? And the photos, too, had been printed. Not sent digitally. No one would have accused Mordechai of being a tech wiz, but he had email, for fuck's sake. Who wrote letters anymore?

The story was strangely sparse, though the letter was three pages long. Max had come back for this past Christmas to find things had become very strange at ye olde homestead. Grandma had become a recluse, Aunt Emily had moved in, and Mom and Dad weren't speaking to each other. Max's younger brother— younger by quite a fair margin, like more than twenty years— had taken to showing up in doorways like some sort of horror movie kid.

And then, of course, all the horses had been shot.

"Jesus." I sat back in my seat, then leaned forward again, hitting Google to figure out where Max and his clan called home. The estate or whatever you wanted to call it was outside of a small town innocuously called "Hooperton," about three hours away by car if there was no traffic.

Like most places outside Chicago's city limits, public transportation was virtually nonexistent. There were no buses to

Hooperton. You could take an Uber, but that would cost like a million dollars, and your driver would probably harvest your kidney.

Granted, Max had dangled ten grand in front of me as if it were nothing. I could call him and ask him to play chauffeur or send one of his minions to shuttle me from the city to his creepy little kingdom. But that didn't feel right, either. For one, I wouldn't have my own wheels, so escaping was an issue. For another, being stuck in a car driven by a potentially possessed guy for three hours didn't sound like a good time either. Max had seemed straight-up normal to me, but I hadn't really looked at him closely. Perhaps there was a reason why the rabbi hadn't met with him yet.

No. I rejected that idea as soon as I had it. Mordechai didn't turn anyone away. And he'd made those random notes on Max's letter in rabbi shorthand, letters and figures and shapes I didn't really understand—didn't want to understand. He'd been planning to meet with Max; he simply hadn't gotten the chance. If he'd been here right now, he'd probably tell me that God had needed him more.

Yeah, well, God was wrong on that count.

I hunched in my chair, staring at the computer. With the additional search term of Hooperton, I was able to pull up a little more information on the Grahams, but not much. There were articles in the local newsfeeds about donations and business sales. There was an old society scroll in Chicago about Emily Winslow, sister of Mrs. Graham and only in her thirties, who might be the aunt flown home to roost. I doubted it though. There was some resemblance to the figure I'd seen in the photos, but this woman was beautiful, laughing, blonde and bright. She didn't look like the type to shut herself away in a moldering Midwestern castle.

None of that solved my transportation problem though.

I chewed on the inside of my mouth. The rabbi's car was definitely out, though that would have been easiest. I didn't want to pay for an Uber.

Steve had a car.

"Yeah, I know," I answered the inner voice before I could stop myself. I grimaced. Talking to a demon was never a good idea, unless you were about to expel it.

I blew out a breath and glanced at the card I'd lined up neatly below Max's letter. Before I could lose my nerve, I flicked to my phone app and keyed in the numbers.

He picked up on the second ring.

"Hello, this is Max." His voice sounded normal, open. Not possessed.

"Hi, Max. This is Delia Thompson. We met the other—"

"Yes." Something shifted in his tone then, and I found myself sitting taller in my chair. "You're coming."

The hope in his voice cut right through me. "I don't know what I can do," I said quickly. That was a lie. He'd suggested what I should do already, but it wasn't a good idea, and definitely not a legal one.

Max didn't seem to care. "Absolutely. Just to check things out. See what you think. Anything would help, seriously. And before you ask, my offer stands. I'll have the money for you when you arrive, or I can send it directly to your account."

That was adorable. Like I was that professional. Still, I liked Max for it. "You can give it to me when I see you, that's fine," I said. I squared the edges of the letter. Monday seemed a little too eager, even to me. And Tuesday would give me time to back down if I wanted. Which I probably should. Which I knew I wouldn't. Besides, I needed to track down Steve. With the right amount of bullshit, it wouldn't be that hard to use his car for one day, right? "Tuesday afternoon work for you?"

"Yes." Pause. "Thank you, Delia."

Thank you, Delia, the creature inside me mocked, both furious with Max for the way he made me feel and needing the guy at the same time. I knew how it felt.

"Of course." I kept my voice as professional as possible, if only to keep from screaming. "See you Tuesday."

TUESDAY DAWNED ALMOST OBSCENELY bright and cheerful. Steve, who shockingly was still taking up space in the duplex, seemed to buy that I was going on a job interview across town, though what upwardly mobile aspirations there would be for deli counter workers, I couldn't guess. He didn't care, just handed over his keys. He'd been weird ever since the rabbi had died, staying out at the clubs later, coming home via Uber or God only knew who. Then again, I'd been acting weird too, I supposed. It was a weird time.

I didn't have a set plan in mind as I headed out to Hooperton. I'd never driven farther than a few miles, always in the city, and generally to the hospital and back if Mom had gotten hurt, or gotten drunk after a shift somewhere, or whatever. I was absurdly excited to leave the city, though, even if I was going to some batshit crazy house in the middle of nowhere.

I was still going somewhere. Anywhere but here.

The drive rambled along without incident: three hours of highway bleeding into farmland, then the town of Hooperton itself—five quaint blocks that looked like they'd been frozen in 1950—then dissolving back into estates and empty fields. By the time I turned onto the final two-lane road, I was surrounded by nothing but orchards, crops, and isolation. The Graham house had no neighbors for at least five miles.

Nothing creepy about that, especially not to someone who'd

lived in a city her entire life. The entire countryside felt abandoned.

Finally, I crested a small rise and saw the house proper.

"Whoa."

It looked exactly like the pictures. Minus the horses of course.

The building soared like some sort of historical monument, all white brick with green shutters and an enormous door. Despite its proud façade, though, the place seemed to sag a little under its own weight. I felt it, then—families layered on families had lived in this house, each more broken than the last.

"Get a grip," I muttered to myself. I only needed to care about the current family, and the demons apparently creeping around them. And I had to say, the place looked exactly like an Airbnb designed for vacationing evil.

As I stared, one of the upstairs windows caught the light, then went dead black—not curtains closing, but a darkness that seemed to press against the glass from inside. A shadow? I blinked, and it was just a window again, reflecting the afternoon sky. My hands tightened on the steering wheel.

There were woods surrounding the house, rolling away on two sides, but they'd been cleared enough to give you an unobstructed view of the back field, the now super-empty back field, which ran a quarter-mile easy before giving way to more woods. A couple of huge barns stood at the opening of another stretch of farmland, with more long grass fluttering in the breeze.

There was no one outside.

My anxiety ratcheted up as I drove toward the house, so I repeated my mantra to myself. "I'm not staying. I'll look, I'll say haunted, I'll collect my ten grand, and I'll leave. That's it. That's all he wants, and I can give him that."

I *could* give him that too. Because there was something definitely fucked up with this place.

I drove up and parked on the wide, curving drive, and there still was no one moving in the front yard or in the paddocks. I didn't look at the windows, because I didn't want to see anyone standing there. I sat there for a second, debating, and then the door opened. It wasn't Max, though.

It was a little boy.

I felt the curl of recognition swirl through me, making my heart hurt. Kids were the *worst*. The fact that demons picked on children always seemed particularly cruel to me, because kids were so open. So forgiving. So tolerant of the other that sought to share space with them that they sometimes didn't even know it was there.

Behind the boy, another figure emerged, and this one I did recognize. Max raised his hand to wave at me, and I forced myself to shut off the car and pop the door open. He wanted actual results for his ten thousand, dammit. More than me just wanting to pee myself. I had to give him something useful. Something like Mordechai would say.

I got out of the car, my hand snaking for my backpack. I didn't want to leave anything behind, anywhere. Part of that was being nervous that I'd somehow be stuck here. Part of it was wanting something to hold onto.

Either way, I got out of the car and walked up to the front porch, which was one of those massive veranda things, with wicker furniture that actually still looked new. None of it rocked on its own, thank God. There wasn't enough breeze for that.

"Delia, I'd like you to meet my brother Sam." Max's voice was a little strained. His brother—who had to be twenty years Max's junior, easy—looked at me with eyes way too old for his face and didn't smile. Still, he didn't start screaming obscenities at me, so: bonus.

"Hey there, Sam," I said. I looked up at the big house. Outside the car, it didn't seem so bad.

"So." Max was watching me, expectation clear. "Where do we start?"

I blinked at him and realized: I had no idea.

Fortunately for both of us, *then* Sam started screaming.

CHAPTER

THIRTEEN

"No, no, no, no, no, no, NO!"

"Sam!" Max grabbed for him, but Sam lurched away from Max and barreled into me, half-knocking me back before running down the stairs and away. Max jerked forward to catch me before I fell down the wide country stone steps as well, and we both turned to watch Sam race toward one of the huge barns that stood, doors open, at the far end of the yard.

When Max didn't shout after the kid again, I squinted at him. "Does he, um, do that a lot? Or is that a normal kid thing?"

Max sighed, then seemed to realize he still had his hand on my arm and pulled away, grimacing. "I guess it depends on context. A year ago, I would say a normal kid thing. A year ago, though, this place was different." He peered up at the building beside us. "You can feel it, can't you?"

He spoke in a low tone, almost a whisper, and I glanced up as well. I really felt like I should have some sort of monitoring equipment on me and regretted not checking out more paranormal ghost-hunting stuff. Then again, Mordechai never needed any of that.

103

You don't need it either.

While I appreciated the vote of confidence, given the source was a monster, I didn't put too much stock in it. I'd spent so long following Mordechai's lead that I wasn't sure exactly how this whole psychic investigation actually worked. But Max was waiting for an answer, so I dutifully narrowed my eyes at the old, stately home. "I feel like it's a little off, yeah."

His smile was mirthless. "A little. Is that all?"

He reached into his pocket and pulled out a slip of paper. A check, I realized. Just like that. He handed it to me, and I felt the most curious urge to stuff it in my pants and run like hell.

Instead, I waved it at him. "I haven't done anything yet."

"Coming out here is something. Getting people to do even that has become nearly impossible." His gaze on me hardened a little. "Rabbi Mordechai sounded like he was willing to help, which is a hell of a lot further than I got with the local priests. Or in Chicago. They gave me some prayers—*prayers*." He curled his lip. "We're way beyond that."

I frowned at him. "So your first stop was the Catholic Church? And they turned you down?" It didn't seem like they should be allowed to do that, but I didn't know all the rules of Catholicism, despite my tenure at All Souls. Oddly enough, proper techniques for exorcisms had never come up in religion class.

"They kept passing the buck," he said, disgust heavy in his voice. "The local priest here—a guy who actually knows my family—he tried to help. He came out to the house and prayed over it. Of course, nothing creepy bothered him while he did it, but it didn't actually accomplish anything."

I squinted at him. "What do you mean, nothing bothered him?"

He shrugged. "The things that happen here...they seemed tuned to us, specifically. To mock us. The worst thing they could do was not show up when we finally got help, and so, that's what happened."

His voice sounded unbearably tired, and I knew what he was thinking. Who knew if the evil lurking here would show itself to me, either?

Oh, it will.

A wave of uneasiness flickered through me, equal parts cold dread and giddy excitement, but fortunately, Max didn't seem to notice.

"Then in Chicago, they referred me to their local priest and asked about my own religious practices, like that had anything to do with anything. Suggested I talk to the cops, as if I didn't have to do that already when all the horses were shot."

I felt his words hitting me too fast, too hard. I wasn't sure where to focus. "That happened this past winter?"

"Wasn't really even winter anymore, it was March. It'd been really cold for a long stretch of days, and we'd gotten a lot more snow than we had in years past. The local cops told me they thought my father had gotten a little turned around." He glanced at me. "It's not a crime, you know. Killing your own livestock. It felt like a crime, but it wasn't."

"And is that, ah, the biggest thing that happened? Anything since then?"

He shook his head. "I took a leave of absence from work and came home in April. That's when the Bells left, our housekeeper and her husband. They took care of the horses. Which were dead, so...I let them go with an extra year's pay for sticking with us so long." His voice was bitter. "The Bells had been with the family for more than twenty years, since before I was born. They were—are—such good people. But I couldn't keep them here. Not when everything had gotten so bad, so quickly."

He looked past me to where Sam had disappeared into the barn. I followed his line of sight. "Is he okay in there?"

"Yeah. Nothing in there anymore that's any different from inside the house. He doesn't usually hurt himself too badly."

Too badly? What did that even mean?

Max waved around. "The official tour is pretty basic. We've got the main house, here, then two other houses on the property. The Bells' house is empty now, but not abandoned, really. They left their stuff, saying they wanted to come back once they could. Once I let them. The other house is more of a lake cottage out back past the woods."

"Anyone live in the lake cottage? Like, full-time?" I didn't know why I asked the question, but Max's glance told me it was the right one.

"Yeah. My sister's old boyfriend, Joe Bell. He's twenty-six now, works odd jobs for Dad, clears the property and trims trees, stuff like that. But he keeps to himself. He went through a lot when he and my sister broke up, and Dad sort of took pity on him and rented the place out to him. He can come and go as he wants—there's a separate road to the place. I doubt we'll see him while you're here. He's harmless."

Nothing about this place felt harmless to me. It was time to come clean.

"Max, I can't do a lot, but I can do what you asked me to do, at least." The obligation of his money dragged on me, pulling me under like a riptide. "I can write up a visit here as if Rabbi Mordechai had been here. Like he had seen this place before he died. And then you could go back to the Catholic people or find another rabbi, someone who would take your case because it was already, you know, vetted."

He sagged a little, though I didn't understand why. "Can't you do something yourself?"

Panic zipped through me. "No, Max. Do I look like a rabbi to you? Or a Catholic priest? I was Rabbi Mordechai's *assistant*."

"But that woman—"

"Fuck Mrs. Klein." I was getting truly angry now, but I couldn't help it. The house seemed to loom over me, pressing on every nerve. I wanted out of there, but I wanted to prove I was stronger than any kind of demon filth. Needed it, like a choking man needed air. "This is the deal. I'll go through the house with you to get the details, then fake a pre-death meeting between you and Mordechai, write it up and forge the rabbi's name, and you can do with that whatever you want. But that's it, Max. If that's not enough, you can take your money back, and I'll leave right now."

"No." Max reached out, stopping himself before he grabbed my arm again. I didn't flinch back, but I had to fight not to flee down the steps, and clearly, he realized it. "Don't go. That's fine." He pulled his arm back awkwardly, brushing a hand through his hair. "It's fine. I guess we should get started then."

He turned to the front door, and we heard another childish scream. This one seemed strangely normal though, as if I was already getting used to Sam and his outbursts. Now the little boy stood at the edge of the open doorway to the barn, staring up at the house. He clenched his fists into little boy rage and stood stiff as a tree trunk. Even from this distance, I could see him practically vibrating with fury.

"No!" he yelled, then tried again, this time stretching out the word in one long, protracted wail. "Nooooo!"

Max turned back to me. "I guess you have a fan."

I managed a lopsided grin. "Kids are my specialty."

We walked into the house. I didn't know what I was expecting, but it wasn't a light and bright farmhouse with wide windows and airy spaces. The walls were all painted in soft pastels, and the floors were hardwood, covered for the most part by huge cream-colored rugs, some with faded patterns, some more modern. The house seemed empty, but not abandoned. More...waiting for a chance to strike. Like a ghoul hiding behind a butterfly bush.

"You and Sam live here alone, now?" I asked, just to break the silence. "The others all left?"

Max snorted a short laugh. "Oh, God no," he said. "Everyone's waiting for you to take the tour, then we'll talk a little on the back porch."

I stared at him. "Your family knows why I'm here?"

He glanced down at me. He seemed taller in the house than he had outside. "I told them you were coming, and why, yes. When they're fine, they're fine. They're open to finding out answers too."

"Oh. I mean, sure." I smiled brightly. "Of course they are."

Max took me through the entire house, which looked eerily similar to my own place in one distinct way: how clean it was. "You said the housekeeper moved out?"

"In April, yeah. I have a service that comes out once a week, or I did until this past week. Then even that..." He shrugged. "Something happened, I don't know what. But the service called and left a voicemail. Said they wouldn't be able to come back. That I didn't owe them for the remaining visits."

"That's why you came to see Mordechai in person."

His jaw tightened. "It's going to get out. Someone's going to talk, and I thought if I handled it—if it was taken care of..." He stopped, shook his head as his gaze shifted to the far wall, as if seeing all the way out to the back porch. "I have to fix this, somehow."

He led me up the grand staircase. Half the doors to the upstairs rooms were closed. Max opened them without hesitation, but the rooms inside were as tidy as the rest of the house. All except one room, anyway. I knew something was up by the way Max opened the door.

I looked inside, seeing the issue immediately. The guest

bathroom was spotless except for the mirror. Someone had written MISS ME? in dusky red ink on the glass, then scrubbed at it—the words were faded but still legible. "This was two weeks ago," Max said flatly. "I keep cleaning it. It keeps coming back. *That's* when I decided to contact Rabbi Mordechai. I didn't want to think about what might get written next."

"Yeah." I grimaced. "I get that."

He gestured down the hallway. "My room's down there. It's messy, but ordinary messy. Sam's been staying with me. It seems to chill him out, but he doesn't like me to straighten up." His smile was crooked, the first normal-guy smile I'd seen on him. "I figure it's one less room to clean now."

I nodded. So Max was the one who kept the place clean. Made sense. "Where did he sleep before?"

Max headed down the hallway, where another door stood half open. That seemed to bother him. "I thought..."

He pushed the door open all the way and stepped back. "Sam's room. I'm sorry about the state it's in, but I wanted to keep it the way it was—so that you could see it. I've taken pictures, and I'll clean it all up afterwards. I just...I just wanted someone to see it."

I swallowed down my sense of revulsion and stepped inside.

Oh...shit.

Literally.

FOURTEEN

Sam's room contained a bed, a dresser, and little else. But the walls made up for it. Crayon markings and the remains of dried feces decorated every surface. All the windows stood open, and enormous fans faced the outside, taking most of the stench away. Most, but not all.

I stared. The chaos should've been meaningless, probably was meaningless to Max, but my stomach lurched at the familiarity. The walls I'd painted in my sleep had carried the same frantic patterns, but not made of shit and colored wax.

It took me a couple of tries to speak. "When did he do this?"

"It was like that when I got back from the city. I'd locked the room's door, told him to stay with Mom and Dad, but obviously he got back in somehow. I was about to start calling shrinks again when you contacted me, so I figured I'd wait."

Shrinks *again*? "He's gone in for therapy before?"

"Yeah. Nothing serious, but he'd have...episodes, every now and then. We thought it was normal kid stuff, especially with him being so much younger than the rest of us, but it wasn't. I just didn't realize he wasn't the only one having issues."

I nodded, looking around. This definitely qualified as having issues. Maybe the housecleaners saw this room, and that was why they ran. "You mentioned an older sister. Where's her room?"

For the first time, Max paused. "Carol Ann, yes. She doesn't live here."

My creep-o-meter pinged hard to the right. "But her ex-boyfriend does?"

"Well, Joe doesn't live here in the house, either. He lives out on the lake, and he never comes around."

Uh-oh. "So where does she live?"

He sighed. "She's in Nebraska, at the Brightwell Clinic."

That seemed important. "The what?"

"It's a mental health hospital, okay?" Max's words came quicker now, harsh and embarrassed as a flush crawled up his neck. "But she got sick a long time ago—like seven years. And she got sick, sick. Not possessed, sick. There was no Exorcist moment like floating people or writing on the walls or anything like that."

I winced, but he was on a roll.

"I wasn't here, but everyone's stories were the same. She had a mental breakdown, and we got her the best care we possibly could."

"And then put up her boyfriend in the lake house."

Another long breath. "Look—Joe's a good guy. He was seriously messed up when Carol Ann had her breakdown. We felt sorry for him, and we didn't think it would be anything permanent. He didn't think it would be either. But time sort of passed, you know?"

"It has a way of doing that." And though I was acting like a hard ass, I did understand. How long ago had it been that I'd walked through the doors of that first little kid's house, dragging all those yapping dogs, only to interrupt Rabbi Mordechai mid-exorcism? It seemed like only yesterday. "Does she have a room where she used to sleep? Like a room you don't use or whatever?"

A sudden thought gripped me. Had the sister originally slept in *Sam's* room? Please, no. I'd seriously puke.

Fortunately, Max pointed to the ceiling. "Yeah, it's another flight up. But I checked it this morning, like every morning. It hasn't been disturbed."

I couldn't entirely shut down my nausea as we headed to his sister's room, but Max was correct. The room looked like the perfect early twenties sorority girl haven: white furniture, Pottery Barn accents in bright teals and pinks, everything neat and tidy. No bloody voodoo doll stuck with pins or Ouija board peeking out from under the bed.

The rest of the tour finished easily enough. Big, comfortable estate house but not rudely extravagant, that felt old, not befouled, at least other than Sam's room. We didn't say anything more until we reached the back of the house. I could see it opened onto a large porch, and then I did stop. We were standing in the kitchen, and all the accoutrements of meal making were there. Sandwich bread, a large pot of good-smelling soup. Vegetables, dip, and little folded-over pieces of deli meat, secured with toothpicks. All of it sitting out, looking homey. Homey and untouched. Like the whole house was holding its breath.

"They're all waiting for me out there?" I asked, surprised that my voice was barely a whisper.

"I'm telling you, most of the time it's like this. There's an awareness that something isn't right, but nobody seems to know when it's going to pop up. Or how bad it's going to be."

Oh, it's going to be very, very bad.

Hearing the creature's voice again so soon jolted me, which I was sure was its point. But instead of feeling anger, an almost absurd sense of giddiness swirled up inside me as we stepped out onto the covered back porch. I wasn't alone out here in the middle of nowhere with all these haunted house demons, not really.

A soft laugh curled through me. *Not yet.*

All my good feelings leeched away.

We carried the food outside. The porch was wide and gracious, gray-painted floorboards setting off white wicker furniture. Still, as I was introduced to the family, I had to fight the shiver. They looked less like people than portraits, their gazes hollow, their secrets pushed down and boxed up, then stuck in an attic corner of this creepy old house where no one could see. They seemed to be there—but not really there at the same time. Absent in their own skin.

I frowned and tried to focus, to glean what tastes and smells I could of their histories, but my intuition wasn't firing on any cylinders. There was the pale, slender Judith, Max's mother, who shivered despite the warmth and made small plates of *hors d'oeuvres* that everyone ate but her. Then came the gracious, expansive father, Frank, a big man who seemed like he'd had the wind knocked out of him recently, his clothes too loose, his skin around his eyes and jaw too slack.

The wispy-bunned grandmother, Kate, glared at me even when I wasn't looking at her, and then of course there was the tousle-haired, seven-year-old Sam, who hovered at her side, almost as if he were standing guard. I didn't know how he'd gotten there, but I'd already decided he was a sneaky little fuck.

I'm watching you, buddy, I thought at him, hard.

Sam pressed closer to his grandmother, and Max glanced around. "Where's Emily?"

"Out," croaked the old woman. I peered at her a little more closely, somehow knowing she was Dad's mother, not Judith's. Like Sam, her reaction to the evil worming through this house seemed a little closer to the surface. Even her eyes had that weird milky look, the encroachment of cataracts making her look crazier than a bed bug.

Max sighed and gestured for me to sit down. Reluctantly, I did.

Then they all stared at me. Not knowing what else to do, I launched in with my questions.

They answered in turns—when trouble started, what the worst part was—but their voices had that practiced quality of people who'd told the same story too many times to too many skeptics. I stopped listening to their words and focused on what I could taste instead: Judith's disappointment, Frank's fear, Kate's…nothing. She gave me nothing at all.

With her last non-answer, though, something *finally* stirred inside me, the same prickling of awareness I felt looking at Mrs. Klein's hangdog house or catching the scent wafting off Claire Bickwell's dickhead boyfriend. The rush and tumble of possibility when I shook Max Graham's hand, Sam's echoing screams as I stared at his disgusting room. Something that was all me, not the demon inside me. Something I understood.

I exhaled with more relief than I expected, but nobody noticed. I could do this, I thought. I was doing this.

And I was doing it my way.

"Everyone experiences difficult things differently," I said, looking around the room. "Can you each tell me what the worst part has been, so far, for you?"

"Covered that," the dad grunted, staring down at his knees.

"Oh, Frank," Judith sighed, staring at me reproachfully as she reached over and squeezed his forearm. I refocused on the grandmother, who was back to glaring at me, while Sam stared at the far wall, his mouth puckered tight.

Then I glanced at Max.

And stopped cold. Uh-oh.

Max didn't speak, but he watched me with a clear and

unambiguous light in his eyes that made me shudder all the way to the core of my being. Working with Mordechai, I'd seen that expression a hundred different times over the years. I'd just never had it directed at me.

Directed at me, it took on a whole new weight.

Hope.

Uh-oh is right. This time, laughter spilled out around my mocking inner voice, filling up my mind, clogging my throat.

"Shut up," I thought fiercely at the thing crawling around in me, the thing I despised but suddenly felt I needed in a way that made me slightly sick. *"Just—chill for a second."*

It fell silent but didn't leave me. Not quite.

Not yet. It ribboned through me like an arch-backed cat, equal parts reassurance and threat. For the first time, I didn't mind it so much. If it was a demon, maybe it could help me. Maybe it was the reason why I'd been so successful at the Klein's.

I didn't want to think about that too much.

Instead, I exhaled, slow and careful, and kept up with my questions. The house stayed still the whole time. There was no moaning or wailing of a host of ghostly corpses, there were no crashing dishes or clattering windowpanes. Even Sam finally flagged, his arms around his grandma, his big eyes watching me, angry and accusing. Eventually, the family's answers ran together in mutters and sighs, their voices flat and echoing, as if they'd been rehearsing these responses for years.

At that point, I knew we were done. I walked back through the house with Max and out onto the wide front porch, grateful that the sun was still shining. The whole place was quiet, save for the breeze rustling in the trees. It looked like what I supposed it'd been for most of its existence, a peaceful idyll in the Midwest. The home of an absurdly prosperous somebody or other, and the birthplace of generations of ordinary people after that.

Until this generation, who'd gotten their asses uniformly kicked.

"What next?" Max stood too close to me, and I knew he didn't want to let me go. But I had to get Steve's car back. I had to get the letter written and inserted into Mordechai's papers, with copies sent to Max and the Rockdale temple, possibly the diocese. Anyone I could think of.

What was more, I didn't know how I felt about Max standing that close. It felt weirdly right yet completely wrong all at once, my nerves jumping at his every glance.

Not only my nerves, either. Deep inside, I felt a strange kind of *awareness*. The kind that had nothing to do with danger and everything to do with how close Max was, how much space he took up in the air between us.

A low, possessive growl murmured far in the back edges of my mind, almost too low to hear.

Almost.

"What, you don't like this now?" I thought with a full-on internal smirk, feeling a sudden burst of energy that had nothing to do with the parasite and everything to do with me. It was powerful—dangerous. It was almost fun.

Then I turned to Max, and the hope in his eyes cut through me again.

"I'll be in touch in, like, a day. Two, tops. You've got my number if anything happens, but otherwise I should have something for you super fast. I won't cash the check until—"

Max waved that off with a curt hand-slash. "Cash the check. I don't care about the money."

I tried to give him a reassuring smile. "It's going to be okay, Max."

He stepped back, as if suddenly realizing that he was

showing his hand too much. He glanced toward the empty paddock behind the house and shook his head. The breeze caught his curling black hair, tousling it. "From your lips to God's ears." He sighed.

Laughter welled up within me, low and sneering. *You wish.*

Still, something seemed a little off with the creature inside me. It didn't like Max, but it did like this house and whatever was inside the house. It was excited, and angry, and maybe angry that it was excited, and all those feelings were spinning around inside of me, giving me strength and draining me at the same time. It was a thing apart from me, but it was also me, I thought. For all that I'd worked with Mordechai all these years, I didn't really know what it meant to feel like this. I didn't want to know.

I was terrified that I knew.

I made it home in three hours flat. Despite my urge to see the place, my desire to help, I was glad to put Max's ever-so-extremely haunted house behind me. Everything was okay at home—Steve was gone, but he'd left a note saying he'd be out of the house for the night. Probably clubbing or hanging around one of the bars he'd picked up coasters from. It was his thing lately. Either way, I had his number if I wanted to reach him.

I didn't. Everything was quiet. I needed quiet.

It stayed that way for about another six hours.

FIFTEEN

I should have known what was happening because I was hot—too hot. Middle-of-the-summer, high-noon hot. Even though the fans were on and the windows wide open, I could hear the blast of the whirling metal laboring in the humid air. But I flung off the sheets and fell onto the floor, streaming with sweat. The nightmare had been real, immediate, and so in my face that I scrabbled across the floor like some sort of crab creature, yanking open the door so I could spill into the hallway.

It was about thirty degrees cooler in the corridor.

I sagged against the wall in the darkness, feeling like I'd been hit by a bus. Everything everywhere hurt, my skin scraped raw, my joints overstretched. And there was a strange smell I couldn't quite identify, but was all around me.

The entire rest of the house was stone silent. There was no sound from the neighbors, no sirens blaring outside, nothing that would have woken me up other than—

A shrill tweeting noise sounded from back inside my room, and I lurched around, staring wildly, trying to make sense of it.

My phone. It was my phone.

Mordechai. I thought the name before I remembered that it wouldn't be Rabbi Mordechai, couldn't be him. Ever again. A wave of loneliness so intense it bordered on nausea swept over me as I crept back into my room, flipping on the light. The phone lay on the tan carpet, and the walls smelled like fresh paint.

No, not paint, I realized, finally recognizing the difference. It was the smell of markers. Sharpie markers.

I blinked and stared, bleary-eyed, but there was nothing on the walls.

My phone chirped again.

I reached out and that's when I saw my arm, really saw it, my arm and my T-shirt, my shorts and—

Oh, *shit.* I lunged forward and hauled the phone up, then race-crawled out of the room again, barely stopping myself before I crashed into the wall. Scrabbling around, I flipped on the hallway light. I cast a long glance down the corridor and saw the first Sharpie, lying on the ground with its cap next to it, like an errant child let out to play.

My phone sounded and I swiped it on, hitting the message app.

It's started again. Max's text read. *What should I do? The horses are the worst.*

Beneath his words sat three rounded squares, arrows in their centers. Video clips. The first showed an empty field. The second had caught an image of Max's mother, Judith. The third showed Sam.

I frowned at the screen, reread Max's text. There were no more horses on the Graham estate.

Sitting alone in the middle of my house at three in the morning with my body covered in the ink of what looked like a thousand Sharpie markers, I figured I could handle an empty field. I clicked the square open.

Then froze at the sound of terrified horses screaming in the darkness.

I stabbed the video off, then turned my sound way down for good measure. No. Way. No way that was actually happening, ghost horses screaming behind a demon-infested house. That couldn't be real. I struggled to my feet, my hands shaking as I tried to walk to the bathroom and type at the same time.

Are you okay?? I texted Max. No way was I clicking on the other two videos.

There was no response. Of course there was no response. The house had probably eaten him.

I flopped into the bathroom and stared at myself in the mirror.

And froze.

A stark, slashing command marked my face. My forehead. Perfectly executed in block letters backwards, so it reflected correctly in the mirror. **GO BACK.**

But that wasn't all. My entire body was covered in Sharpie ink. Pungent fumes clung to me like a second skin, acrid and sweet, making me gag even as my brain scrambled to understand what had happened to me. The refrain of disgusting words that usually adorned my walls was only the start of it. **Slut, Whore, Failure, Loser, Freak, Beast** stretched down my neck, spilling over my arms, so familiar as to almost be reassuring—except for the fact that these were on my own skin, my own body...

I stepped back, seeing more, and my heart lurched sideways in horror, then started beating at a frantic pace. As the scrawled words reached my breasts, my hips, they became different.

Horribly different.

Now you are a broken seal: A scarlet stain upon the earth ran along the curve of one breast. **o! that I could play with you myself little sparrow** curled in a wide circle around my hip. **Then where my hand is set, my seal shall be...**dove deep over one thigh, aiming for—

"What the *fuck!*" I hissed, vaguely recognizing the words as something real— something written by poets or scribes or whatever the hell a million years ago. People who knew what they were doing. But these overwrought outpourings of a bunch of emo dead people had no business on my skin, etched like infernal brands.

I lifted my arms to find more text nestled in my armpit. **The firefly wakens.** And down my ribcage, in shakier script **...in secret, between the shadow and the soul.**

My face burned as I stared at the snaking curves, the sinuous lines. The words scrawled over my too-white skin were *beautiful*. Disturbing and invasive and completely violating, but beautiful. And that made it so much worse. I didn't want to feel anything but rage, but instead my belly twisted with an emotion I couldn't name. Something dark, but also gorgeous. Something—

"What the fuck is *wrong* with you?" I whispered.

Even as I said it, I felt a flutter of something in my chest— not quite an answer, more like a held breath. Anticipation. Need.

Then outrage flashed again. This emotion, at last, felt right; purely, finally, unmistakably *me*. Boiling rage blasted up my spine like a holy fire, clearing everything in its path. Fury knotted up my guts and radiated outward, pulsing blasts of heat and ice.

For one brief shining moment, I was vengeance and retribution wrapped up in a barbed wire ball of get-the-fuck-gone and I was here to *stay*.

Me, not the creature inside me.

"Whoa," I whispered.

I stared at my reflection in the mirror as the moment bled

away, my brows climbing so high on my forehead that my **GO BACK** order looked like a squashed marshmallow. The words on my face and neck stayed flat and stark—but on my torso and legs? They shimmered and jumped, scrambling a little on my skin before settling down again, and they looked different now, shinier...almost pretty despite the desecration they represented.

I couldn't help it. My mouth quirked a little to the side, and a soft, breathy chuckle escaped me. "You didn't plan on writing *that* stuff, did you?" I whispered aloud.

There was no response.

I stepped back from the mirror and squinted down at my legs, grimacing in confusion as the shit covering me switched again—this time to something darker, more desperate. Down the length of my legs to my feet, the writing diverged into languages I couldn't decipher, but I could tell that I didn't want to know what these words and symbols meant. They practically pulsed with a wild darkness that, like the words on my torso, seemed like they'd been poured out in some kind of fugue.

I grimaced. How many markers had I gone through? Everywhere I could reach, I was covered in ink.

Now that the adrenaline was wearing off, I could feel the pain, too, a dull throbbing ache that seemed to blossom up from the seat of my spine. I strained to see my back and winced. *Ouch.* With a sick knot of dread in my stomach, I kept going, curving just enough to see what I'd done.

Black and red bruises snaked down my back, the skin on my right hip half-scraped away. Apparently whatever skin I couldn't easily reach I'd tried to sand off my body out of spite. *Jesus Christ.*

Steve better have left some bourbon in the house. Because this shower was going to sting like a bitch.

I glanced into the mirror again, glaring at the desecration of my forehead, my neck.

"Fuck you," I said to my reflection.

But this time, the thing inside me was ready. A long, slow laugh rolled through my body, spinning through my veins. *Don't tempt me.*

Furious, I wheeled away and stabbed the water on. The shower did hurt like a bitch. I was beyond grateful that I could get the ink off my neck pretty well, but my arms had only gotten down to a faded gray, and my forehead was still a mess before I gave up in the early hours of the morning. Max had texted back only once, that things had quieted down, and it was all I could do not to tell him to never contact me again.

It was Wednesday morning, and Steve would need his car eventually, no matter where he'd crashed. The fact that he hadn't texted me already was a miracle. The bruising on my arms and back had blossomed into teeth-rattling pain, but I still focused on the house long enough to clean my bedroom and the bathroom, then move down into the living room, gathering up Sharpies as I went.

Then I went into the kitchen and saw them.

Every knife in the drawer was now sitting on the counter, lined up perfectly, an arsenal of home-based weaponry. A message? It had to be a message.

And the voice inside me, the messenger?

Definitely. Not. Me.

Not an alt, not a split personality, not even an imaginary friend gone terribly wrong.

No.

I had a demon inside me. A straight-up, horn-headed, swishy-tailed demon. Forget the tortured fallen angel portrait I'd painted on my wall this last time or seen in the mirror at Mrs. Klein's house. Forget the crudely gross bulbous monsters I'd drawn countless times before that. Mordechai had told me that first a demon would try to intimidate, then manipulate, and that was exactly what was happening here.

"Try all the games you want, asshole. I know how to evict you," I muttered aloud to the kitchen knives, then to the appliances, the countertops—anything that would listen. "All I need to do is see you."

The demon inside me didn't respond.

Slowly, methodically, I replaced the Sharpies in their basket in the living room. Then I continued trying to clean the ink off my face and hands. Unfortunately, the ink was a lot more tenacious than it should have been. Especially on my forehead.

In the end, I had to admit defeat. I had things I needed to do. Places to go. Important places where normal people worked and breathed, and I couldn't be walking around looking like the Illustrated Man.

I caved at about 6:30 a.m. and dug through all my shit until I found the card. Then I texted pharmaceutical queen Claire Bickwell.

This is Delia, and I've got kind of a weird problem. For reasons I don't want to explain, I have Sharpie ink on my hands and forehead that is fading with soap, but not coming all the way off. Any suggestions?

To her credit, there was only about a 5.7-second delay before the response pinged back on my screen. *Do you live close? Can you come to the store?*

I sighed, staring down at the phone. Why couldn't anything be easy?

Sure! I typed with a cheer I totally didn't feel. *I'll be right there.*

SIXTEEN

Still blessed with Steve's car, I made it to Reider Pharmacy by 6:50 a.m. Claire was waiting for me at the back door and immediately ushered me inside with a big smile and promises of a miracle transformation.

"Oh, this isn't bad at all," she assured me breezily when she took my hands. "It's kind of pretty, right? Like a henna tattoo?"

"Pretty isn't the word I'd use," I muttered, tracing the letters that crawled like ants along my fingers. I hadn't tried to decipher the Hindi masterpiece etched into my hands, but I'd videoed my whole body for the therapist I'd so desperately need eventually. I'd donned a long-sleeved T-shirt despite the impending heat of the day. I didn't care about my arms, though. I just needed my hands to pass muster. And my face.

Claire's composure did crack a little when she saw my forehead. The fact that she could read the letters at all convinced me that coming here was the right thing to do.

"Hands are easy," she said, giving me a small collection of stuff in a net bag, like I'd checked into some kind of spa. "You need to keep at it, but the best thing you can do is to keep using your hands. There's pumice in there, and a rough cleanser, stuff

I bought for my face a hundred years ago that proved to be too harsh. But for hands, it's perfect. If you can do anything that makes your hands sweat, that's also good. Your face, though…" She sat back a little on her heels and finally took in a deep breath as her bright blue eyes dropped to the ink shadows peeking out around my collar. "Jesus, Delia, what happened to you? Who did this?"

I'd thought about this on the drive over. It wasn't going to work for me to simply tell Claire to mind her own business. She was helping me, and I needed the help. I couldn't tell her the truth-truth, of course. But it needed to be at least fairly believable. "I know, it's terrible. But I help out at a kids' group, and usually it's fine. Last night was art night, though, and I was so exhausted. I fell asleep. By the time the other counselors found me—well, this had happened."

"*Kids* did this to you?" She squinted at me. "You don't expect me to believe that."

"It's true!" I protested, shaking my head. "Normally they're fine. Last night, not so much. But I've got to go places today. I can't look like this."

"Well, that last part at least is the truth." Still, she stopped with the questions. Instead, she grabbed a couple of bottles, one that was clearly baby oil, another some kind of makeup remover. A few minutes later, she, too, gave up. "That's about as good as it's going to get in terms of removal," she decided, peering at me. "Your facial skin doesn't exfoliate as quickly."

"Good to know."

"I'm going to put some cover-up on you, and I'm also giving you some to take with you." She held up a bottle of goop and a little flat disk filled with, I suspected, more goop. "As long as you don't sweat or rub your face a lot, the primer will hold the makeup on. The sponge applicator is what you should use, not your fingers, nothing with heat."

She pressed her lips together in a thin line as she worked on me, and I felt a curious fight going on inside me.

Other than Mordechai, I'd never had a friend. Other than Mordechai, I'd never needed a friend. Setting aside the fact that I was *possessed*, so it was already pretty crowded in my corner of the room, I wondered, for what felt like the first time ever, what it would be like to have someone else standing with me.

Claire and I were nowhere close to being alike, but in another lifetime, in another place, we theoretically could have been friends. Or at least friend-adjacent. Friendly.

But even as I thought all that, I heard myself rejecting it as well. Rejecting it with anger, too much anger. I was possessed! And I didn't even know when it had happened—recently? Five years ago? Ten?

Had Mordechai known?

He had to have known.

"You going into work today?" Claire asked, interrupting my thoughts.

I squinted at her. "No. I can't do that, looking like this. I'd get fired."

"Doubtful, but okay." A smile ghosted over her features as she sat back from me again, nodding. She didn't meet my eyes, but her gaze remained on my forehead as her throat worked, the words looking stuck behind her slender gold cross. I was about to say something rude when she finally spit it out.

"Would you mind—um, can I program a second number into your phone? So you can reach me if I don't answer the first one? You know, if you need me again?"

That made me blink. "I texted you this morning. I don't text that many people. That number's now in my phone."

"I would feel better, though. I worry. Do you mind? You can check out your face while I do it..."

"I—sure." I gave her my phone. She handed over the mirror,

and I watched my own eyes bug out. "Whoa," I said, admiring my reflection. "You did a really good job!"

"Oh my God, this phone is old," Claire breathed, holding it like an ancient artifact. "And I cannot believe you have Find My Friends on this—you!" she giggled, and I grimaced.

"My mom put that on my phone. She died."

That shut her up, but I didn't have the heart to say anything else—that the ancient phone was also a sort of shrine to everything that was Mom, that I was afraid of upgrading and letting yet another piece of me fall away. Stupid shit that no one needed to know, and that I didn't need to think about, not anymore.

I returned my focus to Claire's makeup job, so thoroughly impressed that I didn't mind her keying in her digits as I added a little more powder to my forehead and roughed my bangs up. This would work well enough. This would totally work well enough for what I needed.

Still, Claire didn't let me out of her tiny office without a goody bag of something she called "spa-ceuticals", and strict instructions to look into every mirror I passed for the next five hours to make sure nothing slipped in the heat of the day. I threw the bag onto the passenger seat, hunching a little as I started Steve's car, then bouncing out onto the street. I pulled over a half-block away and checked myself in the rear-view mirror. I'd been right. With my bangs over my forehead and as long as I kept moving, it totally worked.

I headed for the bank.

Cashing a $10,000 check was not the easiest thing you might imagine. Max, in his wisdom, hadn't given me a check-check, but a cashier's check, which helped, but not a lot. I still had to have a long conversation with a nervous bank manager, who only relented when I gave him Max's number, which he called.

The sound of Max's voice, even over the phone, was like a blade sliding between my ribs. My heart twisted in what was, for once, not my fuckhead entity squatting on my guts but my own, honest to God feelings. That was progress, anyway.

Max hadn't responded to my final text the previous night. The fact that he even picked up the phone when the banker called him was cause for an intense wave of relief. I didn't want to set up a bank account, so we settled on a safe deposit box. I put the cash in that, minus a few hundred dollars because I'd never had that much money on my person at once before.

Then I headed to the library.

Ultimately, typing Rabbi Mordechai's fake report proved very straightforward. The Graham family was a God-fearing (if Protestant) group of souls afflicted by multiple levels of demon attack, from infestation to full-on possession. I completely embellished the situation with the older sister, because I knew there had to be more going on with that, especially with good ol' ex-boyfriend Joe Bell still lurking around. Max seemed as yet unafflicted but given that every other person in his household was affected by the infestation to some degree, it was only a matter of time.

By the time I was done, I'd definitely convinced myself that the Grahams were in some deeply disturbing trouble, so I was hopeful I'd convince whoever read this report. I printed out three copies from the library's machines and signed them all with Rabbi Mordechai's scratchy scrawl. I went to the UPS store and scanned a copy for Max as well. He could mail all these off to whoever he wanted and be well on his way to the exorcism he so seriously needed. I'd done everything I'd told him I would do.

It wasn't remotely enough.

I knew it. Max knew it.

My skin, still a light, sickly greenish-gray underneath my long-sleeved T-shirt, knew it as well.

But there *was* something else I could do...it would suck, yes. But if anyone could take care of Max Graham, it was Mordechai.

Or, rather, whoever was going to replace him.

There was only one place I could go to find that person.

SEVENTEEN

Mourners still hovered around Mordechai's house, so I didn't feel too conspicuous walking up the long drive. Just sad. They'd sell this house eventually, I thought. And then there'd be no more reason for me to come back here. There wouldn't be a reason anyway, after I delivered this letter.

I circled the house, but any hope of getting into Mordechai's office unnoticed faded as I saw a woman sitting on a chair in front of it, with the door propped open behind her. The air smelled faintly of tomato soup. The woman looked up and smiled at me as I approached, and I knew her, I thought. I'd seen her on the refrigerator. "I'm sorry, dear, but the shiva is only up at the main house. No one's allowed back here."

"I—I'm Delia Thompson."

If I'd expected this announcement to be met with something other than a quizzical smile, I was doomed to be disappointed. But I didn't have to go inside, after all. I just needed to hand the letters over.

I pulled the shiny new UPS large brown envelope filled with documents out of my messenger bag and held it out to her. "I knew Rabbi Mordechai. I was his assistant on some of his work, and um, I still had these letters in my things. He'd wanted me to prepare them for mailing, but I don't know to whom. He didn't tell me before he—before he—"

"Oh, my, I'm so sorry." The woman came toward me, and it clicked: she was the wife of the rabbi's nephew. Dark-haired and clear-eyed, she tasted of compassion and acceptance. She also had the decency not to look too hard at my face as she took the envelope from me.

"Thank you," I said, stepping back and gripping the shoulder strap of the bag with both hands. "It's important that it goes to, um, whoever should get it. It's a family in trouble, and the rabbi had visited them to help, but he didn't finish the work with them. I don't..." I gave her my best, most hopeful smile. "Do you know if they've assigned a replacement for him yet? Or whatever they do?"

"I don't." Her manner was still gentle and caring, her hold on the envelope firm. The rabbi's nephew had chosen well. "You know he wasn't officially part of the—never mind. I'll give this to Rabbi Ethan. I'm sure they'll forward it to the right person as soon as possible."

"Okay, thanks." I nodded quickly. "But it's urgent."

I turned to leave, but it was already too late.

"Mary? Who are you talking to?" A taller, younger version of Rabbi Mordechai stepped out of the office, and I stiffened reflexively, confused. For the briefest moment, I thought it was Mordechai standing there, Mordechai back from the grave, but this man was sharper, harder. Stronger. Possibly even smarter than Mordechai was, a caul of hard-won cynicism settling over him like one of Mordechai's shawls.

I had to get out of here. He might know who I was—

He knows.

Shut up, I thought desperately. I took an involuntary step back, but Ethan's gaze traveled from the envelope in Mary's hands to me.

His face went hard. "What are you doing here?" he asked harshly.

"Ethan." Mary was clearly surprised to hear him take such a tone, and my heart shriveled a little. In another lifetime, on another planet, I would mourn with these people, tell them stories about their uncle and all the people he had helped. As it was, I just wanted to run.

"You are not welcome here," he said curtly, his eyes flat and cold beneath his bushy brows. "Why do you trouble the—"

"I'm leaving. I'm leaving!" I blurted, then I was scrambling back, turning away as something desperate quaked inside me. "Please—read the report," I managed, over my shoulder. "Those people need your help."

"Get *out*." The force of Rabbi Ethan's anger seemed to hit me square in the back, and I sprawled forward, half falling as I sped around the side of the house.

As I stumbled away, I heard Mary's voice, soft but firm: "Ethan, that's enough."

But he didn't call me back, and I didn't stop moving. There were mourners still showing up, but I didn't slow down for them, didn't slow down for anyone. Even as I ran, I kept flashing back to that bright, new, empty folder. My name, in Mordechai's hand. Cold as the grave he now rested in, under all that dirt.

Why had he created a file on me?

And had anything ever been in it?

I ran for Steve's car, lungs heaving, heart thundering, and slammed myself into the driver's seat, fumbling for my keys. I jolted out into the street almost before I'd shut the door.

It took another seventeen blocks before I even understood

where I was, and where I was heading. I was driving back out of town.

I pulled over to the side of the street and cut the engine, breathing hard. I wasn't going back to Max's. I'd done what I had to do. I'd given Mordechai's nephew the document about the Graham house. He'd know what to do with it. Whether he wanted to work with Max's family or not, he'd know what he was looking at when he read the report. I was done. I was out of it.

So now what?

I needed to go home. Steve would want his car, after all. It was his car. I had to get it to him.

But when I pulled into the duplex's driveway, there was no Steve. The afternoon faded into evening—still no Steve. I texted him; no response. He wasn't my job, he wasn't my responsibility, but a gnawing, growling restlessness tapped at me, poking and pulling, refusing me rest. Steve was in danger, I somehow knew. He was weak, open—too open.

He was also my friend.

Standing in the middle of my kitchen, still covered in demon scrawl, I felt something twist inside me at that thought. Twist and shiver, as if looking for a place to hide.

I held out my over-scrubbed hands, turned them over. Curled them into fists.

"Did you do something to Steve?" I asked the air around me coldly. I turned, confronting the fridge because I had nowhere else to look. "Did something bad happen to him because of you?"

No—the voice began, but I had no patience for it now, because I knew—knew! what was going on. Something *had* happened last night, when I was coating myself in Sharpie ink. Things had gotten out of hand. Wet, pulsing darkness had built up and spilled over, poisoning everything in its path.

"You told somebody about Steve, didn't you?" I stared at my muddy reflection in the fridge, feeling almost incandescent with rage. "You also woke up whatever hellstorm was sleeping in Max's house to get me to go back out there, but you couldn't leave it at that. You had to push."

You needed pushed.

"I *knew* it." I was fairly spitting now. "And to make sure I was, you told somebody—some*thing*—about Steve, didn't you? Who? One of your noxious little fucking demon friends? What's next? Are you going to send Claire a fucking possessed doll?"

Claire wouldn't have stopped you.

All the blood drained out of my face. "Did you hurt him?" I challenged the microwave glass, spinning around to try and get a glimpse of the thing inside me. "You fucking *bastard*."

The thing inside me fell silent, but my mind was off and running now. Steve would be the perfect target for a demon. He was trusting, sweet, gentle. Good—but not strong. Not hardened. And he walked a shadowy line between partier and addict that got narrower with each passing month.

But where the fuck would a demon take him? Where *was* he?

Nearly blind with rage, I tore through Steve's clothes and his backpack, pawing through way too many cards and flyers from bars and liquor stores. One place kept showing up, though, one place that resonated in a strange, sick way. A strange, sick way that wasn't unlike the demon writhing inside me.

But perhaps what I was feeling wasn't the demon, this time. Maybe it was truth coiled up and ready to explode, and the demon would be collateral damage.

Either way, the creature inside me said not a single word as I stared down at the coaster in my hand. Some club called The Descent. Grabbing my phone, I searched for it—and frowned.

Okay, this place was super high ticket. Definitely not Steve's vibe.

Still...

I checked the clock. It was pushing midnight, and my tension ratcheted tighter. I didn't care how the evil shitstorm had found Steve, it had. Because of me.

But I wasn't the kid anymore who'd stumbled across Mordechai while I was out walking my neighbor's dogs. I was no longer the girl who trailed him around, mimicking his every move, memorizing each word and sigh. I was the woman who'd evicted a demon on my own, who'd gotten paid $10,000 to take on a totally different houseful of demons out in the middle of goddamned nowhere. The woman with shit scrawled all over my body and cold hard fury thumping through my veins.

And I was also the woman who was going to kick one fucked-up, Sharpie-loving demon right out onto his ass really, really, soon.

But first...I was going to go get Steve.

EIGHTEEN

As I prowled through the streets of downtown Chicago, letting my intuition guide me in a way I'd never even considered a possibility before, I realized I'd made a mistake, allowing myself to have a housemate. I'd wanted someone to share the loneliness of my mother's home, to mask her absence, to make me feel normal.

But I wasn't normal. I was *possessed*. When the hell had that happened, anyway? Before Mom died? After?

Had her death been my fault?

My hands tightened on the wheel, but I couldn't focus on that now. Steve deserved my full attention. He'd never once looked at me like I was some sort of freak. He should have, but he didn't. I owed him for that. Plus, I was driving around in his car. If he turned up dead, that probably wasn't going to go over too well with Officer Hernandez. I had to find him—him, and whatever was with him. Hurting him.

We can hurt them back, you know.

"That's exactly what we're going to do, asshole."

You shouldn't call me that.

"No problem." I smirked. "How about you tell me your name?"

Silence greeted that request. I parked Steve's car three blocks away from The Descent in a well-lit upscale parking garage surrounded by well-lit upscale cars. I was keyed up, stressed out, not quite sure how I'd ended up in this part of town, and not quite sure how to find my way back home. Those were problems that I'd deal with later. For now, though...

I stopped, squinting down the long street toward The Descent, taking in the winking neon lights, the heavy onyx marble storefront. Despite all the coasters Steve had dragged home from this place, I still had a hard time believing he was actually here.

Steve drank too much, smoked weed, and had probably dabbled in half a dozen other designer drugs in the time that I knew him, but he wasn't really into a darker vibe. And despite its fancy lights and well-dressed bouncers, I knew instinctively that The Descent was about as dark as Chicago ever got.

The club was located in a decent enough area of town, a few blocks off Fifth Avenue. The kind of place that an unwary tourist might stumble into after a show or an overpriced dinner. It touted its music as house and goth, and its neon light show got good ratings on Yelp. From what I could tell from the pictures posted online, the people who writhed on its dance floor were young, pretty, and wound tight with need and greed. That also didn't seem like Steve, but then again, I didn't know everything about him. And I was almost certain he was here.

Jolting myself back into action, I continued moving down the street, vaguely aware that I wasn't dressed like most of the people standing in line for The Descent. I wore dark jeans, a black tank top and hoodie, and the still-fading ink from the night before. I had on boots too. Big, clunky, shit-kicking boots, the kind that could stomp a man to death. I was young, but I wasn't rich, and I wasn't pretty. I also didn't care.

It was that last bit that made it all come together.

I stalked up to the front of the line and stared at the bouncer by the door. There must have been something in my face, my attitude, because he didn't laugh me off the sidewalk, simply stared back at me with his watery, bloodshot eyes. He was a big man, smarter than he wanted people to think. Broken by the death of a brother, the coldness of his mother, or the spiritual absence of a father gone for far too long. He was a mark, I thought, but a harmless mark. And he looked at me with a weary, regretful smile that made my pulse quicken.

Bad things came to The Descent, I knew at once. Tonight, I was one of them.

"Name?" he asked.

I opened my mouth to speak, to say the name of the demon I had released from Mrs. Klein's sister Iris, if only for extra credibility. But something else issued from my throat, the softest sigh, a quiet, unexpected word. "Delia."

He stepped to the side, and I was through.

Utter chaos greeted me, a frenzied pulse of light and music, laughter and dancing, shouting and the stench of humanity too closely pressed together, desperate and fearful and alive. The air inside Descent tasted like panic and sweat, with an underlying sweetness that made my stomach turn if only because of how familiar it was. Not quite brimstone, not quite rot—something in between. Something hungry.

I felt the cool wash of light sweep over me, tasted the sharp tang of liquor and want. But Steve wasn't here. He wouldn't be here under the lights on the open floor. He would be where the others crouched and breathed in darkness, the ones who watched, the ones who took.

I could take too, I thought. I could find these other rooms, enter them, and see the creatures that had dared to go too far. I could save him.

There will always be a Steve to save.

Ignoring my inner dickhead, I headed for the back of the dance floor where two hulking bodyguards stood. I smelled the darkness within them as I approached, but it wasn't possession. It was simply brutality and vice. They were the kind of guys who liked to see beautiful things crushed. And they were on the outside of the rooms they guarded. What was waiting for me in there?

I approached them, and they looked up as one, sweeping me with a practiced gaze, taking in my cheap tank top and heavy boots, my ragged dark hair and ink-stained skin. I was not the norm in this crowd. The first one smiled, not a good smile, and dropped a meaty hand to his belt. "What do you want?"

"I'm the exorcist," I said, my voice abrupt, flat. How an exorcist should talk, I decided. "They're expecting me."

"You're not on the list."

A cold smile curved my lips. "I'm usually not."

Something in my expression stopped them from asking any other questions. The first one turned, keyed the door, and disappeared into the darkness, while the second blocked the door with his foot, but held out his hand to stop me from following. He wasn't as smart as the first one, and he wasn't as corrupted, but he was about fifty percent more jacked on coke. I looked into his eyes. There was no demon inside him...but there didn't have to be. This guy had ensnared himself.

"You don't want to stop me," I told bouncer #2 as more intuitive knowledge flooded me—way more information than I usually got, deeper and fuller, running along the edges of the ink still staining my skin, sinking into my bones.

"Sure, I do." He grinned, his lips peeling back from his too white teeth. His body was large, his black shirt stretched tight over pecs he'd worked hard to blow up in the gym, and I knew his story too. Knew it and used it, as I stared into his too bright eyes.

"Your dad's losing hope," I told him, getting right up into his face. "He thinks you're going to die up here in this city of filth. Your mom drinks too much, and now he does too. He needs you. He's not good at this."

He flinched back. "Who the fuck are you, cunt?"

I leaned in closer. "You were too dumb to stick with school, but you aren't too dumb to work, to fight. Don't fight me. Not tonight. Fight the asshole who wants to nail your sister after the game tomorrow night. He'll hurt her."

"The fuck he will." With a heavy push, the guard shoved the door open and stepped aside. "Your boy's in cell three. Four is the exit. They try to get you into two, they're gonna hurt you. If you're lying to me, *I'm* gonna hurt—"

"I'm not." I was already past him before he could finish his threat, and the door banged shut behind me. The hallway was long and lit by flickering, neon-esque LED lights, with a half-dozen doors lining one side. Its industrial tile floor had been painted to look like stained concrete, and decorator-quality epithets scrawled both sides of the corridor. All of it fake, of course, but very atmospheric. Someone had taken their time. The lights above the "cell" doors alternated blue, yellow, and red. Cell two was colored red, with two more lights after it. White for three, then blue for four.

I headed down the hallway, and a second later the door to cell three opened, and the first beefy bouncer emerged to lumber down the hallway toward me. He held himself too stiffly, and he didn't meet my eyes. "Three, not two. Three," he rasped, still without looking at me, and as he passed, a new smell assaulted my senses. Urine.

Nice.

I picked up my pace and shot forward, reaching the spring-loaded door of cell #3 before it could snick shut. I slipped in, my eyes instantly adjusting to the low-level red haze that illuminated the room. I smelled Steve's aftershave almost instantly, but I couldn't see him, could only see the table overflowing with drug paraphernalia, booze and food, and a scrum of people jittering to the pulsing, pounding music, all of them eager, jacked-up addicts, their necks punctured with what looked like bite marks, their eyes spinning and wide.

Beside them, a black-suited Eastern-European-looking man with high cheekbones and broad shoulders at odds with his long, lean body stood in an obvious position of power, the lord of all these scrabbling sycophants. He lazily fondled another half-stoned woman who was doing her level best to fuck his right thigh, but his eyes were on me.

Not *his* eyes, of course. His eyes had long-since been compromised by the dark creature that had a stranglehold on his guts. But when those sneaky rat-red eyes met mine, it was game over for the demon. I knew him in a heartbeat.

I wasn't the only one.

Pithius. Of course.

"Pithius," I snapped, as another flood of information washed over me, this time not intuition, but a direct download from my personal demon-GPT, who apparently thought Pithius the fifth-level lust demon was an attention-grabbing whore who damaged dirty when he should just kill. In a flash, I got about eight centuries of the creature's degradation, destruction, and madness—for whom this current victim, Nikolai Volkov, was barely a trifle.

The information dump left me dizzy, my creature's contempt for Pithius rolling through me like nausea. Territorial. Possessive.

I grimaced. If that kind of demon was in *this* guy, I thought, what the hell was fucking with—

"Nooooo…" The panicked groan from the far, shadowed corner of the room jerked my attention over—a section I hadn't noticed at first, a circular conversation pit of overstuffed seats where bodies lay strewn like fallen toys. I saw Steve, finally.

Steve was not doing well.

"*Christ*," I muttered, with enough emphasis to make all the demons in the room hiss. Steve was cut up, tourniqueted, and his blood was spilling out over the writhing bodies of two other partiers—one man, one woman. More red liquid dropped from a bag hung over them, and I didn't know if that blood was real or fake. It smelled real enough, and the pain Steve was in had finally gotten real enough as well to shatter the haze of whatever dope was running through his system.

But Steve's long, anguished groan told me something else, too—namely, he was still Steve. He wasn't held by a demon, only by the foolish handmaidens of a demon. That was bad enough, given the shape he was in, but it also meant I didn't have to play nice at all with dickhead number one.

"Pithius!" I roared, turning back to Nikolai Volkov—only to recoil in surprise as he lunged toward me, his woman cast aside. He reached for my face, fingernails whittled into talons, teeth biting and gnashing. There was metal at his wrists and around his neck, and some sort of hard girdle around his waist beneath his trousers. This bastard was going to be a bitch to take down, unless—

Eyes, Delia.

I didn't hesitate.

My hands shot out as if I'd done this a thousand times before, jabbing out, up—no hesitation, no slacking off. My right thumb missed its mark but the left one struck gold as it pierced the soft, gelatinous orb. Nikolai gave an unholy bellow of pain.

Pressing my advantage, I grabbed the guy by his long black hair and jerked him around, trapping his other eye with my glare, adding my own roar to his cries. With his body already pierced and bleeding, extracting the demon was easy, especially since I didn't need to worry about Nikolai's pain. But between Pithius's screech of horror and outrage and the frozen sweep of evil rushing into the room, the other humans and their minor demon parasites all jolted out of their fugue state.

Panic vibrated through the room, clearly more powerful than the lesser demons trying to maintain control, and the other partiers rushed for the door, leaving Steve and Nikolai behind.

Fortunately, there were half a dozen knives between me and Steve's slowly exsanguinating body, and I scooped two up, cutting and thrashing to get through the tide of humanity. Then I sliced through the lines holding Steve fast, cut the tourniquets and yanked out the ports. He still bled, and he wasn't a small guy, but with a strength I knew I didn't have, I threw his arm over my shoulder and dragged him out of cell three—straight into utter chaos.

The crowd was trapped in the hallway, disoriented and screaming, trying to rush back toward the main club. I stumbled, went down, then another set of hands reached out, pulling Steve from me, then yanking me up as well for good measure. Our impromptu savior hauled both of us in the opposite direction of the club, down the hallway toward a glowing blue light and then out another doorway into the cool, clean night.

The stranger pulled us into the alley and draped Steve over me again, then he stepped back inside Descent before the doorway to hell closed. As he released me, our skin scraped, and renewed energy shot through me, hot and surging. The man smelled improbably of crackling electricity, sex, and expensive champagne. I looked up, staggering beneath Steve, and recognized him.

It was the European lord of the Descent underworld, the one-eyed victim of Pithius—and he was still standing, still alive, despite the rage with which his demon captor had departed his body.

"Thank you," he breathed in a low, sonorous rumble, watching me intently with his one working eye while the other one hung halfway down his face.

I decided right then that whatever drugs the guy was on, they were totally worth it. And despite the gore dripping along his jaw, Nikolai Volkov was *hot*.

The growl from deep within me was almost inaudible beneath the screams from the hallway. Almost.

I smirked.

Then the man receded into the darkness, and Steve and I stumbled off into the night.

NINETEEN

Steve's car was where I'd left it, thank God. I managed to stuff him into the back seat with only minimal additional blood loss. He was going to have one hell of a detailing bill, but that wasn't my problem.

The ride home passed in a blur. By the time we got to the duplex, Steve was waking up again and full-on delirious. He wasn't in any apparent pain, though, so I took advantage of his spurt of energy to get him into the house and onto the couch. Thirty seconds after I covered him with my grandmother's afghan, he was out cold again.

I stared down at him for a long moment, bouncing on my toes. After all the action at the club and the ride home, I wasn't the least bit tired. I was buzzing, on edge, riding high on the night's events. I felt glorious, actually—filled with power for what felt like the first time in my *life*.

Without a specific focus, I drifted into the kitchen, which made my smile tease into a grin. I'd confronted my demon in this room, calling it out, straight up yelling at it. Then I'd gone out and rescued Deadbeat Steve over its objections. And I'd exorcised another demon in the process.

All by yourself?

My grin deepened. "Ahhh, there you are," I said to my muddy reflection in the refrigerator door. "I wondered where you'd snuck off to."

I did a little shimmy, hips swishing. "And yeah, I did it pretty much *all* by myself. You certainly didn't seem to like that hot guy that ol' Pith—"

Don't say his name.

A stab of fear jolted through me, cutting me off, and I blinked with surprise. "Why?" I asked, genuinely curious. Had Mordechai ever repeated the name of the demons he exorcised, once he sent them on their way? I didn't think so, but...maybe?

Either way, my own personal demon didn't seem willing to enlighten me on this point of protocol. Whatever.

Tired of the fridge view, I turned toward my reflection in the microwave, tilting my head coyly, still surfing on adrenaline. I squinted, but couldn't see much, and I *wanted* to see myself, to see the new and improved nightclub-demon-exorcising badass version of me. I wanted to know if I looked as hot as I felt.

I snorted even as I headed toward the stairs. I'd never thought of myself as hot—hell, I never thought of myself as anything, most of the time. Not pretty or ugly, sexy or stiff, fun or boring. I'd seriously never considered the idea of "me" at all, outside of a worker, daughter, roommate, student, assistant to an exorcist, and probably definitely a freak.

Why was that?

Uneasiness quivered inside me, and I pounced on the reaction, batting it around like a cat with a ball of yarn. "Is it because of you?" I wondered aloud as I stopped at the bottom of the stairs, not even bothering to keep my voice low. Steve was beyond dead to the world right now. "Did you do that to me?"

I mean, it made sense. Of course it made sense. What self-respecting demon wanted its host to have actual self-identifying thoughts?

And then there was its reaction to Max—and especially to the random mafia-looking guy I'd just met at Descent. Met and *helped*, though I'd hurt him too. Hurt him a lot, now that I thought about it. Oh well.

But he was definitely a smokin' hot male, and my demon hadn't loved that.

My demon also didn't so much as hiss at this assessment, so I knew I was on to something. I bounded up the stairs, faster than I ever had, my mind buzzing with new connections.

I'd never dated in high school or after—never wanted to date. I'd had a few opportunities, especially at UIC, but though I'd lost my virginity at sixteen and screwed around a few times after that, sex had never really registered on my radar as a desire or focus. There'd always been something else to deal with, something else to do. How crazy was it that I'd never so much as *thought* of a guy in any real way until now? Maybe not crazy at all.

Sex was power, everyone always said.

How much power?

At the top of the stairs, still moving fast, I didn't head for my bedroom with its bare white walls. Instead, I opened the door into the bigger room right next to the staircase, the one my mother had slept in, and then, on very rare occasions and only right at the beginning, Steve.

I stepped inside and closed the door behind me, then flipped on the light. The soft glow illuminated light-blue painted walls, a clean white comforter-covered bed, a white-painted chest of drawers, and threadbare but vacuumed carpet. I'd at least tried to make the room decent for Steve, for all that he never liked it. I didn't like it, either. I sure as hell never slept in here. But tonight, it had something I needed,

Mirrors. Over the dresser and lining the closet walls, positioned so you could practically see yourself coming and going. I never used them; I never wanted to look.

Tonight, though...I wanted to look at *everything*.

Delia.

"Oh, now you want to talk to me." I didn't miss the oddly desperate note that reverberated when the demon spoke my name. It was different than how it had warned me against saying Pithius's name aloud. It sounded more nervous. Uneasy. That was interesting. And new.

So, the thing inside me didn't want me looking at myself? Why would that be?

I marched up to the full-length mirror and stared at my reflection.

For a moment, nothing happened. Then I felt a flicker of pressure behind my eyes. A tightening in my chest that wasn't quite pain. The demon, pushing back. Trying to make me turn away.

I smiled at my reflection and stayed exactly where I was.

Tilting my head, I turned a little to the side. I looked almost pretty, I thought, if you didn't count the smears of blood or the fading vestiges of Sharpie ink on my skin. And for the first time in my life, I wondered what *he* saw when he looked through my eyes. Did he see the same pragmatic, grim-eyed fighter I was checking out? Or did he see something else—something he'd kept *me* from seeing clearly all these years?

The thought made heat curl low in my belly.

For my assault on Descent, I'd dressed up in the most goth thing I could find that still covered me up—black jeans, black tank top without a bra, black hoodie, black boots. I'd shed the hoodie downstairs next to Steve, and my markered-up arms gleamed with their epithets and slurs, but I didn't care so much about those anymore.

Instead, I focused on my hazel eyes, my longish dark brown hair, and my too-pale skin that rarely saw the sun. I was neither skinny nor fat, my body way more functional than curvy, but...I liked the way I looked, I decided. I was fierce. I was strong.

I'd had to be, I supposed, given that I was lugging a freaking demon around.

Suppressing a giggle, I lifted my hands to my temples, pressing my fingers along my cheeks, my neck, and over my shoulder blades, as if memorizing new terrain I'd never mapped before. New, wild, *delicious* terrain.

And I was delicious. Yummy enough to gobble up whole.

Inside me, something shifted. Not quite a flinch—more like attention snapping into sharp focus. Like I'd just walked into a room my demon had been guarding, and now he couldn't look away.

Good.

I dipped my hands farther down my chest and felt him twist inside me—not away, but toward. Like a hooked fish fighting the line.

"You don't like this?" I murmured, staring into my own eyes as I cupped my breasts, feeling their weight and roundness. I kneaded them slowly, deliberately, and heard the hiss in the back of my mind.

But beneath the hiss was something else. A low, subsonic rumble that I felt more than heard. Hunger. Want. The kind of need that had been carefully choked off, starved for fifteen years.

My nipples hardened under my palms—from my touch or the demon's attention, I couldn't tell anymore.

I also didn't care.

My lips quirked into a smile. "Is this why I never felt *anything* for *anyone* before now?" I whispered to my reflection. "Were you cock blocking me, you sack of shit?"

And since when was that a thing? I knew enough from researching possessions with Mordechai that most demons gloried in the sexual depravity of their hosts—driving their trapped humans to ever-worsening acts of debasement.

"But not you?" I cooed as I squeezed my breasts more firmly, then slid my hands down my thin tank top to drag it free from the waistband of my jeans. "That's not your thing? Or maybe...it was all along, hmm? But you didn't want to push your luck?"

When my fingers brushed along the skin of my belly, the demon twisted again, the movement tight, even a little angry. Interesting.

I pulled off my tank in one smooth motion—my brows lifting. I'd forgotten about the words I'd written all over my torso.

No. Not me. The realization hit me cold and sharp. *I* hadn't written these phrases and lines. It had. *He* had. Using my hand, yes, but these weren't my words.

"*Poetry*," I breathed, tracing the shaky letters across my ribs, my belly, circling my breasts like a brand. My skin prickled beneath my fingers, hypersensitive, as the thing inside me went utterly still. "You wrote poetry on me. Here—and here, and here. Why? Is there something you want, down there in the dark?" I whispered the challenge, fingers drifting lower, following the text down to my hipbones. "Something you've wanted for a while?"

The silence inside me felt like a held breath. Like the moment before surrender.

I played my fingers up over my breasts again, feeling my own rising heat—and something else beneath it. His desire bleeding into mine like ink in water, impossible to separate.

"You could have had this any time," I murmured, watching my hands in the mirror. "Fifteen years, you've been inside me. You could have made me do anything...but you didn't."

Without warning, I pinched my nipples hard, trapping

them between my fingers. Pleasure spiked through me—both mine and not-mine, doubled and reflected back. Inside me, the demon made a sound I'd never heard before. Not a hiss. Not a growl.

Almost a moan.

"There you are," I breathed.

No response to that, and I tipped my head back, drawing in a deep breath as I slid my hands along my waist again, following the slight flare of my hips then sweeping them back over my belly.

Slowly, methodically, I unsnapped my jeans and dragged the denim down, exposing plain black cotton panties.

"So boring," I murmured, but my voice had gone husky. The air felt thicker. Charged. "You could have dressed me in lace. Silk. You could have had so much more fun. But you wanted to keep me like this. Didn't you? Untouched. Unknowing. A gift not yet unwrapped."

His presence behind my gaze had never felt so close. So intense.

"So I'll unwrap it for you."

I kicked the jeans aside. My breathing went shallow. And inside me—*inside* me—the demon breathed in too. Harsh. Ragged, almost. Like he was drowning.

Stop.

The word swept through my mind like trash in the wind, desperate and raw. Not a command. A plea.

I smiled at my reflection and slid my hand into my panties.

Drawing in a slow, deliberate breath, I forced myself to focus solely on the touch of my fingers along the soft, hidden folds between my legs, the whorls of sensation that sparked off shivering heat when I dipped inside. Stroking and sliding, I feathered my fingers along my clit like the brush of a hummingbird's wing. I gusted out a heavier sigh, shimmying my body again, undulating against the force of my hand.

I couldn't look at my eyes in the mirror anymore, couldn't risk breaking my focus. Instead, I stared at my hand and imagined it was someone else's hand, someone subtle and sure in the darkness, strong and sly. I could feel the pressure building, spiraling up, and I dipped in again, spreading myself.

It felt good—wild. A little profane, but that was the whole point, wasn't it?

Yes, it was.

The pleasure was mine, of course, but threaded through it was something else—a thrumming curiosity that couldn't be squashed down anymore. It wasn't separate from me, but full and hot, woven through every sensation.

My sighs turned into longer, deeper moans, and at some point, I lifted my hand to plant it on the mirror, leaning in, my body closer to my own reflection, but my eyes fixed on my hand, my fingers, the deep and rolling pleasure as I touched and explored, skimmed and fondled. Time seemed to slip away, lost on the escalating heartbeat, as I got closer—closer.

Every stroke of my fingers sent shockwaves through me— through both of us—and at some point he stopped trying to pull away. Instead, his presence shifted, a reversing tide. It flooded through me, no longer fighting or resisting, but riding each cresting wave as I went up...up, up...before plunging down the other side.

For the first time in fifteen years, we weren't at war.

My breath shuddered out at the thought of that, which somehow pushed me higher, closer, my heart pounding raggedly at the idea of this creature who yearned as I yearned, slid as I slid. My neck arched as I swept my fingers high again to the nub of my clit, stroking and pulsing before dipping deep again. Slick heat coated my fingers and the scent of my own arousal swirled around me.

I felt the dark energy twist up in a sharp wet coil, then pulse, pulse, the want becoming need, the need becoming its own living thing. The line between us dissolved completely and I felt the demon within me reach down, embrace me, then shove me up again.

I shattered, built, shattered again...and built higher. I wanted this, needed this—needed *him* to feel it with me.

The pleasure crested—and it was ours, not just mine, not just his. Ours. For one blinding second, we were the same thing. We were—the—same—

I jerked my head up, directly meeting my own untethered gaze in the mirror, and in that one-brief-moment-*yes*!

Yes!

"*You*," I breathed out as my gaze filled with the creature inside me.

A suggestion of wings, massive and dark.

Eyes that weren't eyes but points of light in a shape that had once been beautiful and was now...broken. Hungry. Ancient.

And looking at me like I was the only thing in all of creation that mattered, as its quivering, shivering desperation vibrated with something that wasn't just lust or violence—not entirely. It was panic. Shame.

Need.

The broken, starving thing beneath the monster. An image of utter desolation and vulnerability that seared itself into my—

A force that seemed to blast out from the mirror itself jerked me three full inches off the floor and flung me backward across the room as an enraged roar exploded in my brain, loud enough to make my ears bleed. The bed caught me in the back of the thighs, and I flipped straight over it, smashing into the wall and crumbling into a heap on the floor, a discarded doll.

But I wasn't a fucking doll.

Not anymore.

"I saw you!" I seethed as I lurched to my feet, scrambling back up on the bed again as I glared at the mirror across the room. I didn't know what I expected to see staring back at me. The unholy nightmare trapped behind my eyeballs had been more shadow than form, and if it leaped out of the mirror at me right then I'd probably die on the spot.

I didn't care, though. In this particular moment, I didn't care about anything other than that I had won—*won*! I'd lured the creature out because it wanted me, needed me, and at the very last second, I'd looked up and I had *seen* it.

And seeing these fuckers was the first step to booting them straight back to hell.

I stared at the mirror for another long moment, the pain of my impromptu body slam against the bedroom wall beginning to break through my euphoria. But nothing flickered in the mirror, nothing murmured in the back of my brain.

My demon, for the moment, had nothing to say.

But I could still feel him. Coiled tight in the deepest part of me. Not angry anymore.

Hiding.

And for the first time ever...I wondered if he was afraid of *me*.

The thought should have felt like victory.

It didn't.

Moving slowly, never taking my eyes off the mirror, I gathered up my clothes and backed toward the hallway.

Thirty seconds later, I closed the door to my mother's room behind me and sagged against it. Then, fatigue and pain finally catching up to me, I stumbled back to my own bed.

CHAPTER

TWENTY

Steve left on Saturday morning, three days after the Descent attack.

He'd mumbled something about his folks needing him, but he still wouldn't meet my eyes when he took his keys. His car had bloodstains in the backseat we both pretended not to see.

Either way, I let him go. We didn't need to see each other, I supposed, not anytime soon. Maybe never again. Some shared experiences were hard to come back from, and this certainly qualified.

I texted him a couple times over the weekend—explaining where I'd taken his car earlier in the week, how I'd tried to help the Grahams. Asking if he was okay.

He never responded.

Sunday, I slept until 2 p.m. When I woke up, my body felt like it had been beaten with hammers—delayed reaction from being thrown across Mom's bedroom, probably, or the cumulative toll of the past week catching up. I shuffled downstairs, made coffee, and found myself standing in the kitchen staring at the spot where the knives had been lined up.

The demon inside me remained silent. Completely, eerily silent.

Again, I should have felt relieved. Instead, I felt hollow. Like I'd found myself but lost something I didn't know I needed.

I hadn't been back to my mother's room since that night. Hadn't looked in a mirror, either. Couldn't bring myself to.

Sunday afternoon, I texted Max. He responded quickly—thrilled a new rabbi knew about the problem, even more thrilled that Wednesday night had been completely quiet. No ghost horses, no screaming. Everything settled.

I didn't tell him about the Sharpie attack or Steve. What was the point?

On Monday, I couldn't stand the silence anymore. I needed to do something, learn something, *be* something other than stuck in an empty apartment haunted by a quiet demon.

In truth, I hadn't realized how much I'd come to rely on Mordechai sending me on this errand or that, to research old houses or apartment buildings, to look up genealogies. Half the time I'd been pretty sure he'd just been coming up with stuff for me to do, but it didn't matter. With him, I'd had a purpose, a plan. Now I was nothing.

But I sure was learning a lot about the work he did. That was good, right?

The demon inside me didn't respond.

Claire found me at the library Tuesday evening, sliding into the chair across from me with her own stack of pharmaceutical journals.

"Pathways that connect heaven and earth => fault lines that can be corrupted." I copied down dutifully, glancing up at her with a smile.

Ever since the Sharpie incident, she'd started texting me on the daily. Given that everyone else had abandoned me, I didn't mind that so much. In a moment of weakness, I'd told her about Mordechai, how I'd helped him as an exorcist's assistant, and eventually, about my research at the library. So I shouldn't have been surprised when she showed up to join me here quietly reading her own research texts on pills or whatever, her little golden cross glinting in the overhead light.

I still was, though.

The internet in incognito search mode proved a willing teacher on all sorts of subjects, even some that were surprisingly dark to be delivered on a library's server. I found myself buried in new information about demons—more disturbing things in a way—about how they were essentially part of the cosmic balance, a sort of "left-side" of power that was neither bad nor good, but simply necessary. I learned that iron could bind them, that names could, too, and that there was a hierarchy of command among these assholes, from first to seventh levels. I took notes like my life depended on it, because maybe it did. Right now, I was reading about how a particular class of spirit, the shedim, could appear human—

"You know, I've been doing some thinking," Claire said abruptly, smiling when I glanced up. "You should do this work professionally. Exorcism work. Like, as your job."

"Mmhmm. I'm not actually an exorcist, Claire."

"But you kind of are, right?" She pointed at my research pile. "You do the work. People pay you. That's literally a job."

"Right."

"I'm serious." And it was true; Claire had her serious face on, the one that usually preceded a lecture about drinking more water, going to therapy, or finishing college. In that order of importance.

Now she pointed at her own laptop, one not owned by the library. "I've been looking up stories online, and they all say the same kind of thing you told me about when you went to the Klein's house. An exorcist goes in, confronts evil, hoovers it out, and leaves. The people have to recover and heal and all that, but you can *do* the hard part! You provide a real service that people would definitely pay for. Max's money isn't going to last forever, you know. This is a way to make, seriously, a whole lot more."

"I guess," I grumbled. "But it's not as easy as that. I'm not, like, a priest or a rabbi. That's kind of part of the package."

"So you're a freelancer!" Claire declared, bouncing a little in her seat. "And your lack of religious affiliation means you can do the stuff a priest or a rabbi won't do. You can specialize that way."

I squinted at her. "Do you know how bad evil would have to be to make a rabbi or priest shy away?"

"I'm *serious*," she said again, completely missing the fact that I was being serious too. Still, her excitement didn't just unnerve me on a surface level. Deep in my gut, something slithered and coiled, whether in fear or excitement, I couldn't tell. Not excitement, I didn't think.

"Something you afraid of in there?" I thought, using my inside voice. *"Or do you not think I'm strong enough?"*

My demon didn't answer. Instead, my phone beeped loudly, the unexpected sound following so quickly on my thoughts, I nearly jumped out of my own skin.

Claire flinched too. "Is that Max?" she squeaked as I grabbed for my phone, punching in my code because my face never worked to open it anymore.

"It's gotta be Max," I said as I stabbed open the app. "Who else would it be?"

Then I stopped as I squinted down. Blinked.

It wasn't Max.

It was Officer Hernandez.

Need to talk about Rabbi Mordechai's death. New information. You free?

The words blurred. I read them again.

New information.

About the cemetery, the night he'd died. The night I'd run.

CHAPTER

TWENTY-ONE

Claire insisted on driving me back to my house for my "talk" with the cop. Not an interview or an interrogation, Officer Hernandez assured me via text. She just wanted to swing by and catch up. You know, like cops did.

It was hard for me to turn down Claire's suggestion, since she had a car. She was also a woman on a mission. By the time Hernandez showed up at the front door of my duplex, Claire had not only swept through the entire first floor like an avenging Molly Maid, she'd warmed up the cookies she'd insisted we buy at a bakery along the way and had set out take-out coffee in real-life mugs as if I actually had a coffee maker in my house.

By this time, Claire was practically bouncing off the walls with excitement.

I got the feeling she didn't have enough going on in her life. The thought made me smile.

"Officer Hernandez, this is my friend Claire," I said, when Hernandez stepped into the living room, smelling of questions, yesterday's court appearance, and surprising cheerfulness. "She also knows about Mordechai, though they never met in person. If she can't stay while we talk, that's totally okay."

"Claire…" Hernandez held out her hand, and Claire took it eagerly.

"Bickwell," she said with a bright smile. "Delia and I work near each other, that's how we met. I'm a pharmacist at Reider's on Madison, do you know it?"

I didn't have the heart to tell Claire that Hernandez had probably already run her license plate, but Hernandez, to her credit, just smiled.

"I do. Nice to meet you." She shifted her attention to me as we sat, all of us ignoring the cookies. "I understand you had a run-in with the rabbi's nephew after Mordechai's death."

"Rabbi Ethan?" I frowned. "I did, but that was two weeks ago. I haven't been back since, I swear."

She nodded. "He said the same thing, but he still didn't seem too pleased with you when we spoke yesterday."

"Well, I didn't know what else to do," I said, hearing the defensiveness in my voice. "I guess I shouldn't have tried to return the documents I had of Mordechai's so soon. But I felt bad, keeping a hold of them."

"I understand." She studied me. "He asked a lot of questions about you."

That made me go a little cold. "Really?"

"Yes. Said he knew about you, from his uncle, of course, but that you were nothing like he expected."

I tensed, then picked up my mug of coffee to cover the movement. What exactly had Ethan been expecting? "Did he tell you something about me I should know? Did he file a complaint or whatever?" My eyes widened. "Is that why you're here?"

"Slow down, it's nothing like that." She held up her hands with a smile. "I just found out more about Rabbi Mordechai's passing this morning, and after I shared it with him, I wanted you to know as well. Talking over the phone felt...not good enough."

"Oh." Relief washed through me. "I mean, yes. Totally. Thank you."

She nodded, but both she and Claire watched me closely. I sipped my cooling coffee and tried not to look possessed. "The doctor said the results of the autopsy were conclusive. Death was due to cardiac arrest. Your Rabbi Mordechai had partial blockage in one of his arteries and nearly full blockage in the second, so a heart attack was more a matter of when, not if."

I frowned. "But he never seemed sick." Not exactly true, of course. Mordechai *had* struck me as appearing weaker, recently. I'd noticed it. Had I said something to him about that? I...I didn't think so.

Why hadn't I said anything?

"With cases like these, sometimes there aren't any symptoms." Again, Hernandez seemed gentle, almost reassuring. I shifted a little uneasily in my chair.

"What about his hands?" The question came out before I really knew what to do with it. I set my cup back down. "You were worried about his hands—they were blistered, you said."

"Blistered?" Claire piped up, but Hernandez shook her head.

"Not blistered. Apparently, Mordechai had a skin ailment, sort of a dermatitis, the doctor told me, that afflicted the fingers and had become inflamed, possibly as part of his body's reaction to the heart attack."

"Oh." Curiously, I felt both reassured and anxious at once. "Well, I'm a terrible friend, either way. I never even noticed his hands."

"But you wouldn't have, right?" Claire nodded to Hernandez, who now regarded her with more than mild interest. "I mean, not necessarily. I'm a pharmacist, so I know a little about what might have happened. Rabbi Mordechai's hand condition might have been pretty mild until his heart attack, and then when that happened, it reacted right along with the rest of his body."

"Exactly." Officer Hernandez nodded, then looked back at me. "The head injury was never really explained, and I still haven't figured out what he meant by the word he wrote on the ground." She reached for her pocket, pulled out a worn-looking notebook, and flipped it open.

My blood seemed to ice over, and I stiffened so sharply, I'm surprised my back didn't snap. "I haven't either," I said quickly, shaking my head. I could feel Claire's startled gaze shift to me, but I didn't care. "It may not be safe to talk about that."

"Safe?" Hernandez peered at me. "Why not?"

"I don't know—it's just—" I shook my head harder now, my vision seeming to blur. Suddenly, I could see another person in front of me, another scene. Rabbi Mordechai, yelling at me. Only instead of telling me to run, to get away, his words were much more specific. "Go!" he'd yelled. *Go!*

Darkness exploded in the back of my brain.

"...Delia?"

I blinked my eyes open. Everything looked out of whack, upside down and off-center. In less than a second, I realized I must have fainted. I was on the carpet, next to the couch. Claire and Officer Hernandez stood over me, their faces tight. Hernandez had her hand on her phone, lifting it to her ear.

"No! God, sorry, I'm fine." I sat up quickly, but not too quickly—the room didn't spin. "I'm good. I...I'm sorry. Please—don't call anyone. I don't have insurance. And I'm okay."

Looking unhappy, Hernandez pocketed her phone. "You eat anything today?"

"She's so *bad* about that." Claire harumphed as they helped me back up onto the couch. "Here, there are all these cookies, and—" She picked one up, but when I waved her off, she scowled at me. "Why didn't you tell me you were hungry?"

"I'm sorry." I put my hand on my belly, where something still writhed and twitched inside me, even as the darkness bled away. Not hunger, though. Not even close. "I just got busy. Sorry to freak you guys out, I sort of freaked myself out too, I guess." I laughed shakily.

"Do you have someone who can check up on you?" Hernandez asked. "Your housemate—Steve, right? Is he around?"

"Oh. No. He moved out." I steadied myself. "I'll just get something to eat."

"We'll get something to eat. Besides cookies." Claire sat down next to me.

Hernandez seemed satisfied. She said more words, inconsequential words, but not the one word that hovered just on the edge of my awareness, taunting and teasing me before slipping back into the dark.

Still, I didn't really start breathing normally again until long after she left.

It wasn't until another week after I called that I finally got a text from Max—fully twenty-four days since I'd been to his place the first time.

When it popped up, I was working at the deli. I'd planned on quitting after the influx of his ten thousand dollars, but I'd found I couldn't bring myself to do it. I couldn't bring myself to thinking of the money as real, as final. That the job was finished.

So I was in the middle of filling a tub with chicken salad

when I heard the breathy chirping of my phone, and I somehow just knew. Knew it wasn't Claire, though she'd shown up every day at the deli to have chummy "business planning" lunches with me like she was some venture capitalist and not a pill pusher. Knew it wasn't Steve, telling me he wanted to come back to my couch. It wasn't even Officer Hernandez, who now had her own ring tone. Which meant it had to be Max.

Unfortunately, Max didn't have much to say.

I can send a car tomorrow—Saturday. Time?

I texted back as soon as the lunch line died down. *Any time after nine. What happened? Are you okay?*

His next text took a long time to come. And when it did, it was only four words. *I'm fine. Joe's dead.*

TWENTY-TWO

The car Max sent was a rental, with a stout, gray-haired driver whose smile was kind and his eyes direct. He smelled like ginger tea and sourdough toast, worn couches and a comfortable wife. He asked no questions and needed no conversation. I liked him on the spot.

More importantly, he wasn't Claire, who miraculously had not been around to hear Max's ping, which meant I hadn't had to explain where I was going or why. As far as Claire knew, I was spending the weekend at home, safe and snug 'til my next deli shift. I was glad for that. Never mind her insistence that she help me launch an exorcism business; she didn't need to clock this level of crazy with me.

The car Max had sent for me wasn't a full-on limo—more like a nice sedan—but I knew I was giving the Soos a show as I walked outside with my backpack and black overnight bag. I looked like I was being taken off for questioning by the CIA.

I got in the car. The driver confirmed our destination, and I agreed, then we both shut the hell up. I found myself retracing streets that I couldn't quite remember, finally reaching countryside that I didn't quite recognize. I'd been driving and pre-occupied, but shouldn't some of this look familiar?

None of it did.

The closer we got to Hooperton, the more nervous I became. I'd left the house with nothing but a change of clothes to come out to the middle of nowhere, where no one knew where I was? Had I completely lost my mind?

I pulled out my phone, unsure of what to send to whom. If I told Claire Bickwell where I was, she and her shiny blonde hair and earnest face would probably call the national guard—or come out here and appoint herself as my deputy. And while the idea of anyone I knew besides me being possessed used to amuse me quite a bit, now, after Steve, not so much. There was only so much therapy I wanted to be held accountable for.

Ultimately, I texted Mordechai's number to Claire and told her I'd be cleaning up an old job we'd worked on for the next week or so, and if she couldn't get a hold of me, to call this number.

This text served a couple of purposes. First, it gave me a reason to check in with *someone*, which seemed unreasonably reassuring in a post-Mordechai world. Secondly, if I didn't check in with Claire and she got worried, which she probably would, she would call the rabbi's phone. Chances were good that either Rabbi Ethan or his wife would answer, or she'd be referred to someone at Rockdale Temple. Either way, eventually they would connect her with me, and me with the rabbi, and the rabbi with the envelope I'd left on my kitchen counter, which contained everything anyone needed to know about where I was and what I'd be doing. So, in the event I was in trouble, and Claire took the initiative to help, she could show up with people who could actually, you know, do something.

This all seemed like a good plan. Then again, I was about to go confront a houseful of homicidal demons with nothing but a few psalms and a bad attitude. I wasn't exactly the poster child for careful planning.

At my request, Max's driver pulled over on the north side of Hooperton at a convenience store and gas station. He refilled his vehicle while I went inside for supplies. I immediately caught the attention of the plump woman behind the counter. She was talking to a man working the register, but they both shut up and smiled as I came up. I'd been marked as a stranger. I could feel their interest, their curiosity, and I wondered if they'd been talking about the death out at the Graham estate. Would anyone even know? Surely there'd been cops, a coroner's van. Joe hadn't been a regular figure at the house, but he'd died, presumably, on their property. Was there any way a secret like that wouldn't get out in such a small town?

"Here you go, dear," the woman said, handing me back change for my twenty. "Do you have gas too?"

"Um—I think we paid at the pump." I suddenly felt the downside of the woman's curiosity. My driver looked like a driver—not a family member, not a boyfriend. Would she put the two together, know where I was going? "Thanks," I said and hurried out.

My guy came out a few minutes later. I was already in the car, my provisions stowed, my stomach sour.

The rest of the trip was different. He took us around the small town on what passed as an outer belt, and I found I missed seeing the quaint village square once again. Had Joe lived in this town his whole life? Was he as much of a fixture as the courthouse and library? Was his family here?

Why did he die?

Not how. How was a given. If Joe had been killed in some ordinary way, like by an ax-wielding serial killer, Max wouldn't be sending a car to come fetch me to the countryside, he'd probably be calling his lawyer. So Joe had to have taken his own life in some way, or fallen sick in some bizarre fashion, or had some sort of strange accident. I was betting on it being option one or three, and I couldn't stop the morbid curiosity that swelled up inside me as I considered all the angles.

An accident? Maybe, but the timing seemed a little questionable for that. It was way more likely to be suicide, but suicide how long ago? Max hadn't exactly been keeping tabs on Joe. He hadn't come to our little family meeting. So how had anyone figured out he was dead? I was pretty sure that if he'd killed himself, he'd probably used a gun. Out in the sticks like this, people were lousy with guns.

We continued into the countryside, and my nerves ratcheted up as each mile felt darker, more intense. Trees pressed closer to the road, their branches forming a canopy that turned the sunlight green and strange. I saw a dead deer in the ditch, its belly swollen, and then another a quarter-mile later. The third one was still alive, struggling to stand on broken legs as we passed.

"Jesus," my driver breathed, but he didn't slow down.

When we finally reached the Graham estate, though, I was relieved to see that I wouldn't be the chief form of distraction for the family: the cops would be.

The driver didn't miss a beat but parked the car discreetly by the large barn that used to hold the horses. "Do you need to see Max before you leave?" I asked him.

He turned and smiled at me, meeting my eyes with a soft, compassionate gaze. "Not at all. Mr. Graham already paid for both the trip and a tip. But looks like there's quite a bit of excitement up there. Do you want to make sure you want to stay before I leave?"

I was so startled by the offer that I blinked, then shook my head quickly. "Thank you—I'm only staying for a few days. To, um, help out."

"Here's my card." He handed back an official heavy card with a driving service insignia stamped on it. A step above Uber, for sure. "You need me to come get you, you call. It's a long way from the city, and you shouldn't be out here without a way back."

For some reason, the guy's random kindness made me want to cry. Even if he was simply angling for future business, I didn't care. "Thanks." I took the card, then got out of the vehicle, dragging my bags with me. There were two cars in the driveway besides Max's and the two police cruisers. It was a full house in Crazytown.

And I was walking into it.

"Delia." Max's voice was so loud and relieved that it startled me. I jerked my head up, stopping short as he emerged from the house and trotted down the stairs. "I'm so glad you're here."

He approached me with long strides; his face fixed into a cheerful smile that only looked a little like a death rictus. "Please hug me," he murmured intently.

"'kay." I dropped my bag and stepped into what I thought was a credible hug. "What's going on?" I asked into his shoulder.

"As far as the police are concerned, you're a friend I met while in grad school. You're absolutely *not* an exorcist."

I patted him on the back, trying to stamp down the laughter bubbling up inside me. "Glad to hear it."

He turned and grabbed my bag, still talking quickly. "Joe was found by my aunt Emily yesterday morning. She swore she'd seen him alive and healthy—well, as healthy as he ever got—last week. But when she found him yesterday, he was behind the lake house, off into the woods. He'd shot himself, but the official story is that he died by hanging. That's what everyone in town will be told."

Gun. Called that.

I clamped down on the shiver that rolled through me, wondering if my demon was waking up again. Now wasn't the time. "Any idea when?" I asked Max.

"The coroner is ruling that the death happened within the last couple of days, but she won't be more specific yet. Apparently, there'd been some animals in the area..." He tightened his jaw. "It's hard to tell exactly when. And so far, there's no reason why."

I winced. "Was he unstable?"

Max's glance was grim. "He'd been living in seclusion since Carol Ann was committed to an insane asylum six years ago. Does that count?"

"I mean...yeah." I nodded at the cars. "Are you guys, like, in trouble or anything?"

"Not really, but we're not making any friends with the cops, that's for sure. The last time the cops were out here was to question my dad in April about twenty dead horses on the property." He grimaced. "And at least we still had the Bells on the property then. They could offer some reasonable amount of assurance that the rest of the family wasn't batshit crazy. Or a threat to ourselves."

This time, I didn't miss the name—why hadn't I noticed it before? "The Bells? As in, related to Joe Bell, please tell me no?"

"As in his aunt and uncle, yeah. Though, to be fair, they'd pretty much written him off after everything that happened with Carol Ann. But I think they were grateful to my dad for giving him someplace to live." Max winced, his skin seeming stretched a little too tight across his face. "And now, someplace to die."

"You said Joe wasn't connected to what happened to Carol Ann, though. That's what you said, right? Was that not the case?"

Another wince. "He didn't cause it or anything, no. No way.

They dated for years before she got sick. He worshipped the ground she walked on—she was the rich girl in the county, he was the hired help, that sort of thing."

"Your family didn't have a problem with that?"

"Carol Ann was always a little...flighty," Max said. "Joe wasn't. He was normal. Nice. Good with the horses, gentle as anything. Easygoing."

I looked at him. We were almost at the house now. "And this is the guy who took his own life."

"Yeah, well. It's been a rough patch of years."

We climbed the steps to the house, and I felt my skin ice over, like the temperature had dropped a good ten degrees between the grassy front yard and the porch. The sensation fled as soon as it came, but I still held my arms close to my body, my hand curving around the strap of my pack.

I felt not one stirring of the demon inside me. Probably a good thing.

Right?

"Officer Michaels, this is Delia Thompson," Max said, refocusing me. "I told you she was coming for a visit."

Officer Michaels was a stocky man, but his uniform fit him well. He hadn't gone soft recently; he was just big and fleshy in the way I expected most small-town cops to be. He nodded to me, his face impassive. "Did you know the deceased?"

"No, sir," I said. "Max had told me about him, but I'd never met him."

"How long will you be staying?"

"I don't know." I tightened my hand on my strap. "Um, should I not be here? Am I causing a problem or anything?"

Fortunately, the cop was already shaking his head. "No, no." His gaze slid to Max's, who put a protective hand on my arm.

"I told her Joe was dead," he said firmly. "That—that we

didn't know what had happened, but that it looked like he'd hung himself."

Officer Michaels looked at him for a long moment, then seemed to collapse in on himself a little, like a turtle withdrawing into its shell. "Hell of a thing," he muttered, glancing back into the house, where I could hear other people talking. "I've known your dad a long time."

I fought to keep my face steady. What did that have to do with anything? Unless…"Um, is there any possibility that Joe *didn't* do this to himself?" I asked, eyes wide and hopefully guileless. "That there's someone else out there in the woods or whatever—"

Michaels's sigh was gratifyingly dismissive. "We don't have a reason for it, but there's always the possibility that someone else was involved, talked Joe into doing it. But—and I know we'll tell the other story in town, but Max has never been able to lie to me in his life. I know you know, and I appreciate your discretion."

He didn't seem to notice me gaping, just kept on rolling. "But the gunshot injuries were clearly self-inflicted. The coroner will have her report on that pretty fast. Possibly later today. The body will be available for burial after that, unless she finds anything." He quirked a glance at Max. "You taking responsibility for the body, or should I contact the Bells?"

"I've already spoken with them. Ware Funeral Home will take care of the body once it's released from the morgue. We'll bury Joe in the Bells' plot." He gave me an additional explanation. "Joe's parents disowned him a long time ago, moved out of town, God only knows where. The Bells were sort of his guardians."

"Oh." The more I heard about Joe, the sketchier he got. Not that anyone in this family made any sense.

"Right." Officer Michaels nodded firmly, as if he'd come to

some decision. "I might have more questions, but this is almost certainly going to be ruled suicide or, at best, accidental death. The latter would be easier for everyone, but we'll have to see what the coroner says. Max, if you don't mind—"

I let them draw away from me as my attention was pulled to the far side of the porch, where it graciously wrapped around the house, giving ample view to the now-empty paddock stretching beyond. A couple stood shoulder to shoulder at the fence, looking out over the vast space. The wind lifted the woman's white hair and blew it back from her face; the man wore a ballcap pulled down over his forehead, though it looked like he had no hair at all. The Bells, had to be.

I closed my eyes, guilt washing over me as an unexpected thought assaulted me. If I'd have stayed here all those days ago, would their nephew Joe still be alive? Had my willingness to abandon the Graham estate, to run back to Chicago and act like everything was going to be okay, somehow left him unprotected? Why hadn't I asked to see the lake house when I'd come out here? I'd gotten a creepy feeling about it without even seeing it. Would I have been able to identify the signs of affliction in that house?

Probably.

The sudden return of the voice in my head made me jolt, and I hitched my bag up on my shoulder to cover the movement, my eyes flaring open again.

"They're good people, you know. All of them."

I about flung myself off the porch at the raspy voice. I turned and stared down at the old woman who'd somehow managed to walk up to me without making any sound at all. Max's grandmother, Kate.

"I'm sorry?" I managed, trying not to shriek.

She gestured to the couple by the fence.

"The Bells. Bob Michaels, that nice policeman you just met.

Even Joe." Her mouth pursed, adding even more wrinkles in the webwork of fine lines traced over her face. "Poor dumbass Joe."

I blinked, fought the smile. "Why was he a dumbass?"

"I know why you're here, you know." Her voice went a little lower, like she was confiding a secret to me, and her black eyes were cold, shrewd marbles sunk deep in her head. "Why you're *really* here."

A flush of embarrassment swept through me. "Max thought—"

"Bully with what Max thought. Max is a sweet boy who should never have gotten sucked back into the sins of his family."

Sins? But before I could ask her, she continued. "You're here not because you can help, but because you couldn't stay away. You couldn't leave it alone. But I've seen your type before, missy."

I squinted at her. Embarrassment bled away, replaced by curiosity and something deeper. Sharper. "You don't want me here?"

"Actually, I do," the old woman retorted, surprising me. "Been long overdue, you ask me. This whole place is a boil waiting to burst."

I flinched at that image as she turned to stare at the Bells.

I stared at them too. I had no reason to talk to the couple, but that was where I was drawn. Max and his people were enclosed, insular, boxes within boxes. I'd have to pull those boxes apart if I ever expected to understand what had happened here. But the Bells were like an orbiting star. The Bells and Michaels, the policeman. The coroner too. The large animal vet. All these people who circled the lives of this privileged house, touching it for a moment before spinning away again. How much did they know? How much could I ask them?

How much would this old woman tell me?

I glanced down at her. "If you knew things were getting bad here, why didn't you do something about it?"

"Who's to say I didn't? You're here, aren't you?" She cackled at my expression, shaking her head. "Oh, honey, you're going to need to do better than that. Max seems to think you've got the blessing of God on High upon you. You've made him a believer for sure. All I have to say is, he better be right."

"Yeah?" I asked, my tone challenging. I gripped my backpack tighter. "So what do you believe in?"

She looked at me sharply, as if surprised at the comeback. I was surprised too, mainly because I really wanted to know her answer.

She swiveled her head away. After another minute of staring out at the Bells, she spoke again, softly. "I believe we were put on this earth to fight."

TWENTY-THREE

The cops left about an hour after that. Max had come for me when he'd realized his grandma had trapped me, and he showed me to my room. To my unutterably great relief, it was on the first floor. It was a sort of extra, unused sitting area that had been converted to a guest room, I figured, since there was no closet. Instead, two huge armoires stood at either end of the room, flanking picture windows that looked out onto the horseless paddock. There was a bed in the room and a bathroom down the hall, so other than being a billion times nicer, it wasn't that different from home.

Idly, I wondered if there were any Sharpies in the house. Or cans of craft paint.

"Wanna go for a walk?" Max stood at the door, his hands in his pockets.

"Where is everyone?" I turned toward him, forcing myself to leave my pack where it sat. I was here for the duration. Whatever that meant.

"Mom and Dad went into town with the cops, and Grandma, who knows. Ditto Aunt Emily. I'm just glad she kept it together long enough to get the cops out of here."

"I saw the Bells outside earlier."

"Yeah. They want to come back, if you can believe that. Clean out Joe's house. They think—it's like they think things are going to get better now." His mouth twisted. "I thought that too, last week, after everything quieted down again. Now I don't know what to think."

"No word from Rabbi Ethan?" This had begun weighing on me more and more, for some reason. If the rabbi took an interest, it would be the best of all possible worlds for Max and his family. And yet, now that I was here, I felt like I needed more time to figure things out myself.

"No word. Do you have his direct contact information?"

"I'll give you Mordechai's. I have to think that's as direct as you're going to get now."

"K." But he didn't ask for the digits, didn't pull out his phone, and I didn't either. We left the house by way of the back door, crossing the wide veranda to thick wooden steps. An ATV sat at the back paddock gate, which stood open, and I glanced at him.

"Quickest way to get to the cottage, and I wanted you to see it."

"Isn't it a crime scene or whatever?"

"Not the house. Joe—where Joe was found was quite a bit off from it, and the house itself has already been gone through by the police, as much as they could. They told me not to touch anything, but that I could go through it and take pictures for insurance purposes, make sure nothing gets taken while everything is in limbo."

We got into the ATV, and I clutched the sidewall as he started the machine. I'd never ridden on an ATV before, but it felt like what I expected a souped-up golf cart would feel. Wobbly and reckless, a grown-up's toy. Unexpectedly, my mind went to the only true child in the house. "Where'd Sam go?"

Max sighed. "He's with Mom and Dad. He's been fine since that thing last week, but they don't want him to have some sort of relapse if they're not around to do something about it."

"Oh." Shame burned through me. I'd only watched the videos of Max's mom and brother once—and without sound. Their faces had been enough. At first, I told myself that the screams of the ghost horses had been more than enough to convince me that something was seriously wrong at the Graham house. I hadn't needed any more motivation to get "Mordechai's" report done and to his office.

But after that, I didn't listen to those videos out of simple fear. Fear of hearing Sam's terror, or his mother's. I didn't even *like* the mother, had felt her coldness almost immediately when Max had introduced us, but that didn't mean that she should be left alone to fend for herself.

Because I'd known something wasn't quite right out at the big, remote house. Wasn't quite right, or wasn't quite finished, either way. And I'd left.

We traveled the rest of the way to the lake cottage in silence. It was a pretty trail—wide and manicured, not at all the grown-over, enchanted-woods scenario I'd been imagining. The trees were flush with early summer growth, and the woods were cool without being chilly. Enough bright sunlight peeked through the overhang to make it seem normal instead of gothic.

The lake was bigger than I'd imagined it would be as well—I could see the other side of it, but at a distance, and we passed a dock with a pontoon boat on it, canoe snugged up beside it. It was all quite pastoral; the kind of place you'd want to bring friends to. It was nice, for a hotbed of infestation.

The lake house itself was also far more impressive than I'd expected. This wasn't some "cabin in the woods" setup with weathered planks and a moldy roof. The Graham's lake house was a long, rambling ranch home perched about three hundred feet above a lake that was easily a half mile wide from what I could see. It curved out of sight around a forested bend in the shoreline. A large, grassy yard ran down to the water, and at the water's edge sat a delicate gazebo atop a picture-perfect dock.

A small motorboat and two jet skis bobbed in the water. They both looked clean and well cared for. Everything about the place looked well cared for, actually, except the water itself. From here I could see the lake's surface, and it was completely still—no ripples, no movement, like a sheet of hammered metal reflecting the sky. Even the boats at the dock sat motionless despite the breeze that lifted my hair. Nothing disturbed that water. Nothing living, anyway.

I shivered in the suddenly cool breeze.

"When's the last time you were out here?" I asked Max.

"When I first got back, two months ago." He cut the engine and sat looking at the house. "That sounds pretty negligent, I know, but I figured Emily would let me know if there was anything amiss. She's here, by the way." He gestured to the edge of the driveway, and I noticed for the first time the back of a car visible behind the house. "She comes out here a lot."

I frowned. "She's not going to take anything, is she?"

Max's smile was weary. "I wish she would. Joe wasn't much for getting rid of things. The house always seemed clean when I went inside it. But it was...crowded. C'mon, let's get this over with."

He didn't bother to knock on the door but opened it wide while shouting out Emily's name. Immediately I understood his "crowded" reference, and I stopped short, causing Max to bump into me. "Whoa."

"Yeah."

Ex-boyfriend Joe Bell was a hoarder. Not a disgusting one, exactly. I didn't think that I'd find the desiccated corpse of a cat underneath all this mess. But that didn't make it any less of a mess. Every catalog delivered to this place over the past fifty years looked like it had been neatly stacked up in piles along the walls. In addition to the catalogs, there were ducks—dozens of them everywhere, the kind of low-rent sculpture that hunters used or country people displayed on their hearths to show that someone in their family at one time hunted waterfowl or thought they *might* hunt them some day.

"Um, I guess he was a collector—and an artist too."

Max snorted. "Yeah. Hang on." He shouted Emily's name again, but when there was no answer, he took off, leaving me in the middle of Duck Dynasty. It looked like half the carvings were commercial quality, while half were in varying stages of homemade, all the way back to Joe's earliest attempts, if the strange wooden lumps by the hearth were any indication.

The other thing that stood out was the guns. Four separate gleaming cases filled the far wall of the room, with shiny rifles inside. Exclusively rifles, and all of them looking, once again, like hunting guns vs. any sort of Civil War replica stuff. Not that I'd really know what a rifle meant for hurting a human would look like, or if it would even look different at all. But though the guns were excessive, they didn't have a desperate feel to them, not like the surrounding catalogs or the ducks did. It was almost like they were part of the background, silent sentinels awaiting their turn.

One of the cases was missing a gun.

I stepped over a pile of duck bills and moved toward that wall. The lock hadn't been broken or the glass smashed or anything. The case was closed. Like Joe had simply selected that morning's gun the way Claire selected her shoes, then gone out on his date with destiny.

The air near the gun cases felt colder, and when I breathed out, I could almost see my breath.

Then I felt it. Not quite possession—this was something

else. An infestation, tied more to place than person. House familiars, they were called in the old texts. The presence hung over the room like fine mist, and once I sensed it, I could feel its shape and size. It knew I was here too. Something quivered in the corners, a shadow slipping out of the way.

"You need to go," I whispered.

My hands had started to lift when Max shouted from deeper in the house. "Oh, Jesus. Emily!"

"Max!" A peal of laughter sounded as I heard a loud splash deeper in the house, and I turned to pick my way back through the stacks of catalogs and ducks, making it only halfway when Max strode into the room. He looked both furious and embarrassed, and he held up his hands. "Probably not the best time for us to—"

"Who's out there with you? Oh, Max! You brought a *girl* here?"

I jolted straight as a woman dashed out of the hallway, her hands clapping together with childish glee when she caught sight of me. She was beautiful, and I recognized her from the pictures in the house as Emily Winslow, Max's mom's sister, the small-time actress and model who'd been living with Max's family for the past few years in between shows or gigs or whatever actresses and models did. She was dressed in a silky pink robe that almost reached her knees, and her hair was in a high, blonde springy ponytail. Water dripped from the tip of that ponytail onto the hardwood— dark drops that seemed too thick, almost black in the dim hallway light.

As I stared, she fumbled with the robe's sash, securing it more tightly. "Well, don't just let her gape at me, Max. Is this your friend from the other day? The one who upset Judith so?" When Max couldn't seem to find the words, she finished lashing her robe to her voluptuous body and strode toward me, her hand out. Somewhere in this town there apparently was someone who did manicures.

"I'm Emily Winslow, you might have heard of me? I was in *The Family Five*—the daughter. Everyone knows me from that one."

"Oh my God, of course," I agreed. I shook her hand quickly then pulled it back to cradle it against my body, as if I was awestruck. It seemed to be the correct response. She flushed with delight and turned again to Max.

"I fully approve."

"What are you doing here, Emily?" he asked tightly.

"I preferred it when you called me Auntie."

"I preferred it when you acted like one."

"So serious." She pouted, then turned back to me. "Are you going to liven him up?"

"*Emily*."

"I was taking a *bath*, Max. What did it look like I was doing?"

"You had to have heard me coming through the house."

She winked at me, a little 'just between us girls' move that sent another jolt of uneasiness through me. "Maybe I wanted to surprise you."

"Something wrong with the bathtubs up at the main house? Jesus, Emily, Joe just died."

"Well, he didn't die here, give him credit for that." She looked around the room as if suddenly seeing it. "And at least now we can get rid of all his *stuff*. He was always so sensitive about his *stuff*. Like his *stuff* was going to bring Carol Ann back. So tragic, isn't it?"

My gaze jumped to Max's as she turned on her heel and flitted through the room, and it was everything I could do not to look for hidden cameras. Because she was putting on a show, right? She was every boozy housewife in every Hollywood movie since *The Great Gatsby*, only she was standing in a dead man's living room.

Virulent whore.

The thought was thick with revulsion, disgust—and it blossomed up out of me so strongly I tasted copper and ash. My demon's flavor, not mine. But the hatred felt like mine, the judgment, the contempt. For a moment I couldn't tell where I ended and it began.

Emily's head swung around toward me, her mouth curving into a smile. "Why are you here, little girl?" she asked.

"Jesus, Emily." Max practically groaned as my brows climbed my forehead. "Have you been drinking?"

"And what if I have?" Emily's transition from siren to wronged victim was instantaneous. Her eyes widened piteously, her mouth wobbled. "Joe is *dead*, Max, as you so helpfully pointed out. The only one of *all* of you who understood me, and he's dead."

Whoa, whoa, whoa. I lifted my hands as she swayed toward me, but Max was way ahead of me on this. "What do you mean, he understood you? Joe didn't talk to anyone long enough to understand them. He barely set foot outside of this house."

"You think so?" Emily had shifted back to sultry vixen and was drawing her hand along a pile of jumbled carvings. "You think you knew him in the, what, three times a year you bothered to come out and check on him? The boyfriend of your dear, somewhat departed sister, Max, tsk tsk. You'd think you would have shown him more compassion than that."

"We let him live here out of compassion."

"You let him live here out of *guilt*." Emily didn't hiss the word, but she imbued it with the same silky intensity that she packed into her gaze. "You didn't know what role he played in little Carol Ann's sickness, but you were sure he had to have done something. Maybe he fucked her a little too hard?"

I jolted at the vulgarity, but Max took a long step toward Emily, who cringed away from him with a squeak.

"Don't hurt me!" In the blink of an eye, she switched again, this time from seductress to little girl. "You always want to hurt me!"

Max's face was a mask of bewildered frustration, and he lifted both his hands. "I'm not going to hurt you, Emily. But don't talk about Carol Ann that way. She got sick. Joe had nothing to do with it. End of story."

"You *do* want to hurt me. You *always* wanted to hurt me." Emily had wrapped her arms around her waist now, almost rocking. Max's shock transformed into helpless confusion, and I bit my lip. He was completely out of his element. I knew what this creature was, but I wasn't in much better shape to respond to it than Max.

I couldn't take on this demon, I thought. *Demons*, if there were more than one, which I thought there would be. Two demons living in collusion in this house if not in conjunction, suffering each other's presence. It was a rarity. Demons were solitary creatures. One of them had slithered into Emily, but was it always there? Or was it in the house, taking up residence in visitors as it suited them?

"Why are you so mean to me?" Emily's wail pulled me out of my own thoughts, and I gaped as she flung herself into Max's arms. Max who was her nephew, even though she was only in her mid-thirties and he was in his late twenties—her *nephew*. Her total abandonment of social standards was classic textbook possession, yet so blatant and insidious, it took my breath away.

"Emily, c'mon. Pull yourself together. We need to understand why you're here. Why here, specifically? Why now?" With a move obviously born of long practice, Max set her away from his body as she attempted to compose herself. "The cops didn't see you here, did they?"

"*Them*." Emily pouted again, back to working the cute little girl angle. "They didn't want to listen to anything I had to say. And the coroner is old. Probably doesn't even know her job, all the advances they've made with forensics. I saw this show where—"

"What did you tell them?"

"I said Joe was the nicest man I'd ever met. That he wouldn't hurt a *fly*." Emily burst into tears, throwing me off my game yet again. "I don't know why he took that gun out there, Max. Why would he do that? He had everything to live for!"

I forced myself not to look around at the evidence of what Joe had to live for, but Max was paying closer attention. "Tell me you weren't out here this past week, talking to him."

Her eyes got huge. "It's not a crime to talk to someone. Joe and I were friends."

"Okay, then what did you two talk about? Did you tell the cops you were out here?"

"They didn't ask." She sniffed. "And I certainly didn't suggest that he kill himself, if that's what you're saying. Joe and I were *friends*."

"You described Joe as a 'shut-in hoarder' up until three months ago. So I don't think your friendship was all that deep."

"You don't understand," she whined. But even as Max rolled his eyes and turned toward the kitchen—presumably to continue looking through the place—I realized that he did understand. There was something about the way he moved, the way he watched everyone, that told me he understood a *lot* more than he was letting on.

Which was all well and good...but understood what, exactly?

What hadn't he told me?

I didn't ask him. Not because I didn't want to know, but because it didn't matter. I was here now, and I wasn't going to leave until it was over. I couldn't run away from this place, not again.

Maybe never again?

The softest whisper of a laugh curled through me, silent and distant.

Maybe.

CHAPTER

TWENTY-FOUR

Dinner that night was about as lonely and quiet as the ones I'd spent at home. A tray of lasagna had appeared in the refrigerator with cooking directions, and Max had gratefully thrown the thing into the oven as soon as he'd discovered it. Sam and the parents came back while it was baking, but after they ate, the parents went upstairs without speaking to me, and Sam sat with his grandmother, staring at me with dark distrust.

Right back at you, asshole.

Emily was all smiles and giggles, then tears and recriminations by turns, lamenting Joe's death. By the time she started on her third glass of wine, she'd transformed him from depressed shut-in to tragic martyr to unhinged monster and back again.

"What he did was *terrible*," she said, pushing lasagna around her plate. "I mean, Joe was in on it from the very beginning. That's why he was so fucked up afterwards. Such a shame, too. He really was the *sweetest* guy."

The grandmother's hand tightened on Sam's. "Emily."

"But some things you can't undo, you know?" Emily's eyes

found mine across the table. They were bright, fever-bright, and I felt something inside me twist in recognition.

I knew that feeling. I had that feeling. Some things you can't undo.

"He helped her conjure *spirits*," Emily continued, her words a breathless giggle. "He'd do anything for Carol Ann. They even met in that house—the lake cottage. Why do you think he couldn't leave it?"

I leaned forward. "Why now, Emily? Six years in that house. Why did he kill himself now?"

"Well, I'm sure I don't know." She fluttered her eyelashes, then took another drink.

The rest of the night didn't get any better. Max and I did the dishes in silence, then stepped out onto the back porch.

We were settled on the large wicker furniture in the next few minutes, and I looked out over the darkening expanse of the empty paddock. The breeze was gentle, taking the edge off the evening's heat, and the entire place seemed...peaceful. I could almost imagine the snuffling of horses in the far distance, picture the sun coming up over the trees, announcing a new day. This must have been a really pretty place once, I thought. And by "once" I didn't mean a hundred years ago, I meant something more like six years ago.

"So what happened, exactly?" I finally murmured. "With Carol Ann. And what did you actually see, versus hear about later?"

"Oh, I saw all of it." Max sagged back a little in his own chair. "I was home from college for what I thought was going to be the last time for a while, what with law school on the horizon and then work at a firm. It was the summertime. Carol Ann was graduating high school, and everything was going her way. We weren't close, not really—she was five years younger than me, and a girl. But we got along well enough, and she was smart and funny and a little badass—the perfect little sister. University of Chicago, Joe planning to follow her there, the whole future mapped out. Then she hit puberty and turned dark. Goth phase, scary movies, occult websites, you name it. We didn't think much of it. What we didn't know, though, was that Joe got her whatever she wanted—the Ouija Boards, black magic supplies, all of it."

I figured as much. Again, darkness didn't need much of an invitation, but it was always happy to accept one if offered. "And Joe helped—"

"She had seizures?" How many times had I seen this, working with Mordechai? Stupid, stupid people and their stupid, stupid arrogance, thinking they could tap into the kind of power they didn't have a prayer of understanding.

"Yeah. It started out with her shaking uncontrollably, saying the most horrible things. She screamed until she was hoarse before we could even get the doctor all the way out here. Then she lashed out when he arrived, so he got to see her at her worst. And when I say lashed out—she went at him like she was going to gouge his eyes out. We barely got her restrained when the seizures started. Full body, eyes rolling back, mouth foaming. She caught the room on fire just by standing there."

I stared at him. So this was the missing piece—what he hadn't told me. "Max. I thought you said she didn't act possessed."

"Well, I lied." He sighed and hunched over, and it was like the entire family's misery sat on his shoulders, weighing him down. "That's why we had to send her away—far away. It was like nothing I'd ever seen. Sam was even worse off—he was in his bassinet the whole time, watching. He was practically in shock by the time it was done, shaking uncontrollably, not uttering a sound. We'd sort of forgotten he was there."

"Did you sedate her?"

"We didn't have to. She started speaking in a language we couldn't even understand, but it sounded like curses in Latin or Greek or God only knew what. And then she just—went limp."

I remembered this phrase from Mordechai's reports. "Catatonic stupor."

"Yeah. All the bones in her body seemed to melt, and she crumpled, her face slack, her mind totally gone. She's been like that ever since. The next day, Joe showed us the entire carload of shit she'd been into, and then he had his own little breakdown."

"I bet."

"The Bells were horrified. Dad was shell-shocked. Mom cried a lot. But we all assumed Carol Ann would get better, eventually. We sent her to that hospital, and she was clean, comfortable, you know, cared-for. We thought she'd snap back." Max shook his head. "She didn't."

"I don't suppose you had an exorcist come in back then?"

"Not at first, no. Not even after they moved her to Nebraska and put her under twenty-four-hour-a-day care. Mom and Dad weren't exactly religious, but it was bad enough to have a daughter who was mentally incapacitated. That somehow was better, though, than a daughter who was possessed. We just, well...dealt with things. It worked—here, anyway. For a while."

I nodded. "And when did things change for the worse? The horses?"

"For me, it was this past spring. I'd been gone since Christmas and coming back—it was as if I hadn't really seen everything for what it was until I'd escaped. Mom and Dad acting so weird, Sam looking like a hollow-eyed shell, and Emily—Jesus." He gestured helplessly. "That stunt with the bath today, I'd like to say that was out of the ordinary. She's lived at the house off and on since I was in college, whenever she's between gigs, but she's gone completely nuts with the sexual stuff in the last year or so. I swear to God, I half expected her to hit on me when I came home in April, but by then she'd seemed distracted. I just didn't realize it was with Joe. And now..." He shook his head. "Now I don't know what to think. I don't want to imagine that she had anything to do with Joe's death, but, well, it's not like I can ask him."

I thought of all the things I could tell him, all the things I knew. About infestation and compulsion, oppression and possession. About how to go about identifying and then removing the darkness from his home and his family.

Tomorrow, I thought. Tomorrow I'd say what I needed to say, begin doing what I needed to do.

The house didn't give me that long to wait.

A SCREAM JOLTED ME AWAKE, and I scrambled upright, my arms spasming around me. What was on me? It took me another twenty seconds to process the blanket, the porch. I'd fallen asleep on the porch in my chaise, Max lying five feet away from me, also huddled in his own blanket, like two kids on a sleepover at their grandma's. Only Max's eyes were open and big as saucers.

"You heard that too?" he asked. "I was hoping I imagined it."

Another scream rent the night, and we were both on our feet. "Sam?"

"Mom!" he yelled back. The voice had sounded too young, too childlike to be his mother, but okay.

One thing I appreciated about Max: he was not one of those people who skimped on electricity. As we ran through the house, he flipped on every light in every room we entered, and those we passed as well. The whole bottom of the house was lit up like a Christmas tree by the time we hit the second floor, and I heard a door slam upstairs—the third floor, Grandma's room.

"Sam will be with her," Max said grimly. Emily stood in her doorway, lolling against the doorframe, mercifully clothed though clearly drunk out of her mind. She grinned at me as I ran by.

"*Boo*." She giggled.

Max didn't stop at his parents' closed door. He opened and pushed it wide, bounding into the room. "Dad!"

I didn't know what to expect when I came racing into Max's parents' bedroom, but it wasn't his dad standing on one side of the room, vibrating with rage, and his mother on the other side, shrinking away from him. They'd seemed like the quintessential American couple—uptight but used to it and each other, willing to suffer in tandem until the bitter end.

Not anymore. A shotgun lay on the bed between them, looking oiled and dangerous even though no one stood closer than five feet to it. Mr. Graham turned as he registered Max's arrival, his face a mottled red.

"She brought that gun into this house. That bitch—she brought it!" He whirled on his wife. "And you just continue to stand there like everything is fine and it's all going to be fine, and it is *not* going to be fine. What Joe did—none of us is ever going to be fine again."

"It's not Joe's gun, Frank!" Judith pleaded. "Emily wouldn't do that. It *looks* like Joe's gun, but it isn't. You know how she is."

"I know she's your fucking sister, and she's done nothing but ruin everything she touches since the moment she came back here." He swung around like a wounded bear, looking for something to maul. "She should go."

"She *can't* go." His wife wailed. "She's hurting, Frank, you know she's hurting."

"She's fucking hurting all right."

Hearing the f-bomb come out of the mouth of the upright Mr. Graham pinged my creep-o-meter hard to the right. There was scared, there was crazy scared, and then there was Frank Graham cursing.

"Dad." Max rushed toward him, stopping short as his dad swung around again. As tall as Max was, Frank was bigger in almost every way—burlier, tougher. Certainly more desperate. "Dad, it's okay. I'll take the gun."

"Don't you dare take that gun," Frank seethed. He looked at the rifle like it was a coiled serpent on the comforter. "Everyone who has touched that gun has come to harm or done unspeakable things. Including your *slut sister*." He turned again on Mrs. Graham, and she crumpled back, looking legitimately terrified.

I stepped forward more quickly than anyone expected, even myself. I walked right up to the gun. I'd never handled a gun before, especially not a rifle, but I could tell which end the bullets came out of. "I'll take it."

The words came out of my mouth almost strangely, and everyone stopped for a moment as I snatched up the weapon. It was lighter than I expected it to be, but more dangerous too, and the power that flowed through me like unfurling satin when I pulled it to my body had nothing to do with the supernatural and everything to do with knowing this gun—this *thing* could kill someone. And I held it in my hands.

"Where, Max?"

"I'll take it—"

"No!" Frank, Judith, and I all screamed the word at the same time, and Max dropped his hands. Stunned.

"My car," he said quietly. "Lock it in my trunk. Keys are in the kitchen."

"Got it."

I turned and left the room. Emily, thank God, was no longer in the doorway of her bedroom, and I didn't stop to knock on her door. Part of me thought it was the same gun, no matter what Mrs. Graham thought. But that couldn't be right. Surely the police had confiscated that gun. What if it was the gun Frank had used to shoot the horses?

My stomach turned as I thought about that. I needed to get out of the house, and I picked up the pace, rattling down the stairs even as another cry went up, this one more familiar, but all the worse for it. Sam's voice, reedy and high, screaming at the top of his little boy lungs.

"No!" He shouted as I hit the first floor of the house, heading for the kitchen and Max's keys, then banging my way to the front of the mansion and out onto the wide, gracious porch. "No, no, no, no, NO!"

CHAPTER

TWENTY-FIVE

I stayed outside with the gun for a long time. I didn't mean to, not really. But I couldn't figure out how to pop Max's trunk, and the gun looked so dangerous, sitting in his car all in the open. So I sat and waited until the bedroom lights went off, one by one, and a sweep of porch lights replaced them, soft and hazy in the warm summer's night.

Max came out another ten minutes after that. He didn't come all the way to the car at first, but sat on the steps, watching me watch him. It took me a minute to figure out that he didn't know what I was going to do with the gun. I put the keys in the ignition long enough to roll down the windows.

"I'm not going to shoot you," I called out across the yard.

"Glad to hear it." Pause. "You okay?"

"That sort of thing happen a lot?"

He rubbed a hand through his jet-black mop of curls. "Time to time."

"You don't think I'm, I don't know, triggering it?"

That made him straighten a little. To his credit, he didn't answer right away. When he did, though, it was to ask another question. "Is that why you're out here?"

"Could be. Or maybe I'm just scared."

His teeth flashed in the light. "You really think I believe that?"

"I'd believe it." But I was already opening the door to the car. Still, it took a lot more effort than it should have, and when I stood, I wobbled. "I couldn't open the trunk."

"Sorry. The button sticks sometimes." Then Max was at my side, and he pulled the gun from my hands along with the keys. A soft thunk of the trunk opening sounded behind us, and Max walked behind the car and put the gun away. When he returned to me, he reached out for my hand, which was a little surprising. What was even more surprising was that I let him take it.

He turned me toward him then, and we studied each other in the sweep of porch lights. He smelled of expensive soap and leather, of quiet rooms with gleaming furniture where men and women talked to words in books the same way I spoke to the creature inside me. His eyes were dark and earnest in that glow, so achingly sincere, and I knew what he wanted from me. He wanted to feel safe and whole again, normal. He wanted to stop seeing things he couldn't unsee. Things I was destined to see for the rest of my short and doubtlessly crummy life.

I squeezed his hand. "It's going to be okay, Max," I murmured. "I know what to do. I'm just working my way up to doing it."

"I know," he said simply. He gave me a little half-smile. "I kind of want to kiss you now, but I don't want you to think—I mean, with the way Emily acted—"

I didn't let him finish. I stood up on my toes and tilted my head just enough that I could press my lips to his surprisingly full, soft mouth. For the barest moment, I allowed myself to taste the traces of panic, despair, and wine that lingered after the chaos of the evening. I started to shift back, only to feel Max's strong, steady hand snake up behind my head, firmer than I would have suspected, surer. He held me long enough to deepen the kiss, and something raw and wild cracked open inside me, lighting my insides on fire.

He stepped back and gave me a crooked smile in the porchlight. "Hey there, Delia Thompson," he murmured. "I'm Max Graham, and I have a demon problem."

For a moment—just a moment—something hot and violent cracked open inside me. Not desire, or not only desire. Something rawer. Hungrier. The urge to bite down, to break skin, to mark him in ways that would never heal.

I pulled back sharply, my breath coming fast.

Inside me, the demon was growling.

"Hey, Max Graham." I grinned back, punching down the violence, the chaos, the hot, aching need deep within me. "There's a lot of that going around."

TWENTY-SIX

The next day, Max and I went into Hooperton to return Emily's gun. There was only one place she could have gotten it, Max said, in a tone that meant that anyone who'd lived around here for more than two seconds would know this information, and he was none too thrilled to be included in that a small, sad subset.

The gun shop was located on the other side of town, and we passed through the cute town center to get there. "Did you guys come here much when you were growing up?" I asked him. "Or did you pretty much stick to yourself out in the country?"

"We were in town more than you'd expect. Church, mostly, back when I was young. Before—everything." He stopped talking, not needing to say much more. Eventually, we turned onto a beautiful street with giant weeping willow trees hanging down almost to the sidewalks, and stately old homes beyond. Like the Grahams' but built on a city scale. "Dad ran an office down here for a while, something tied to the county exchange office, farmers' coalitions, like that. It kind of petered out too. Since Carol Ann got sick, we started keeping more to ourselves."

His lips tightened. "Carol Ann's illness changed everything.

It was too much, you know? Too much to happen over just one thing."

"Yeah." But it wasn't just one thing, I knew. Possessions that begin in a place and extend to the people who live there are a layered rot that crops up in unexpected ways. I also didn't miss the fact that Max never—not once—referred to Carol Ann's affliction as possession, but a sickness. Like he thought she could get better on her own? Wake up recovered from demonic flu?

I twisted my lips, refocusing. "Did you ever figure out exactly what Carol Ann did to trigger everything? What specifically she was trying to do with Joe and the Ouija Board or whatever?"

He winced. "Carol Ann and that fucking board," he muttered, the phrase sounding like a well-worn epithet. "No, not exactly. Joe was willing to tell anyone who would listen, but he was half out of his head after he saw what happened to Carol Ann, and none of us took anything he said too seriously. After a while, he didn't say much at all. Here it is."

We got out of the car, and I squinted up at the sign above the squat building. "Mills Farm & Fleet?"

"Yep. It's where all the cool kids hang out." He grinned at me, and it was like he held my hand in the soft night again, though we weren't touching. "The gun shop is technically a separate entity, but Mills sells all the gun accessories, so it pretty much feels like the same place. And more to the point..."

He narrowed his eyes in the bright sunlight as he surveyed the far end of the parking lot. "Yeah."

He popped the trunk and took the gun out. "They'll know about what happened out at the house, or at least the official story, but they won't mention it, not specifically, and not to my face. They'll act like they haven't heard anything—especially because John Bell is here today."

I blinked. "He is? He went right back to work?"

"Looks like." Max shrugged. "Not much else he could do, you know? Working is what he does. He picked up retail after we couldn't keep him out on the farm, though Dad still gives him some kind of stipend, I think. But he works here most days now."

"And Mrs. Bell?"

"She gardens." His smile went a little sad. "She and Grandma Kate were pretty much best friends. Now they can't even speak to each other, really. Everything's just too terrible."

Instead of entering the store, Max took me down the sidewalk to a side entrance that I hadn't even noticed in the sunny glare. A small placard announcing "Sam Smith Firearms & Training" hung next to the door, with the hours of operation and an official-looking warning about carrying unlicensed weapons.

"This is the place?"

"This is it." Max pushed the door open into the small space, and I stepped in after him, not knowing what to expect. The shop wasn't large. Glass cases dominated the center sections and lined every wall, with an entryway to the right to Mills Farm & Fleet marked above a doorway, so that everyone would be clear when they left the domain of weaponry. Max walked in with confidence, but it didn't look like anyone was manning the station. Before he got three steps, however, a short, no-nonsense-looking man poked his bald head out of the back.

"Can I help you?"

"Max Graham." Max held up the gun. "I think my aunt, Emily Winslow, might have purchased this from you in the last couple of days, and I wanted to bring it back."

The man frowned. If he knew who Max was, he didn't give any indication. Regardless of Max's statement about the small-town code of 'betray nothing', I got the impression that Sam

Smith wasn't the type of man to give away much of anything. "You have a receipt?"

"I don't. And I don't so much care about the money. I just need you to verify that it was purchased here, if you can do that, and for you to log that I brought it back." The man's frown only deepened, but Max put the gun on the table. "I also need to know if she bought ammunition. It's not loaded now, and it doesn't look like it's been shot, but..." He let that trail off.

The guy looked at the gun, then back up at Max. His eyes had sharpened a little with curiosity, and I took more notice of him now. He tasted of gasoline and gunpowder, open fields and baked-in heat. He was as much a piece of the ground as the dried-out summer harvest, and he was only human. Not much happened in Hooperton, and apparently the 'don't betray anything' rule wasn't airtight. "Emily Winslow is your aunt? She doesn't look much older than you."

Max grimaced. "Yeah, she's not. She's also unstable, which you would have no way of knowing, but I would appreciate it if you'd take the gun back. Lock it up in a box for all I care or call the cops and have them impound it. But she shouldn't have bought it. And if she comes back looking for it, you can call the cops then, too, for any charge you can think of."

The guy nodded, his lips tugging into a smile that could also be a frown if needed. "Her ID checked out. Didn't have any reason to expect she might be trouble."

"Sorry about that."

"No problem at all. Happens." He squinted at Max again. "So, it wasn't the fellow's birthday last week?"

Max stopped. "What?"

"The guy she got this for. She said it was a present, that he'd eat it up."

Max froze. "When did she buy this gun, exactly? I thought it was yesterday?"

"Oh, heck, no. Hang on." The guy turned around and checked his computer. "Week ago, today. Why?" He took in our faces. "Why's that relevant?"

"Well—no one had a birthday. Like I said, she's a little around the bend." He stared at the gun. "It hasn't been shot, right?"

The man looked at him funny, but obligingly picked up the gun, looked at the barrel, and opened the chamber. Empty. "Nope," he said. "It's as clean as it was when it left here. She didn't buy ammo—said she had plenty of that herself."

"Right. Well, good. Thank you."

Max practically pushed me out of the gun shop and into the main area of Mills Farm & Fleet. I felt queasy, my legs barely seeming to function, and yet I had the worst urge to laugh, like Emily hadn't said something to a complete stranger sick enough to make me want to puke.

"I can't..." That's all Max could say. Just those two words.

I let him wander, and we made it to the tack section of the store quickly. The entire place smelled like leather and warmth, and I felt the tightness in my body ease. Max seemed to relax too, and then a familiar face came around the corner—and, thankfully, broke into a weary smile. Mr. Bell.

"Max, hey. How are you doing? How's your dad holding up?"

"Mr. Bell, I'm glad you're here." He and Mr. Bell shook hands, and the man's easy smile didn't waver.

"Well, I'm always here these days. Beats working with Mother and her damned potted plants, I will tell you that. I swear she'd stick me in a ceramic vase if I didn't keep two steps ahead of her." He turned to me, his grin still easy. I found myself liking him instinctively. "John Bell. Used to work out at Max's farm, hope to again one day soon."

"Hi, I'm Delia." I shook his hand, reassured by its weight and solidity. "I'm a friend of Max's."

"Mr. Bell..." Max hesitated. "I asked Delia out here because she's done some work with situations like—well, like Carol Ann's and, well, now Joe's too, I guess. I know you're working..."

"Ah-yup." Mr. Bell looked around. The place was deserted except for us. "It's okay. I can talk. I'll let you know if my number gets called." He cocked a glance at me. "You know his story better'n I do, though. Why do you need it from me?"

"I tend to remember things a little differently," Max said. "It'd be a big help to get a perspective that's not mine. I don't mean to trouble you. I know it's got to be a shock."

"Oh, well, no," Mr. Bell said, surprising me. He stared down at the ground for a long minute, then glanced up at Max again before nodding at me. "Poor Joe hadn't really been with us for a long while. Much as it hurts me to say it, he's at peace now. I truly believe that."

Max sighed, then rubbed his hand over his forehead. "I have to think you're right," he finally offered.

John Bell nodded again, then clasped his hands together with the air of a man who'd told this story too many times, in too many places.

"Joe loved Carol Ann from the time they were babies, you know?" he began. "She was the dominant one, the show-off. He worshipped her."

He sighed, and I sensed Max's impatience almost at a soul-deep level. Mr. Bell must have too, because he straightened, refocusing on us both. "When Joe finally upped and proposed to Carol Ann, Mother and I like to've died a thousand deaths. She'd gotten different, over the years. Still lovely, 'course, still a Graham girl and that made her family. But you know, strange. Like some kids do when they hit high school age. Figured she'd grow out of it. Joe wanted to go to whatever fancy college she got accepted to, but he knew he needed to stay and work. He knew what he wanted, though. Proposed to her on the first day of summer, right in front of us. And she laughed—laughed. Not a mean laugh, either. She actually seemed happy."

He shook his head. "It all went to shit after that. We found that out later, 'course. All that nasty business she had him buy. And I know, I know, that makes it sound like she's all to blame, when surely Joe had a brain as well, but—" He offered me a rueful smile. "You just had to know Joe. There was nothing he wouldn't do for Carol Ann. It's like she operated by an entirely different set of rules."

"Do you know what she was trying to do—what she was trying to get at, with the stuff Joe had bought for her?" I asked quietly. I was still missing something critical here. "I mean, usually when people mess around with the occult, there's a reason for it. Some wish they want to have come true, some wrong they want righted. Did Joe ever give a reason for Carol Ann's requests?"

"None that he ever told me," Mr. Bell said, shaking his head. "She wanted to feel powerful, he said."

I frowned. "Powerful? What do you mean? I thought she was the Queen Bee at her high school?" I looked at Max, and he spread his hands. He'd been in law school when all of this had gone down.

"Well, yeah," Mr. Bell said. "She was everything a seventeen-year-old girl could want to be, but she wasn't Queen Bee that summer after graduation, you remember." He smiled a little grimly at Max. "Your Aunt Emily had just had that TV thing come out, and that was a big deal when she came back to visit that year. 'Cording to Joe, it's all Carol Ann ever talked about, how Aunt Emily was stealing the show, how Aunt Emily thought she was better'n the rest of you all, like that. Typical teenage stuff, but when you're going through it, seems like the biggest thing in the world. So, anyway. She waited until the picnic and—boom. Everything else you know."

They both fell quiet, but I clearly didn't know. "Picnic," I echoed.

"Fourth of July," Max said. His voice was worn down, scraped raw. "I mean, Aunt Emily was there, sure. But she was still on the pageant and parade circuit at that point. If she was on TV back then, I totally missed that."

I didn't like the numb look on his face. "The Fourth of July was when Carol Ann played with the Ouija Board or whatever she did?"

Mr. Bell picked up the tale. "After the picnic. That night. That part even my tired old brain could remember. Joe was so happy that whole day, and I remember, Mother and I were worried that he'd gone and knocked up Carol Ann without waiting for the wedding. That was what we worried about back then." He shook his head. "Seems crazy now."

But I was only half listening. Ouija Boards were more popular now than they'd ever been, but they'd been causing problems for over a hundred years, to hear Mordechai talk. Of all the various ways people tried to tap into the spirit world, Ouija Boards held a particular energy that seemed to go straight for the shadow side. I knew he'd had a call four or five years ago on the subject, but that was one of the ones he hadn't taken me on. Had he recorded it in his files, I wondered?

Mr. Bell's words pulled me back to the present. "That's pretty much all it seemed to be, though. Young girl, jealous of another girl's success, tries to either bring more good stuff down for her, or, okay, some bad stuff to Emily. But Emily didn't seem affected in the slightest, whereas Carol Ann..." He looked at Max apologetically. "Well, maybe she'll find her way back soon."

"Find her way back?" The phrase hit me like a physical

blow. I'd heard it before—Mordechai had said it. Multiple times. About multiple people. But what did it mean?

"Something Joe would say when he got drunk," Mr. Bell explained. "That Carol Ann just needed to find her way back."

Back from where? I wanted to ask. But the look on Max's face stopped me. He was white as a sheet, staring at nothing.

"We still hold out hope for that," Bell finished softly.

Max managed a smile as I tried to corral all the research I'd done, parse out every word that Rabbi Mordechai had ever uttered. "What about more recently?" I asked him. "Did Joe give you any indication that he might be thinking about hurting himself?"

Mr. Bell blew out a long breath, and Max fielded the question. "Joe kept to himself," he began, but Bell waved him off.

"We saw him, from time to time. Mother would bring him food, they'd talk on the porch—never inside. He never wanted her to set foot inside the place."

Given what I'd seen of the cottage, I wasn't surprised. But Bell continued. "But to answer your question, no. He seemed—I don't know, almost happy, of late. Coming out of it. We never would have imagined he'd take this path."

Once again, Mr. Bell's words hit me oddly. Like I was missing something, something I needed to understand. Something I needed to learn more about.

But Max was starting to shake with his own impatience, filled to the brim with too many questions and nowhere near enough answers. "We need to go," he said abruptly, turning away. "Thank you, John—we'll...we'll be seeing you soon."

"Yeah, I reckon you will," Mr. Bell said. But there was no joy in it.

CHAPTER

TWENTY-SEVEN

"You think you can, I don't know, cure us? The house, I mean? The family?"

The question startled me out of my sun-glare reverie. "Yeah, I do," I said. I shouldn't be so bold, I knew. Despite all my work with Mordechai and my brand-new research into demons and how to expel them, I was still seriously new at this. But I felt it in my bones that I could take out the mix of demons plaguing the Grahams once I got them to share their names. And I was good at getting demons to reveal themselves. Really good.

"Carol Ann is harder, since she's not here," I continued. "But if you can get the house and Joe and everything settled, prove what happened here, maybe her treatment could include some spiritual help as well. To get whatever's inside her, you know... out."

Or perhaps I'll pay her a visit.

I didn't even fight the cold chill that rolled over me—I'd been waiting for it. Hoping for it, if I were honest. "Anyway," I said. "What about you? Will you go back to Chicago? Keep lawyering and all that?"

He chuckled a little grimly. "That's the plan, yes. Assuming Mom and Dad are okay. Which after last night, man. That's kind of hard to imagine."

I remembered the violence of the Graham's bedroom. Contained, but not controlled. "That was new too?"

"Him yelling at her? New for me. I mean, I wasn't here when the horses were killed. But no one acted like there was any rift when I came home the next week. Mom was super tense, so was Dad, but they were just—upset. You know. I didn't realize it was at each other."

"It's got to be hard when you don't know why you're doing things. When things sort of seem to happen without you directing them. And then your aunt…"

Max groaned. "What she *said*." His hand tightened on the steering wheel. We hadn't talked again about what the gun shop guy had said about Emily. I still couldn't quite believe what she'd said, either, and I'd heard some things. "Who does that?"

He shot me an intense, almost pleading look, before staring back into the sunshine. "Because she's not insane, you know," he said tightly. "Or not insane like you would expect. She's rational. She makes her own decisions. She drives. Eats dinner in restaurants. She does everything everyone else does. She's not some creepy horror show victim who shuffles around for half the movie and then randomly starts attacking people."

I smiled. "She wouldn't necessarily be that way."

"Well, she should be. If she's possessed by fucking *demons*, then she should act a little bit more like it."

The absurdity of his statement, even blurted in desperation, caught us both off guard. I squeaked a short, harsh giggle that I couldn't quite keep contained, and Max coughed a separate bizarre, truncated laugh. His shoulders came down for the first time since the gun shop, and he sagged back against the driver's seat. He shook his head. "I just don't understand how this got so out of hand. I don't know what we did wrong. What Carol Ann did that was so...wrong."

I grimaced. "She didn't have to do anything wrong, Max. Not really. That's not how it works."

Max didn't say anything for a moment, and I found myself not wanting to look out the window or stare at the road. I needed to look at him, another person, when I made this statement. Even if he couldn't look back at me.

I angled in my seat toward him. "Evil doesn't need much of an invitation, okay? It prefers one, because it's much easier that way. But it doesn't need one. It doesn't hang out waiting for a basement to get extra creepy or an attic to short out its wiring. It's everywhere, all around us. It's in churches and cemeteries. Nurseries and gardens. It's in prisons and asylums, sure, but it's also in kindergartens. It's as much a part of creation as flowers and bunnies are. You can't escape it by being good or by hiding from it. There are all sorts of nuns and priests who've been afflicted. If you want to go that far, Job in the bible, arguably one of the best human beings of all time, was afflicted. Life sometimes sucks that way."

Max glanced at me, fear in his eyes. "So there's nothing you can do?"

I shrugged. "Prayer helps. Blessings. Loving someone, letting them love you back. But you're right—none of that's foolproof."

I gave him a reassuring smile. "The good thing is, once evil makes its move, it's almost always easier to combat. It's shown its hand, and in the case of a possession, it's generally trapped inside the person its possessing. Which means it can be addressed directly and expelled. Ditto for a house or space that's infested. You can identify it. You can learn its name. Once you do that, you have more control, because names are powerful."

"Yeah, I guess." Max sighed. "Except you'd probably need a whole phone book for my family's problems."

I smiled, and it felt like a normal smile. A natural smile. It felt strange, but also right.

We made it back to the house when the sun was beginning to set over the woods of the Graham estate. It was beautiful in a simple, unforced way, though the house looked too still and the paddock behind too empty. We pulled into the drive and parked behind a full contingent of cars, which made my heart sink and my stomach flutter all at once. "They're all here tonight, it looks like."

"Yep. At least we won't have to sit through more lasagna though. That's a bonus."

"True."

The house was weirdly quiet, even with the television going in the front room. A quick look showed both parents staring at the screen, and Sam on the floor in front of them, equally trans-fixed. Emily sat at the kitchen table, staring at her phone. The grandma wasn't on the first floor, but Max seemed to have some sort of senior citizen sixth sense about her and glanced up. "She's listening to music. I created a playlist for her." He smiled. "The fact that she's upstairs and Sam is down here is a very good thing."

By common accord, we walked back to my room on the first floor. I didn't want him to go, but that of course, wouldn't work. It was one thing to fall asleep on the back porch together, this was different. And yet, it wasn't his mom poking her head in to shoo us to our rooms, in the end.

"Hey there, lovebirds."

Max visibly recoiled as Emily's unctuous coo sounded from

the door, which we'd deliberately kept open to avoid anyone being an asshole.

Emily giggled at his response. "What? I was just going to let you know that your mom and dad's show is about done, and you can bet your dad will be checking the doors and windows, as if there weren't a million different ways in and out of this old mausoleum. But you might want to be safely tucked in your own beds before that happens, is all I'm saying."

"Thanks, Emily." Max's tone betrayed too much, and both Emily and I glanced at him. He hadn't talked to his aunt since early that morning. It'd been a long day in between, and he wasn't about to let it go. "I gave the gun back to Bill at the gun shop. If you go back in there again, they'll call the cops."

"The *cops*," she giggled again. "Oh, Max. I don't need guns anymore. I've got Delia now. That's more than enough entertainment, wouldn't you agree?"

Max stood and looked at me. "Good night. Feel free to lock the doors. Or sleep in the car. If Emily bothers you, you can call the cops too."

Emily pouted as he brushed by her, then looked at me. "He's always so angry, you know? It's because he never gets laid. I thought you'd help with that, but you're just as boring as he is."

"Goodnight, Emily," I said, watching her as she rolled her head. She had a way of moving that made it so I could never really get a fix on her eyes. "I'll see you in the morning."

"And I'll be so glad to see you too. It's been so *dull* here." She smiled and slipped out of the room with a graceful wave.

I watched her leave, that graceful, boneless way she moved. Like her spine was made of water. Like something was operating her from the inside, pulling invisible strings.

The door clicked shut, and I was alone. Or as alone as I ever was.

After that, there was nothing more I could do except go to

sleep. I didn't change out of my clothes. I kicked off my shoes and socks and popped the back of my bra, then climbed into the bed and scooted all the way back until I sank into the pillows. It was a ridiculously comfortable bed, but I didn't think I was going to be able to fall asleep on it.

Wrong.

TWENTY-EIGHT

I never really paid too much attention to my dreams. Given my life, what I did, it was reasonable that I'd see things at night that didn't quite make sense, things I didn't want to fully understand. Mordechai and I had this discussion more times than I could count. He was a big fan of spirit messages. For good or ill, he believed your dreams weren't just a matter of your synapses processing your day's experiences and emotions physiologically so your body's systems could better react to the stresses of it. He believed that God sometimes talked to you in your dreams. Which sounded nice.

Except tonight, I saw my demon in my bedroom. In the flesh.

This couldn't be real for many reasons. One, we weren't in my bedroom at Max's, or even at my house. Instead, we were in a room in some palatial hotel, with golden papered walls and a bed approximately the size of Rhode Island. Secondly, I was standing in front of a mirror—and I had no reflection. But the demon looming behind me did.

"Hello, Delia."

. . .

I GLARED INTO THE MIRROR, memorizing every detail, even as my mouth twisted into what I hoped passed as an amused, offhanded grin. I couldn't speak at first; I didn't want to speak. I only wanted to stare.

The demon—my demon—wore the shape of a man, but no man had ever looked like this. He was dressed like the European kingpin from Descent in an expensive black suit and crimson, open-necked shirt. Dark hair spilled across his shoulders, catching the lamplight as though it were spun from shadows. His cheekbones were sharp enough to cut, his mouth lush and dangerous, his eyes the same fathomless pools I'd painted on my bedroom wall...eyes that could drown me in ancient grief or burn me alive with longing.

"You wanted to see me," he said. Not a question.

"I want you gone," I retorted.

"But I've only just begun to explore the possibilities here."

The room tilted, half opulent, half wrong. The damask wallpaper seemed to pulse with my heartbeat, the bed looked too vast, the sheets too smooth. My breath caught, despite myself, and I struggled to keep my heart rate even.

"Mmm." I narrowed my eyes at him. "I know what you're doing, you know."

It was his turn to smile, and I steeled myself against the torrent of naked longing that poured through me. "Do you?" he murmured. My God, he shouldn't be so hot.

"I totally do." I went on the offensive. "I mean, it clearly must've pissed you off that I thought Volkov was hot, yeah? But what if it wasn't the guy's great shoulders and the way they filled out a suit that I liked so much? Maybe I just liked the eyeball hanging out of his head."

Unperturbed, the demon strolled closer to me. Shadows rippled behind him, almost wings, almost nothing.

"I like this new Delia," he murmured. "Think of the fun we could have together if you just let it happen?"

I snorted. "Let you happen, you mean? To me? I'll pass, thanks."

"To you…" He lifted his hand and a breeze spun up between us, though there were no windows in this room. It chased across my cheek, lifting my hair, curling around my neck like a promise. With the pulse of its cool touch, my body formed before my eyes, so that there were now two reflections in the mirror—his and mine—with mine coming into sharper focus now, pale skin, dark hair, huge, skeptical eyes.

Eyes that faltered a bit as the demon spoke again, and a swirling heat passed between us.

"For you…" This new sensation skated over my shoulders, diving down between my breasts, and more of my body formed. In my reflection, I could see that I was still marked with the poetry he'd inscribed on me. Only the words were moving now, sliding across my belly, curling beneath my breasts, diving down—

"In you," he finished, and I didn't miss the raggedness of the moan, hated the way my body responded as he stepped closer to me, the air now scented with jasmine and plumeria and dark, heady notes of bourbon-soaked chocolate.

"Sweet, powerful Delia," he whispered, and somehow, he was right behind me now, his tall, powerful body dwarfing mine, his hands coming up to curl around my shoulders, turning me toward him. "Tell me," he whispered, as his dark eyes stared into mine, ancient and powerful and sure. "Is it agony you fear…or ecstasy?"

Bringing his hands to my face, he brushed back my hair with the softest flick of his fingers. Then he bent down to kiss me, his mouth an inch from mine—

The dream shattered. Not because I woke—because something else interrupted.

A different memory, clawing its way up from whatever dark place I'd buried it.

Mordechai. The cemetery. Blood on his face.

And me, standing over him, laughing.

I awoke like a shot, my eyes wide, my heart too large for its spot in my chest, my lungs stretched to bursting. My hands scrabbled at my belly, but it hadn't changed, wouldn't change. I turned and felt the thing turn with me, I scrambled back in my bed and felt it shift back as well. It filled me full, pressing into all the broken places, pushing apart all the scars. It filled me, and it knew me.

It was me.

"Get out," I tried, but no sound came out of my throat. Nothing moved or fled into the night. Mercifully, nothing else clattered in the house beyond me either. The demons were quiet. Waiting, I thought. Watching. Wondering what was going to come out of this room tomorrow.

I felt the blackness press me down again, and I stumbled back to bed.

Somehow, I must have slept. Because when I opened my eyes, Mordechai was there. It was that last night in the cemetery, all over again. Mordechai was there and he was healthy and whole, staring at me with his wise, gentle eyes. He turned and walked with me down the path of tombstones, clasping his hands in front of him, as he always did.

I snuck a peek at those hands, old man's hands. I liked his hands. They were gnarled and rough with age, but worn down too in all the right places, from holding hands and comforting shoulders and placing a benediction on the bowed heads of the faithful. They were good hands, a rabbi's hands.

They were not blistered in any way.

Standing beside him, I found myself wanting to reach out and touch Mordechai, hold his hand the way he'd held so many others'. But he stepped away as I raised my arm, his gaze swinging back to me. Understanding. Knowing.

The thing inside me began to shiver. Not with dread, but with excitement.

I didn't understand, but I knew something was wrong.

We walked on until we came to the little courtyard, and my demon began to dance.

"No," I whispered.

Yes. You know what you did. You've always known.

The cemetery solidified around us. Not a dream anymore. Memory. And I couldn't look away.

"No," I said again.

Yes.

Suddenly Mordechai turned to me, regarding me with all the earned wisdom of his years in his eyes. But he had changed, somehow. Standing there, he seemed more stooped, more ancient. Weaker. Had the blockage already started forming in his artery? Had the blood already started to cease its easy flow?

That's not what he died of. Stop lying to yourself.

I knew that truth suddenly too. Knew it with the resigned certainty of someone who'd read the plot of the movie before even setting foot inside the theater. But I couldn't stop that movie from unspooling before me now, playing out horribly in front of my eyes.

"Delia, do you know why I've brought you here?" Mordechai asked.

"To tell me about the boy in the house?"

That part was true, real. That part I remembered. But in this reality, Rabbi Mordechai kept talking, his eyes steady on me, as the lines on his face sank deeper.

"I have prepared all I can," he said. "Look at me—"

"No," my shout seemed ripped out of my lungs, the cry of a wounded animal. He must not speak; he must not speak! I stared at Mordechai, knowing I needed to get away, but my feet wouldn't move.

"Why do you trouble this young woman, blessed by the Creator?" he demanded of me—of the thing inside me.

But I wasn't the one who answered him. Instead, the demon within me spoke, harsh and mocking.

"She is blessed by no one!" I opened my mouth too wide to laugh. I felt it, and it hurt, but I couldn't stop the words pouring out of me. "Her mother was a drunken whore when this one was conceived. But she prayed, oh how she prayed to let birth pass her by. She prayed first to God, then she prayed to the angels. Then she prayed to any god who would have her, did you know that? She wouldn't, couldn't take responsibility herself, was too damned stupid to kill it, to let this spirit sicken and die like so many others did. In the end, she gave birth. And she regretted her words, regretted her prayers. But it was too late by then. We *always* listen."

I was hissing the words now; they felt like steam and fire in my belly. "*Always.*"

"The Creator listens too."

"Not as closely." Laughter curled and twisted. "As you well know."

Mordechai bristled, his face going redder. "You are wrong. This choice you think you made? It was made for you. But no more, servant. Begone!"

. . .

"Oн, now you want me to go? After all this time?" The demon's words were out before I could stop them. Out of the mouth of the me I was watching in my dream, and out of my memory before I could clamp down hard on the impossibility, the horror of it.

Rabbi Mordechai didn't flinch, didn't back down. He nodded. *Nodded.* "I hoped you would not grow beyond the tiny seed of doubt and darkness placed within such a strong soul."

"And yet you didn't root it out?" I demanded in my own voice. "You didn't take it from me when you had the chance?"

I couldn't understand who was talking now, the me in the dream or the me in my mind or the me who was sleeping in the bed, tears beginning to leak down my face as the horror of truth slowly filled me.

"You knew?" I squeaked, and this time my voice was high, thin, manic. I clawed at my own belly, thinking of the writing on the walls, the writing on my own skin. It wasn't possible—it *couldn't* be possible. Mordechai had known me for fifteen years! Had I been possessed all that time?

"Why did you really want me around?" I demanded. "Why did you stay my friend, why did my mom—" All of the air whooshed out of me. "She *knew*, didn't she? You told her."

"Delia."

"She knew," I said again, my voice raw. A lifetime of my mother's fear clicked into place—the drinking, the distance, the relief when I left with Mordechai. She hadn't been protecting herself from the world. She'd been protecting herself from me.

My tirade should have penetrated Mordechai's benevolent exterior, but nothing seemed to. It was like rainwater battering against a steel door. But the last accusation made something shift in his expression. Something hard and fierce. And betrayal warred with crowning achievement in the deepest, darkest part of me.

"You *needed* me, didn't you?" The thing inside me accused, my words coming out in short, gasping fish breaths. "You trapped me."

"I didn't know your name. Didn't know that Delia could identify you." Mordechai shook his head. "I know it now, though. And understanding is all it takes."

I smiled in the dream. I could see myself. It wasn't a good smile. "Not all."

Mordechai held up his hand with its gleaming shofar. "Begone from her."

"And how shall I leave?" My voice channeling the demon was silky smooth now, my shoulders back, my hands loose. Not like me at all...or more like me than I ever understood. "How shall I leave this dear girl. Through her eye? She would be blinded. Through her hand? She would be crippled. How would you have me leave this vessel you have allowed me to fill for so many, many years?"

Fifteen years—and that was just the years that Mordechai had known me. How long had I been carrying the spark of this evil inside me, the seed that was growing into rotted fruit? No friends. My own mother afraid of me. The one adult to ever care about me actually using me for—

"Is it true?" The voice that spoke was mine again, only I sounded young, way too young, and Mordechai looked deep into my eyes. I didn't know what he saw there, but he didn't bend. He wasn't weak. I may have been breaking apart in front of him, but he stared at me with eyes that were not intended for the supporters of the afflicted, but for the afflicted herself. And when it got to this point in the exorcism, the afflicted saw what I now saw. A soldier of God.

"You have done this before, dark one," he said, his voice like distant oceans and faraway shores. "You and your brethren but especially you. And now you shift, you turn like a snake in the grass, rooting out your own, sending them into oblivion, crippled and fleeing. I know you do it. I've *watched* you do it."

I smiled, my voice like polished ebony. "Do you want to know why?"

Mordechai raised his hand. "I do not. Your time on this earth is through—"

"*No.*" The word was sharp, a slap, and I looked at Mordechai in amazement. These were new words, words I didn't know. The rabbi banished demons from mortals but he didn't send them back to Hell or wherever demons went when they died. He simply let them go. So what was he doing here? What was he trying to prove?

Mordechai kept his hand held high. "Return to the abyss, foul one, and trouble her no longer." And then he started saying other words, Latin words that I should have known, should at least have been able to remember, but a horrible grinding noise filled my ears, my mouth, my lungs, and I couldn't stop the agony of it from carrying me along its tide.

Mordechai thrust both hands toward me, and I felt a tearing in my gut, my stomach cramping hard enough to make me cry out. But I didn't fall back, I didn't crumble. Instead, I reached for his hands, relishing the moment when our fingers connected and I grabbed hold of him, his eyes going wide and his mouth stretching open in a snarl of rage and surprise.

"Begone from her!" He shouted, and I *laughed* at him, feeling my own heart swell as his body matched itself against me, frailty against youth but not just youth; youth bolstered by unspeakable knowledge and truth. Mordechai's face darkened to a sickly reddish gray, and I threw him from me, hard—harder than I'd ever thrown anything in my life. My head was full of words, then, words and anguish and pain.

"Get away!" Mordechai yelled. "Begone! Leave!"

I saw the scene for the last time etched into my brain. Rabbi

Mordechai, still alive—still alive! Scrabbling on the ground, his hands shuddering and twisting in the dirt. I wanted to spit on him, the disgusting weakling. There was blood on his face, and I reveled in it. He hit his head on something when he fell, one of the feeble stones of his beloved people, marking the end of their short, tragic lives.

Marking his end too.

He scratched a word into the dirt with shaking, bloody fingers. PALE...

And finally, I saw it.

In the memory, I saw what I'd obliterated with my foot as I'd scrambled away—the rest of his message. PALEMERIOUS. Mordechai had named my demon—or I'd given him the name somehow. And with his last breath, dying in the dirt, he'd handed back to me the weapon I needed to fight the thing inside me.

While I'd destroyed the evidence. Scraped it away as I fled.

"Begone," he'd whispered. Not commanding the demon this time. Just begging me to run—to flee.

To live.

And so, I ran.

I JERKED AWAKE A SECOND TIME, clutching the pillow, then spun around, trying to understand where I was. The clock on the bedside table was the only light in the room. It blinked at me, 2:37. As I stared, the numbers seemed to blur, rearrange, shift. 37:2, then 2:12. Then I blinked again, and the clock steadied. 2:12 a.m. Two o'clock in the morning.

I stared at the four walls of this room and felt a strange calm drop over me. Sitting in the house of horrors, I felt curiously apart, even safe. I reached out my hands and looked at them as if I'd never seen my own body before. I stood, turning around.

There were things in this house. I could feel them now, more than ever. They scrabbled around, preying on the minds of those who lived here like parasites, sucking out their lives bit by bit. They hung in the darkness, chittering with excitement, drinking in the pain, the fear. Not just of the weak and the infirm but of the strong. They were noticed here, they were given their due.

The entire house felt not like a gleaming, pristine home of the affluent, but a dark, dirty hovel. Hunched over on itself, squalid and broken, as if it hoped one day it would collapse into a pile of cursed stones. And then the evil would leak out over the earth, slithering away to do its bidding on the back of someone else.

But I could face these demons now, I thought. No matter how bad it got, no matter what I needed to do, I could face this evil.

Because I was worse.

The thought should have broken me. Instead, I felt cold, clear, and ready.

I stood in the dark room and whispered the name aloud for the first time, tasting its shape in my mouth: "Palemerious."

Inside me, the demon went utterly still.

"I know what you are now." I smiled. "And I know what I am too."

TWENTY-NINE

"You okay?"

Max was eyeing me over a breakfast of something that looked like a yellow cake made out of corn. He'd taken two pieces off the griddle and put them on a plate, a plate he was now handing to me. I took it and sniffed experimentally. Yup, corn.

"Why wouldn't I be okay?"

"You were crying."

The voice who answered wasn't Max, but Sam, who sat at the kitchen table with his own plate of corn cake things. Sam had added about fifteen thousand calories of syrup and butter to the concoction, but he was staring at me. My face, anyway. Still didn't want to meet my eyes.

Clever boy, Sam.

"You heard me crying all the way from your room?" To tell the truth, I felt lighter than I had in days. Weeks, actually. I was pretty much the scum of the universe, after all. I might not have killed my mentor and very best friend in the whole world directly, but I sure as hell hadn't done anything to save him. That made me at worst, a murderer. And at best, a murderer.

I put the plate down on the table, sliding into my seat.

"You cry really loud."

"Sorry about that."

Max came to the table with his own plate, but I knew he could sense that something was different as well. I wasn't just keyed up, I was furious. Furious and ready to go blast something to hell. "What is it I'm missing?"

"She cried."

"I got that, Sam." Max's gaze never left mine. "I didn't hear you."

"God doesn't trouble the sleep of the blessed. No offense intended, Sam." I offered the boy a hard smile, and he dropped his gaze to his corn cakes.

I turned to Max. "I think we should get started today with something easy, don't you? Something that needs to be done anyway. It'd be a help to your folks."

"Okay."

I didn't say anything more, and he glanced toward Sam. Understanding flickered across his face, understanding and a sort of queasy awareness that things had just taken a very decided turn. Fortunately, we got through the rest of the meal like three normal people having a typical breakfast. Max's parents were already gone, their car missing from the lot. Grandma was out on the back porch. There'd been yelling, I remembered. A lot of yelling. I'd heard all of it distantly, after I'd awoken in the middle of the night. I wondered if Max had heard any of that, too.

We left after we cleared the dishes. "Where to first?" Max asked, and I held up a couple of water bottles I'd pulled out of the cabinet.

"Church. We should probably call the Bells too."

It was another two hours before we got to the lake cottage. Because we'd driven to the Episcopalian church in town first, we had Max's car, so we approached the house the more direct way. Took longer, but that was just as well. Max was already freaked out. He'd stayed quiet until now, but the words couldn't keep from bubbling out, a bottle stoppered too full.

"This is seriously the way you did things with Rabbi Mordechai?" he demanded, his tone patently disbelieving. "You walked into churches and stole their holy water?"

"We didn't need to steal it." I should have been more freaked out with the whole theft thing, too, frankly, but I had too much anger built up inside me. If a minister had come out and interrupted us while we were dunking our bottles in the fonts, I think I might have thrown something heavy and holy at him just to work off my nervous energy. "Mordechai was a rabbi. You don't really retire from that. That gave him instant access to every sort of religious tool he needed." I wasn't going to use the word 'prop' anymore.

"And he wrote out those house blessing things?"

"Mezuzahs, yeah. But I don't have any of those. And plus, I'm not a rabbi. So that wouldn't work so well coming from me."

"Well, what are you then?"

I looked up at Joe's little cottage, squatting on the hillside, for once in accord with my innermost thoughts. "Pissed."

We slammed the car doors perhaps a little too loudly, as if we were both eager to announce our presence. Max strode ahead. The house was unnaturally still, and he must have been thinking the same thing I was, because he looked over his shoulder and smiled at me. "I think I'd be just fine if we walked into this place and it was completely empty."

He opened the door, and of course, we weren't that lucky. In fact, a terrible funk came out of the kitchen, and he groaned, heading that way. "That's not evil specters. That's milk. Goddamned Emily."

I stood in the middle of the front room without him, looking out over Joe Bell's domain. I knew what we had to do, but it would take hours. Still, might as well get started. When Max walked out of the kitchen toward the front door, I called back to him. "Prop it open."

The lake cottage wasn't a large place—three bedrooms on the edges with three central rooms besides—kitchen, dining room, living room. All the bedrooms but Joe's had been stuffed completely full of catalogs and cardboard boxes and crap. The kitchen, living room, and his bedroom were partially clear, but I wasn't worried so much about the cardboard. I was worried about the ducks.

"Get rid of anything paper to start, unless you want to throw out all his carvings."

"You think we should?"

Yes. I shrugged. It wouldn't be as easy as that, though. "Some of them seem pretty. Are they any good?"

"Oh, merciful heavens." The sound of a woman's voice turned us both around, and I squinted. I'd never met Mrs. Bell, but she almost looked like her picture. A little more worn, a little more frazzled. Like all of us. "Oh, *Max*, your family's beautiful cottage—"

"We can clean it all later." I startled everyone with the cold command in my voice. "Right now, focus on this room. It's the main problem."

Max made his introductions, and I smiled as he upgraded me from "friend" to "someone who does house clearings." Mrs. Bell's eyes widened, but she didn't object. Meanwhile, I pointed to the piles of ducks, barely viewable past the mountain of catalogs and old cardboard boxes. "Any idea if those are any good?"

"Well, I...I just don't know."

Mrs. Bell examined the pile, and her expression turned

reluctant. "Some of these are actually quite well done, once you get them away from the trash."

I was afraid of that. "Right. Well, take all the best ones outside. Kitchen, living room, bathroom, bedroom—anywhere Joe actually lived. Leave the crappy ones."

Max rubbed his jaw. "Should we clear out all the rooms in the house?"

"Not like these. The other bedrooms? Opening the doors should be enough. Show Mrs. Bell."

They both nodded, comforted by my certainty, the tasks I was setting them. That was good. *Props*, Rabbi had said. Well, maybe props had their purposes after all.

I picked up another box of paper, and Mrs. Bell scrambled to her feet, following Max into the back of the lake cottage. The first door he tried was a closet, the second apparently another bathroom—one Emily hadn't been taking baths in. "Oh, my God!" was all I heard. A rapid succession of doors opening and closing followed. They came back looking a little stunned.

"Well, be glad there wasn't an attic or a basement," Max said.

"But where did he get all the paper?" Mrs. Bell protested. "Some of that—I mean, that had to take years to collect."

I shrugged. "Is there a distribution center or Walmart anywhere close? He had to go somewhere to get his duck supplies. Wouldn't take a man too long, if he was committed. And Joe was definitely committed."

"I had no idea." Her voice was hollow.

"C'mon. Let's keep moving— Paper first, then any ducks we can find except the very best of them. Again, those you can put outside. The rest can just go in a pile."

In the end, it took us four hours to clear the paper out of the main rooms of the house. I didn't care about it being clean; I cared about it being more or less empty. By the end of it, I was satisfied.

And I hadn't even done anything significant yet.

"You, um, want us inside the house or outside of it?" Max asked. I could tell he and Mrs. Bell had pow-wowed a little more closely over the past few hours. She looked at me the same way I'd seen too many people look at Rabbi Mordechai over the years: with hope, doubt, and desperation.

But I could feel the stirring inside of me, and what was more, the house could feel it. Joe's pile of suckier-than-average carved ducks sat in a jumble in the center of the room, so much less malevolent now without the stacks of crap everywhere around them. The whole place had an air of overhanging murk, the windows cloudy with dust and grime. Now that the walls had been cleared, I could see why Joe had blocked his view of them.

It was like my own room—Sam's too—but a million times worse, because from the looks of things, Joe had never even tried to clean off the layers of swear words, occult symbols, crude drawings, the bubbling wallpaper and paint, or the bodily fluids. Every exposed surface of the place seemed to pulsate with violence and outrage. And it stank as if it had all been drawn on yesterday, not probably years ago.

"Poor, poor Joe," Mrs. Bell whispered.

"The walls can be cleaned and painted. I'm a fan of Kilz," I said. Max looked at me oddly, but I powered on. "As to what's next, you can watch if you want to. It's not really that dramatic." I blew out a short breath, pitching my smile to deliberately bright, almost manic. Fooling Max and Mrs. Bell, I hoped.

But they weren't the only ones I wanted to deceive.

"I don't know." Max looked around. "This already feels kind of dramatic."

I picked up the second item I'd stolen from the church. I

knew Grandma Kate back at the house had a bible. Hell, she probably had six of them. But I didn't feel right stealing one of hers. And given how messed up she clearly already was, I didn't want to think about what she'd done to the insides of those bibles.

"So, what are you going to do now?" Max asked.

I shrugged, hefting the bible, feeling its heat in my hands. "Use my props. That's why I brought them."

"But Joe wasn't a practicing...anything, so far as I can tell. He wasn't a believer."

"Yeah, well. You see where that got him."

I picked up the bottle of water, then splashed some on myself, savoring the burn. I wasn't wholly good, but I was still in control of this situation. Holding the bible in one hand, I walked around the edge of the room, sprinkling holy water and reciting the rabbi's benediction for a blessed house.

The windows started to creak a little. I smiled, ignoring how my fingers stung. I opened the bible and began reciting the psalm Rabbi Mordechai most often used for this purpose, Psalm 91.

Everything started happening pretty quickly after that.

CHAPTER

THIRTY

The revelation of the lake house demons was subtle at first, almost a knowing more than any real sense or presence. But the floor seemed to shift beneath my feet, to give a kind of rolling shudder. Mrs. Bell and Max squawked and took several steps back, and I got the sense that they were holding each other, fingers wrapped tightly around each other's arms, unselfconscious in their panic. Fear, the great uniter.

Then the walls grew wet. All of Joe's words, his repetition of letters and numbers, his crazy Ouija symbols and crude, foul drawings. They seemed to shimmer and writhe out of the walls as I spoke, undulating with misery. As I stared at them, certain ones flared, bright and bold, words I didn't know, couldn't understand. *AgramonBalban* slid together, streaming down the walls. *AbyzouNaamahAshtaroth.* And then, another line, a word all on its own, prideful and fierce. *Sonillion.*

How many demons' names had Joe learned over the years? And which one had kept him trapped in this unholy well of pain?

As I stared, the words scrambled again, running together.

243

The letters swelled and burst, draining onto the floor, and hissing when they came into contact with the holy water.

The walls were crying, I finally realized. The walls were giving up their burden of darkness—and crying. Tears upon tears flowed down and over the floor, and I felt the knowing swell inside me, the reality of what had happened here. It wasn't any old demon infestation—not here; not for Joe. It was so incredibly worse.

And since I didn't know any one name, I'd have to banish them all.

"*Shedim,*" I said, remembering the collective word from my library reference books—and the flow stopped. A wailing sound and loud crying swept up and around the room, wrapping me in its misery. The ducks themselves started to shake and splinter, some of them, coming apart as if from the inside. But the shedim were not possessing this place, they were infesting it. They needed to go. They...and whoever led them. Because there would be one solitary leader, I thought. One with the power over the rest.

What was that demon's name?

The silence inside my head mocked me. For ten years—fifteen? longer?—there had always been an answer waiting. Knowledge I didn't earn, understanding I shouldn't possess. Now there was only my own ignorance echoing back at me.

I stared grimly at the writhing names on the walls. *Agramon. Balban. Sonillion.* They meant nothing to me. Without Palemerious, I was just a twenty-five-year-old with a high school diploma trying to read demon graffiti.

Willing the understanding to come to me, I pressed on. "Shedim, begone from troubling this place, this man's still-tethered spirit. He was never yours to claim. You know that. You have always known that."

I should have seen the next thing coming. There had been

all those catalogs and cardboard boxes in high stacks, every-where. They were neat and orderly, stuffed to the ceiling in rooms other than this. There had to be a reason for them. I'd taken them to be insulation, and they were, in a sense. But they were also protection from what else lay buried in those walls.

Knives. Whether Joe had papered the walls over after driving the blades into them, or if his words and symbols and drawings had merely covered over the gouges, he had tried to fight the walls himself, at least for a while. And he left his weapons intact.

The first blade hit me broadside, flat against my shoulder. The second was better aimed. As it sliced into my skin, the shedim's cries grew louder, more harrowing, their demand for blood, for sacrifice thrumming through me. They would leave but they would have their due, I realized. Carol Ann hadn't died. Joe, in the end, *had* died—but not here. They wanted death, these creatures, these byproducts of whatever the hell had happened here. They wanted blood.

Right now, they wanted my blood.

Another slice across my forearm made me gasp. The blade bit deep—deeper than it should have. I felt it scrape bone. Hot blood sheeted down my arm, spattering the floorboards. The shedim shrieked with joy at the smell of it.

I saw the shadow loom larger in front of me. A cut ripped through my leggings, the knife clattering off my shin. The wounds bled freely, too heavily for what should be shallow cuts, and I realized I hadn't prepared for this—I hadn't *prepared*.

Rabbi Mordechai hadn't taught me the ways of the exorcist; I wasn't an exorcist. I didn't know his rituals and protections. I didn't even really know his God. I only knew the tiniest portion of the exorcism process.

Enough to take out these assholes, yes.

But I wouldn't be taking them out easily—or well.

Palemerious, they whispered, with a hideous giggle. *Palemerious…*

My eyes snapped wide, sudden clarity jolting through me—

"Fuck!" Pain seared across my chest as something much more real and pointy than clarity stuck me in the shoulder. Another projectile slashed across my face, and another nearly punched through my shoulder, spinning me around.

I flashed with anger, full and bright. "Begone, shedim, and take your brethren all. Fill this place no more and never come back. This place and these people are barred from you and all who serve you and all you serve!"

The laughter started then, long and loud—rich and bold—but somewhere, deep within it, there was a kernel of desperation. A tiny ember of fear, of doubt. I latched onto that ember, blew into it with a mighty breath that had never blown a shofar, had never cried in unison with holy men, but which burned—*burned* with the righteous fury of the power that raged within me. How dare anyone—anything!—defy me when I would have them leave. How dare *anything* keep me from breaking that which demanded to be broken? *How dare any creature born of evil try to defy my—*

Within me, something opened wide, eyes bright, jaw huge, staring into the shadow creatures who writhed in wet agony before me for a moment more.

And I knew their leader. Just like that.

"Sonillion," I gasped, as the truth blasted through me with fire and rage, a wind whipping up out of nowhere. "Begone, Sonillion, and take your servants with you."

Another round of chaos raged. All Joe's suck-ass carvings were lifted off the low table in the middle of the room and thrown at me, like I was being stoned. I stumbled back, crouching down behind a couch, so they hit the far window, breaking it.

The roar of the wind grew louder as it screamed over and out of the house, a houseful of creatures banished not to hell, never to hell. I didn't know where the demons went, but mine was not the power to rid this earth of them. Just from this *place*, for all eternity. Only this place.

And also from me-who-was-in-this-place, me who was power and truth.

I dragged myself to the shattered window, leaned out. Because I wasn't done yet. I still had one more demon left to exorcise.

"Begone," I whispered into the howling wind, my heart a stone lump in my chest, my hands numb, my blood slow and sluggish in my veins. "Begone, Palemerious. You must leave now, too."

My mind seemed to crack wide open, and with my inner eyes, I saw a different storm, a different night. I was back in the cemetery next to Mordechai, who raised blistered hands as I backed away from him in horror. And I was here, in this broken house, confronting the thing he left behind.

"Begone," I said again.

Time stopped, hung, and quivered in abject terror and pain. In a moment of brutal clarity, I saw what awaited me without the demon I carried. It was a world of emptiness. I would see only with my own eyes, I would feel only with my own touch. I would relate to others only with the experience of a woman who knew nothing about anything, whose experience with the world failed in every way, circumscribed by poverty and ignorance and bone-crushing loneliness.

Mordechai was dead, and it was not as if Ethan was going to let me work with him. I would be cast aside, adrift, as cursed at twenty-five as I had been at seven months, my mother bending over her swollen belly, pleading for God, the angels, for anybody to deliver her from the sin that was my corruption in her body, the life force that was even now ruining hers, sucking it dry, using it up, leaving her to face decades of privation and fear because of something she wanted no part of.

"Begone! You cannot stay here!" I still cried out, a thin, high cry, the cry of a child. The shift in my belly was like my stomach being scraped out from the inside. The rush of anguish in my blood nearly dropped me to my knees, but I couldn't stop— couldn't back down. I had no other choice but to move forward, or I'd never be free. "Go!"

For one terrible, infinite moment, I felt him hesitate. Felt something in him reach back toward me—not with rage or possession, but with something I had no name for. Something that felt almost like—

No. I couldn't think that. Wouldn't.

"Go!" I roared again.

It went. Through one of the countless wounds on my arms, my belly, with a screaming, howling rage, a blowing wind of a thousand storms that punched up and through and out of me, Palemerious burst into the broken world, blending with the shedim, screaming through the lake house and out into bright and endless day...

And all was lost.

"Delia!"

Max was at my side, and I felt something unchunk from my shoulder, pain lancing me back to awareness as he threw something away from me. He pressed a thick pad of cloth over a dark and wet place on my shoulder, and I looked at him, afraid to speak. Dreading what might come out of my mouth.

"Delia, what is it? Talk to me."

I blinked up at him.

"They're gone," I finally rasped. *He's gone. Forever gone and away from me. Empty. Wrenching. Gone.*

I blinked harder, this time desperately trying to keep the tears that burned behind my lids from falling. But my thoughts were mine, no one else's. My heartbeat was only heard by me. My skin stretched too tight over my own hollow shell, and I was alone, my demon vanquished and evermore gone.

I had won.

I had lost.

Everything.

"I can see that. Jesus." Another person squatted down beside me, her worry and concern flowing over me like an unexpected balm. A person I remembered—but didn't know right away, as ancient names and places rippled through me, cities and villages, castles and kings, flowing through me and out of me in a spreading stain, whisked away by the wind.

"We need to get her to a hospital," the woman said gently.

"No...no," I managed, pulling myself to a sitting position. I'd started to shiver uncontrollably, but I welcomed that new, harsh pain, focusing on it while the whispers and knowledge of a thousand years swept away from me. "Just a church. And a...a Catholic one, this time."

CHAPTER

THIRTY-ONE

The Catholic church in Hooperton was prettier than I expected, but then, Catholic churches usually were. This one had been built in the 1800s, according to its stone sign. It soared over a well-manicured space with trees and flowerbeds and lots of shade and benches, next to a former high school that was now, apparently, a grade school for local Catholic children.

We sat in the back of the church, near the confessional boxes and an alcove that boasted a statue of Jesus with dozens of small votive candles in metal stands sitting before it. About a third of the candles were lit, which I thought was kind of impressive for a Thursday morning.

Max and Mrs. Bell had gotten me cleaned up reasonably well. Joe had ended up having an impressive first aid kit in his kitchen, the reasons for which I didn't want to think about too closely. He'd lasted seven years with the shedim plaguing him. Typically, those demons hung around gravesites, drawn to the newly dead. That wasn't exactly the case here, but there were parallels. Joe and Carol Ann were supposed to have gotten married, and Joe had interred himself in this gravesite of their relationship, the lake cottage, out of grief and guilt. Two powerful pulls for dark forces.

Max approached down the long central aisle. It was quiet. I liked quiet. Churches always made me sleepy, and right now, I felt like I could lie down and sleep forever, rather than face another trial.

"You gonna make it?" he asked as he paused beside my pew. Not waiting for me to respond he glanced over to the Jesus statue. "Father Neismeth agreed to come here, to speak with us, even though I haven't darkened the door of this place for Mass since forever ago, to hear him talk."

"Is he the same priest you spoke to before? Who wouldn't help?"

"No, it's an older guy." Max sat in the pew in front of me, angling to look back. "He's apparently the younger priest's boss or whatever, or he was, but now he's retired, living in the priest-house thing. He was the first priest I found when I went looking. I explained to him what you did, and he got really nervous. Said he didn't have the expertise."

I smiled crookedly. Beneath my bandages, my wounds weren't getting any better, though I wasn't going to share that with Max. In fact, they were actively worsening, letting the emptiness leak out of me for all the world to see. Best I could tell, blood trickled out from about six puncture points on my body. It wasn't a great feeling. "That's a slightly different story than you got before."

"Yeah, well. Before this morning, I'd never seen a flock of wooden ducks come to life as vicious projectiles and start puncturing me and my friends. It changes your ability to sell your story. But he said he's not really a priest anymore."

"I don't think you stop being a priest, actually, unless you quit. Which if he's living here—"

"Well, he won't come out to the house, I guess, is the bottom line."

"Oh! Max." I turned as Mrs. Bell called out, alerting us to her presence before she hurried up the side aisle. She was almost breathless when she reached us. "That was Frank. He finally got my text." She scowled down at me. "Honey, you don't look so good."

I smiled a little. I didn't feel so good either.

"I'm just—drained."

That was an understatement. In my thoughts, in the dark back corners of my mind, I kept reaching for something that wasn't there anymore—that voice, that presence, that terrible certainty. How many times in the past hour had I started to ask my inner voice—my *demon*—a question before remembering the silence? How many times had I turned inward, expecting knowledge, and found only my own shallow understanding?

How much of what I'd thought was me remained, without Palemerious inside me anymore?

"Mmm. Well, Frank said he'd go check on Joe at the funeral home like you asked, bless him. Said he'd let us know if anything seemed...strange there. Stranger."

"Good." I hadn't done enough for Joe. I hadn't tried hard enough, when he'd still been alive. I'd been afraid.

I probably would always be afraid, no matter how many times I did this.

Blood trickled down my arm beneath my shirt. Grimacing, I pressed my palm against the worst of it—the puncture in my shoulder. When I pulled my hand away, my fingers came back red. Not good. I gripped the edge of the pew to steady myself as dizziness washed over me. The emptiness inside me made the physical weakness worse, like I was bleeding out from two different wounds at once.

"Hello, hello." A short, slender man, far younger than I would have expected for a Catholic priest, especially a retired one, called from the altar as he emerged from the Sacristy of the church. He wore a clerical collar, black shirt and pants, and he moved with brisk assurance as he trotted down the steps. He had a fringe of white hair and an open, kind face. I didn't know how this would go.

Something else the rabbi had taught me: Demons *believed* in the soldiers of God. Even if those soldiers didn't believe in them.

"Thank you, Father David, for coming in here to meet us," Max said.

"God's house is open to everyone." His eyes rested upon me. I could feel their scrutiny. "You are no longer afflicted," he murmured.

"I'm not." I looked up at him, taking him in a little more carefully than my first glance. He was older than I thought, his gray hair now more pronounced in the shadows. But he was fit and healthy, smelling of green grass and scudding clouds, and bitterness born with humility.

Bitterness?

"Why did you retire?" I blurted. "Doesn't the church need priests?"

If I offended him, he didn't show it. "Alzheimer's disease, early onset. Nasty business. I tend to forget myself and then forget what I've forgotten." He smiled at my widened eyes. "Today's a good day, though. I do what I can on good days. Who hurt you, child?"

I didn't have time for that. I already felt the itch to leave, or to pass out. Or, ideally, to leave and then pass out.

"I need to borrow blessed objects from you, but they *have* to be blessed. Crucifixes and rosaries would be nice, but water, a bible, anything will work. Whatever is sanctified."

"I see." He tilted his head, regarding me somberly. "Max here told me what you did in that house. I believe him, because

I'm called to believe him. But that doesn't make you equipped to do more."

"I don't have a choice."

He smiled gently. "There's always a choice."

"That's beautiful. But in this particular situation, *I* do not have a *choice*. A man died because of my fear." Something in my voice must have changed, because Max glanced sharply at me. The priest seemed to notice it too.

"There are people who can help, people who are trained." He shifted his glance to Max. "In Chicago. I will contact them personally." His expression had turned wintry now. "My memory is affected, but not yet my mind. They trust me. They will come and do this work."

"Good," I said, with equal frost. "That's good. In the meantime, I still need whatever you can spare. Anything that's blessed will do." I felt tears unaccountably start up in my eyes, and I pressed a hand to my stomach. "Seriously. Anything."

"But I don't see how this can help you—"

"It's not for me!" My voice was like a whipcrack. "It's for *them*. The people in that house. The ones the demons are preying on. *They* need it. They need you, more than anything, but they don't have you, so they're stuck with me. But at least you could help give them some weapons to carry into the battle against evil that they're fighting every goddamned *day*."

That little speech took more out of me than I planned, and I drew in a raspy breath to give me enough ballast to launch into a new tirade. That was the only reason the next words I heard were so clear and sharp, they seemed like they were banging my head like a bell.

"Helloooo! Anyone home?" Everyone turned as a sensible, square-tipped set of pumps clicked up the main aisleway. "It's really so—"

Claire's voice cut off sharply, then revved up again. "Oh my

God, Delia, what happened to you? You're bleeding through your shirt!"

I stared as she rushed toward me, my head starting to spin. She was still wearing her clothes from the pharmacy—thin sweater, stylish slacks. No white smock at least, but the aura of it floated around her, a nimbus of assurance probably provided by the drug companies as a freebie with every large order of pills.

"And who are you, dear?" Mrs. Bell asked while I made fish movements with my lips. Claire's smile brightened to include the whole group as she shook the priest's hand.

"Claire Bickwell, Delia's best friend," she lied crisply. "You have a lovely church. The courtyard in particular. Do you also have a hospital? With actual doctors who have tetanus shots?"

The priest gaped at her. Claire could do that to the best of people.

"I'm fine, Claire. I cut myself on some chunks of wood, that's all." I hauled myself a little straighter in the pew. "Why are you here?"

"You don't look fine. You look terrible." She held up her phone. "I got a bad feeling, and I wanted to check on you, so I tried to call you. You didn't pick up, and neither did, um, anyone. I wasn't going to call a dead rabbi more than once. So I went to your place and met your housemate, Steve. He's so nice! He preferred to wait in the car—churches make him nervous, apparently. He brought me."

"Steve?" Max asked, but I could only peer at Claire.

"You—what? Steve came back?" I tried to focus on her as the priest murmured something and stepped away. He opened the door of a confessional chamber and went inside it. I envied him. I think I'd lock myself in a box on a regular basis if Claire stuck around. "This really isn't a good time."

"Of course it is. Hello, Claire, is it? I'm Max, Max Graham."

Max held out a hand and Claire took it, straight-up batting her eyelashes at him. Oh geez. "And this is Mrs. Bell. We live a bit outside of town."

"I've heard," she said meaningfully, then looked around with bouncy expectation. "And you all decided to bring Delia to bleed here instead of a hospital—why?"

"God's house is always open."

We all jumped and refocused on Father David. He had returned from his hidey hole and now held a large, padded envelope out to me.

"Gifts for the family," he said, and I glanced from him to the confessional box. Was there, like, a secret doorway back there into a Catholic cabinet of curiosities? "And I will place the call to the archbishop when I return to the office. You were right in coming here."

When he gave me the envelope, his hand touched mine. My gut spasmed, and the clot in my shoulder popped again, blood breaking through its thin healing membrane. I winced, gritting my teeth, but I didn't feel bad, really. More...electrified by the holy man's touch. What was that about?

"Thanks," I managed, but when I looked up, the priest's eyes were strangely clear. He gazed at me with a fierceness I wouldn't have expected in someone so old and sick.

"God protect you, Delia," he said. "You were right to come here, and you remind me—you remind me of who I am. Who I am, still, no matter how I may forget sometimes."

I drew my hand away sharply, clutching the package. My wounds felt—itchier, somehow. As if the skin had already begun to draw together. "Thanks," I said again.

I sensed his gaze on me the whole way out the church. Early onset Alzheimer's, he'd said. So, could be I'd helped him too. Me, or God. I didn't so much care who got the accolades, if the result brought hope.

Everyone deserved hope.

Back out in the courtyard, Claire smiled brightly. "Mind if Steve and I join you guys, Max?" she asked with the air of someone who always got her way. She waved vaguely to the street, where I saw Steve's beat-up sedan.

Something warm and easy uncurled in my stomach, and my heart's thudding slowed. He'd come back to the duplex. He'd brought Claire here. That was good, right? He'd be okay?

"Delia?"

I glanced over to see Claire squinting at me. "Are you seriously okay? Or should we take you to whatever passes for Urgent Care here?"

"I'm *fine*," I stressed again. "The cuts were from flying wood splinters and some knives and things that came up during a house exorcism, and demonic wounds heal faster in churches. Way better than Urgent Care."

The silence of the group made me grimace, and I looked up to see drawn faces and horrified eyes. "Well, you asked," I groused as Claire stepped forward. To get it over with, I let her pull the back of my shirt up so she could gape at my back. She fussed over me for a solid sixty seconds until I batted her away.

"Well, you won't die, anyway," she decided, with determined cheer. "And this is the *cutest* little town I think I've ever seen. Where is good for lunch? You haven't eaten yet, have you?"

She swung her gaze to me, her smile a little forced, her eyes a little desperate. For the first time, I felt Claire's need to be needed—to be wanted. I couldn't understand it, but, for once, I didn't mind it. She and Steve had come all the way out here, and perhaps together they could help fill the deep cavern I'd opened up inside myself. I stuffed down my own fear, then released the breath I hadn't realized I'd been holding.

"Lunch sounds good, actually." I looked at Max.

"I know just the place. You have GPS, Claire?"

And, of course, she did. She also had clearly done something to my phone, so we could have lunch in Nashville, and she'd probably find me. Still, I offered to ride over with her and Steve to the restaurant Max chose for everyone, while Max and Mrs. Bell went together. Because ground rules would be necessary.

"What exactly did you do?" Claire turned toward me the moment we pulled away from the curb, while Steve stared at me in the rearview mirror. I wasn't imagining it though—my cuts did feel better. Like, unreasonably better, after just a few minutes with a real holy man. That still didn't mean I wanted to hash through the whole story again with Claire. "How many knives are we talking here?" she demanded.

I pressed my lips together, all my good feelings ebbing away. This was wrong, this was stupid. I could seriously put them both in danger. "Claire, this isn't a good time for you to be nosing into my life."

Steve snorted from the front of the vehicle, and Claire's eyes went wide. "Well, somebody should be, clearly. You're *hurt*. And Steve said there are terrible things out here."

"Oh?" I met Steve's gaze as he flipped me a glance via the mirror again. Steve probably would know.

I didn't say those words out loud, but I didn't need to. Steve flinched and refocused on the road ahead. But he didn't stay quiet. "I can feel things, now," he said simply, his long fingers flexing on the steering wheel. "Things I'd rather not feel. And the energy out here...this is some serious shit. Worse than the clusterfuck at the club."

"What *club*?" Claire demanded, her gaze swiveling back to me. "Since when do you go to clubs?"

"I...fuck." I muttered, swallowing back the taste of copper in the back of my throat. I still couldn't sit back in the seat without my back complaining, so I perched on the edge, ignoring the belt. Steve followed Max, who never went above ten miles an hour in town, so I wasn't in danger of being flung around. At least, not for a minute.

"Fuck is right." She scowled. "How bad is this, Delia?"

I glanced out the window, watching the houses slip by. "You're not going to believe me."

Her dry chuckle drew my attention again. "You showed up last week with the word 'Cunt' scrawled on your collarbone, remember? So, what did you exorcise this morning, exactly? Out of whom? And if you look that bad, how bad does the other guy look?"

I couldn't avoid laughing, which made the cut on my shoulder twitch. "Today, there wasn't anyone. It was just a house."

"A *house* did that to you?" Steve demanded from the front seat. "A house. You exorcised a haunted house."

"It was a very unhappy house." I liked this, I realized with surprise. I enjoyed having this special skill. This ability. Even if I didn't yet fully know what I was doing.

Except that wasn't really true either. I *was* good at what I did. Maybe not in ways I fully understood, but I had called upon whatever it was within me to help Mordechai. And whatever it was within me had responded. Had leapt at the chance. It had looked into the eyes of the possessed and it had called their tormentors by name. By name! And then stood by and made sure the darkness had left. It had done well. I had done well.

And then, on the heels of our greatest joint success, I'd booted it straight out of me.

I suddenly didn't feel so great again.

Steve pulled into the restaurant's parking lot, and we stared at the place, a cute wood-timbered café with bistro tables out front, set back from a busy street. "This, um—this place isn't infested, is it?" Claire asked as Max and Mrs. Bell pulled in behind us. "Or possessed or whatever?"

"Claire, I can't exactly tell that from out here." I winced. "That's not how it works."

"Pffft," she said, re-engaging the locks on the doors. "Give me your phone. I'm going to text Max that this option for lunch is no good. Steve, keep driving."

CHAPTER

THIRTY-TWO

We ate at the next restaurant down the street and got the call from Frank a few minutes later. Joe's body at the funeral home hadn't been disturbed by anything, except for the birds. About a hundred of them had landed in the backyard of the home all at once about the time we were clearing his house, and walked around. Then they'd flown off.

None of them were ducks. I asked.

Lunch was surreal, with Max and Claire nattering on about the town, Steve watching me with eyes that seemed a million years older now, and Mrs. Bell murmuring encouraging words at me to eat. I was starving, but also kind of sick to my stomach. I managed.

Claire also informed the group that she had decided I should go professional, and that she'd even picked out an office space for me and my emerging freelance exorcism business. I'd laughed dismissively. No one else did. Steve had watched me with solemn, certain eyes. Max's expression remained alert and focused, and Mrs. Bell just looked frightened.

Claire simply pulled a folder out of her bag and started discussing logos.

After lunch, Steve drove Claire and me to the lake cottage, and Max once again drove Mrs. Bell. We went there in part to get Mrs. Bell back to her car, and in part to make sure the place was still standing. Claire, for all her bravado, was the slowest to get out of the car once we were there, while Steve slammed his door and stared at the cottage angrily. I looked at the building, trash spilling out over the front lawn, the cardboard covering the large hole in the picture window, trying to see it from their eyes. It wasn't a good look.

Max moved briskly to the door, Mrs. Bell right behind him. I followed a little more gingerly, Claire at my side. Steve hung back for a few seconds more, then sighed and moved up next to us.

"This is where you got hurt?" Claire asked.

"Yep."

"And we're going back in?"

"It should be fine now."

And it would be, I knew. Some exorcisms took months— years even, Mordechai had told me. But mine hadn't, not so far. Not Mammon, not Pithius at the club...not my own personal plus one. *Palemerious.* The name danced over my nerve endings, slipping through my veins.

I shivered. Setting aside all that, from everything I'd read, home infestations were like dust bunnies. Once you got the house thoroughly cleaned, and the house or the land beneath it wasn't the problem, it was simply a matter of staying vigilant.

When we stepped into the cottage, it was immediately evident that it was done. The entire place emitted a sense of relief, like a sick person in the first clammy minutes after breaking a fever. You knew you weren't out of the woods yet, but you felt like you were surrounded by a new and overly friendly stand of trees.

"My God. This place is creep central." Claire's voice was hushed as we walked through the house, checking the same doors, finding the same piles of crap. Steve didn't say anything, but he stopped at a point on the floor where blood had been sprayed, his fists opening and closing. Max and I exchanged a look. He didn't know about Steve, what he'd endured, and questions burned behind his eyes. I didn't know the answers to those questions. Steve had always been…Steve to me. I didn't have friends. I didn't have family, not anymore.

But I had Steve. And Claire too, now.

And Max?

I glanced to where he was standing a little too close to Claire and felt the smile tease at the corner of my mouth. Yeah, probably Max too.

Mrs. Bell was already on the phone again, arranging for help to continue cleaning it. When Max tried to protest, she shooed him away. "I had no idea this place looked this bad inside, Max. None. Least I can do is help fix it."

Our two cars made it the long way around the lake and back to the Graham house by about four o'clock. The sky was bright and bold, which boded well for the cleanup at the lake house, but the big house didn't seem to get the memo about the summer day. It squatted like an angry toddler in the middle of the clearing, the wind barely skiffing the tops of the trees and not at all touching the grass or bushes around the house. The whole place looked desolate, though all the cars were lined up neatly, almost precisely along the drive.

"Well, this is nice, at least." Claire didn't seem to pick up any angry demon vibes, which I suppose was a good thing. "Nicer than it looked on Google maps at least. And it's a horse farm, isn't it?"

"Usually," I said. "Not right now, though."

"Oh." She didn't bother hiding her disappointment, but she still peered excitedly up at the house as Steve parked the car. We got out and stood close together while Max parked his vehicle off to the side. "This place has to be over a hundred years old, though, right? Is it amazing inside? Oh, hold on."

She returned to the car and snagged a brightly colored overnight bag from the front seat.

I blinked. "You were pretty sure you were going to spend the night."

She smiled sunnily. "I was! It always pays to be prepared."

Steve, of course, had brought nothing, but I knew from long experience that Steve needed very little. I watched my housemate from the corner of my eye as Max played the host once again, the second time in a week, giving the history of the house, the Grahams who lived in it, even mentioning the Bells as the caretakers of the horses. If he noticed my attention, he gave no indication.

I had so many questions, though. Concerns. Was his blood back to normal? Was he still dizzy? Did he know that he'd been drained out by possessed people living in the heart of our city, as if that was a totally normal thing and not absolutely batshit crazy? Unfortunately, those questions would have to wait. We walked into the house, and Claire got her first blast of the evil that lurked there.

Sam stood at the top of the steps staring down at us. His pupils were completely dilated, black coins in a too-pale face. He wasn't blinking. I'd never seen a child so utterly still.

"Hey, Sam," Max said. "These are a few more friends of mine from the city."

"She should go. Go! They both should." His voice was high and thin, a little boy's voice, but it was inflected with an ugliness that brought us all up short.

Max gave us a nervous smile. "That's not very polite, Sam."

"You shouldn't have brought them here. You shouldn't have brought anyone here. It's a bad place!"

"Sam, honey?" an even fainter voice sounded, high above. Grandma Creepy and her sixth sense of Sam. The little boy turned and trudged away from the stairs, and Claire looked at me with big eyes. "Oh my God," she breathed. "Is he *possessed*?"

I didn't have the heart to tell her all of it. Not yet.

"Let me show you around," Max offered. The tour lasted a little longer than mine had, mainly because Claire was obsessed with the bric-a-brac in every room. At one point, Mrs. Graham drifted in and, noticing Claire's enthusiasm for the crap the family had collected over the past century, took over the tour. Max moved back to me, and I was shocked to feel his fingers entwine in mine as he tugged me back a few steps from his mom, Steve, and Claire.

"You okay?" he asked.

"I guess." I was still bleeding, but...less. "I'm not sure what to do next, though. I feel like it's going to happen tonight, but why? Why not in the middle of the day, like we did things at the cottage?"

He made a face. "Do you think everyone needs to be here? Right now, we've got Sam and Mom, but Emily and Dad aren't in the house. Grandma is, but she always is, so that's not saying much."

"How do you know they're not in the house?"

"Well, we would have been introduced to Emily by now. She wouldn't be able to resist saying hello to the newest pretty girl to come to the house."

Something in his words hit me the wrong way, and I frowned. "What do you mean?"

He looked down at me, startled at the edge in my voice.

"Nothing, just that Emily's never been much one for competition. You managed to escape it—"

"No. Before that. 'The newest pretty girl to come to the house.'" The phrase resonated with me, cold and sharp. "Mr. Bell said Carol Ann got possessed right after Emily arrived—she didn't want a new pretty girl stealing attention." I bit my lip, looking ahead to Claire. "Now we've got another one. What if that's a trigger?"

Max frowned. "You don't think Claire's in any danger, do you? I mean, no one's been hurt-hurt here."

"Except the horses."

He winced. "The horses. That was bad."

"And Joe."

"Well, Joe was pretty fucking unhinged to begin with. Claire seems pretty solid."

"Yeah." We'd moved to the back porch, and Claire's bright voice carried back to us.

"Oh! You *do* have horses!"

Max and I exchanged a look, then hurried out. Mr. Graham stood at the paddock railing, along with Mr. Bell. Sure enough, there was a horse in the paddock. Only one, a sway-back mare that looked a hundred years old.

Mrs. Graham smiled. "Frank just hated there not being horses here. John brought one of the neighbor's horses by. She's on her last legs, poor thing, and the other horses are bothering her."

"Won't she be lonely?" This question was from Claire, and Mrs. Graham turned an approving smile on her.

"They brought some pals along for her as well. A couple of sheepdogs who're friendly with John."

"The horse is going to stay here? Overnight?" Max's concern was evident. Claire crooked him a worried glance, but his mother stiffened.

"She's going to stay here. She'll be fine. John said he's going to bunk down here for a few nights to make sure she settles in okay and see how things go."

"Oh—of course he is." Max squeezed my hand, but there was nothing more I could do than squeeze it back. Part of me was glad that Mr. Bell was on the premises. Part of me rejected that as being anywhere close to a good idea. There were too many people in the house, suddenly. It felt as stuffed as Joe's lake cottage, with nowhere for anyone to go.

"Well, c'mon, Delia!" Claire's teasing voice floated back to me. She was already halfway across the broad lawn. "Geez, you'd think you never saw a horse before!"

I took a step toward her, disengaging Max's hand—and Steve was right there. "I actually haven't seen a horse in person before," he said, his voice a little rough as he stared after Claire. "Isn't that crazy?"

I couldn't link my hand in his—that would be too weird. This was Steve. But I patted him awkwardly on the shoulder. "Let's go be crazy together, then."

The smile he sent me made my stomach burn in sudden, freezing panic. I welcomed that pain though, savored it. It made me feel human.

I needed to remember what that was like, hold on tight to it.

I needed to remember who I still was without him.

The thought sent a spike of something through me—not quite fear, not quite grief. Palemerious wasn't dead. Exorcists didn't kill. So he was just...gone. Ripped out. I'd thrown him out into the bright and endless day, and now I was alone in my own head for the first time in—

How long? When had he first slid into me, defiling me with his manipulation? How many years had he been my closest companion?

I shook the thought away. It didn't matter. He was gone. I'd won.

So why did it feel like losing?

AUNT EMILY DIDN'T COME BACK that night.

At one point, Max called to make sure Mrs. Bell had left the lake cottage safely behind, but she was staying with her sister. She didn't like being alone when John wasn't in the house. There was no message from Emily, no indication of when she'd be back. Mrs. Graham rolled her eyes, her face a little too tight, her smile a little too desperate. Mr. Graham was in a good mood with her sister gone, however, and she wanted—desperately—to keep him that way. I didn't blame her. I'd seen the way her husband had looked at her, the gun between them on the bed. I'd want to keep him happy, too.

In the end, Max just shrugged. "She knows the way here. She'll come back when she's ready."

Steve took a couch in the living room while Claire and I shared the guest bedroom with self-conscious awkwardness. Though Steve hadn't seemed to care, neither of us had any intention of sleeping in one of the more open rooms, or even on the porch. A room with a door was the only viable option.

"So, it's Sam, right? Sam's the problem child here?" she asked.

I looked over at her. I felt worse than ever about her being here, but it wasn't my fault, really. I'd wanted her to know where I was, that was all. I hadn't invited her to come out here —or Steve, for that matter.

Of course, I hadn't texted either of them to keep them at bay. So...maybe I had wanted someone here.

Either way, she needed to know the truth.

"Sam is part of it, yeah. But he's not all of it."

She went completely still, her gaze glued to my face. "The dad?" she whispered. "The dad seems wound tight. The house? Is the house bad too?"

"I don't know," I shook my head. "I'm not some kind of demon whisperer or anything. I wasn't brought in during the discernment part. I just helped with the identification once Rabbi Mordechai had figured out there was a problem."

Her eyes went wider. "But you could tell, right? You were in that lake cottage, and you said you just knew."

My lips twisted in something close to a smile. "Well, a guy shot himself after living as a shut-in for seven years in that place. I had a few clues."

"Jesus." She held her hand to her neck, her fingers grasping the gold cross she wore around her neck. That made me feel unreasonably better. Not for my sake, but for hers. "So, right? It's the dad as well?"

I sighed. "It's—probably the dad. I wouldn't trust the dad, anyway. But the mom doesn't seem to have it altogether, either. And the grandma—I don't know what to think about her."

"Grandma Kate? No way." Claire's voice was firm, absolute, and I blinked at her. "That lady held onto Sam like she was worried he'd be ripped from her arms at any minute."

"Yeah, well. Sam is clearly messed up."

"You're not going to make me believe that the grandmother is. She had a *bible*."

I sighed. "She did. I've never been up to her room, though."

"Well, duh: grandma. You don't want any part of that."

"I thought you were on her side."

"I have a grandma of my own who lives with my parents. My mom's mom. Trust me, you do *not* want to go into any old lady's room. That's totally daughter or daughter-in-law work, not granddaughter." She looked around the space. "You think we should just...go to sleep?"

"Last time something happened, it was in the middle of the night. The mom and dad—well, they got into an argument. It wasn't pretty, but it was loud. And that night, Max and I were out on the back porch."

Her eyes popped wide. "You and Max—wait, what?"

Suddenly, a loud booming sound echoed through the room, like an airplane breaking the sound barrier or a bomb going off. Claire screamed at the top of her lungs which drowned out any response I could have made, but while she curled up on the bed, yanking the covers, I threw them off, racing to the door.

"Where are you going?" she squeaked. "Don't leave me!"

"What?" I turned around and saw her sitting in the bed, her eyes huge, her face white with fear. "Well, come on then. We have to go."

"I can't—" she began, but I waved that off.

"I got stabbed by flying knives already today and I'm still moving. If I can, you can."

My shoulder screamed as I threw open the door, the half-healed wounds spitting fire. I tasted copper in the back of my throat but ignored it.

We raced into the hallway, and Steve was right there—fully dressed. He never undressed when he slept, and the sight of him brought a strange, reassuring comfort that I completely didn't deserve. Another boom had rattled the house again, and Max shot up the corridor, rounding the bottom of the stairs. "Delia!"

"What the hell was that?" I demanded.

"Blunderbuss. I think it's coming from the barn."

"Blunder—are you insane? What the hell is a—"

"Stay inside."

His dad was already halfway across the lawn when we got

to the back porch, and Max took off after him. Claire, Steve, and I were right on their heels, though. With the only potentially sane people in the house on the outside of the building, I sure as hell didn't want to be inside it.

John Bell was coming out of the barn, bounding toward us. He carried an old-fashioned gun low and at his side, but he didn't look like he was going to shoot it anymore. He looked crazed, his hair standing on end, his jacket half pulled on over his T-shirt and jeans. "Get back, boy!" he yelled, his gaze pitched skyward, and Max skidded to a stop.

"Sam—Sam, no!"

We whirled around. Mrs. Graham was leaning out a window, looking up, up—toward the grandma's room. And then farther still.

"Holy Shit," Max breathed. "Sam!"

Walking around the top of the house was the seven-year-old boy. There wasn't any sort of barrier on the roof, nothing to block someone's fall, and we all froze—arms out, legs wide, as if we could possibly catch Sam when he eventually fell clean off the roof. "How in the...how'd he even get up there?" Max gasped, his face ashy in the outdoor lights.

"Kate's room," Judith shouted. "There's a door, but it's always bolted. Always!"

Claire stood clutching her necklace, staring up at the spot where Sam stood. "It's not like he's even looking where he's going. And where's Grandma Kate?"

"The doors to the third floor are locked. I can't break them down," Mrs. Graham wailed. "Frank, *do* something."

"*Shit.*" Mr. Graham stood pole-axed, watching his youngest son teeter on the edge of the roof.

"Fire department?" John Bell offered as he pulled his phone from his jeans pocket. "Police?"

"Whoever is closest." Max broke out of his thrall first, pulling on his dad. "Ladder. We need to get the ladder."

Claire, Steve, and I gravitated toward each other as Max and his father ran for the barn. Phone to his ear, John Bell kept pace with Sam as he tottered on the top of the roof, as if he would somehow be able to catch the kid if he fell. Something kept nagging at me, though. How was Sam even up there? How in the world had he gotten past the grandmother, who was his staunchest protector?

The men were fast, bringing the ladder from the barn and setting it against the wall. It looked impossibly tall, and Mr. Graham moved to go up it only to have Max shove him aside. "Brace it!" he yelled, as Steve bolted forward to take the other side of the ladder.

I pushed Claire forward, too. "Help them."

"Where are you going?"

But I was already heading out. I had to go at this a different way. There was no way that Mrs. Graham would take her attention off her son long enough to batter down her mother's door. But I could. With the right props, anyway.

I took off for the barn.

CHAPTER

THIRTY-THREE

Once I made it back into the house, I was up the three flights of stairs so quickly I was almost shocked to find myself there. Every light was turned on, a chair overturned in the hallway, as if Mrs. Graham had tried fleetingly to beat the door down before giving up and dashing back down the stairs. I tried the handle, and, of course, it was locked. Worse, it was hot to the touch.

Fire?

That would explain a lot.

I took the ax I'd pulled from the barn and heaved it up over my head, then crashed it into the door with all my strength. I reveled in the flow of my muscles, the force I channeled up and through the ax. The world around me suddenly took on a sharper, deeper resonance, like it had in the back rooms of Descent. The crunch of the metal into the wood zipped through me with a visceral satisfaction, the growing smell of heat and something sweet, too sweet, filling my nostrils and lungs and urging me to faster and faster movement.

I was like a creature possessed—only I wasn't, not anymore. I was me, Delia. I was alone and I was enough.

For this, anyway.

The door was heavy and old, but it was still made of wood, and the Grahams had kept their tools well-sharpened. It took only a matter of minutes for a hole to appear, large enough for me to reach inside. I turned the lock easily and pushed the door inward.

Smoke billowed out. It smelled heavy and dank, though, not like a brightly burning fire, but as if—

Fireplace.

I ripped off my hoodie and held it over my face, then dropped to the floor, scrabbling forward. The lights were off in this room, making it impossible to see, but it didn't take me long to find Max's grandmother. She was on the floor by a couch, moaning Sam's name. She seemed impossibly tiny.

The smoke seemed to press down harder as I reached for her. I heard sirens, and suddenly a great pounding noise sounded behind me. "Delia!" I heard Max shouting, from some-where far away.

I hooked my hands under the old woman's armpits, straining to pull her out of the room. She was wet with some-thing that eventually stung my fingers, and I dropped her again, as gently as I could. Some sort of acid or cleaner? I couldn't place it, so I wrapped my hands in my hoodie and hauled on her some more. For a small woman, she felt like she weighed a thousand pounds.

I was halfway to the door when I felt someone behind me, then large hands slipped beneath my armpits as the hiss of white mist burst out over top of me. I was dizzy, falling, and let myself be dragged free of the noise and soot. Wanting to stand, I reached up—and collapsed.

What felt like only seconds later, I snapped back to aware-ness in the front yard, disoriented by the sudden change of environment. My fingers still burned, though—a deep, bone-ache burn that felt different from the smoke damage. Holy water, I realized dimly. Grandma Kate had been soaked in it. That was significant, but my smoke-addled brain couldn't quite figure out why.

"Sam?" I coughed.

"He's fine, he's good. They got him down. Take a deep breath." The EMT had a stethoscope on my chest, and she was looking at me worriedly. "There was a lot of smoke in there. You were lucky you didn't inhale more of it."

"Gran—" I sat up.

"She's out of there, too. She did inhale too much, but she's a tough old bird."

"Delia." Max was at my side, looking at me as if I was a ghost, Claire beside him. She was holding his hand tightly, and he was letting her. Relief swept through me at the sight, but I didn't know why. Then Steve squatted down beside me, and awareness crackled deep in my belly. Not romantic awareness, either—simply human. I needed humans, I was pretty sure. Lots of humans.

"I'm okay," I croaked, peering at Max. Something was seriously wrong with my voice. My throat felt rough and scratchy. "I'm okay—your grandma, though."

"It was the damper," Max said, his mouth moving but his voice sounding weirdly muted. He and Steve helped me get to my feet, both of their hands dropping away faster than I wanted them to. "She'd forgotten to open it and built a fire for some reason, though it's generally hotter than hell up in those rooms. The smoke built up before she could get the thing open and she must have passed out. Sam, disoriented, woke up in the middle of this and headed for the only exit he could see. Unfortunately, that one led straight up to the roof."

"Oh." That all made sense. It even seemed realistic. But Grandma Kate had an oxygen mask on her face and was being put into the ambulance, and something about that struck me as very, very bad. "She going to be okay?" I asked as the doors slammed behind her and the engine gunned.

"They think so. She's still out, but her pulse is strong."

"What about Sam?"

"He got his own ambulance. They think they can keep them both at the local hospital, no need to go to the city. It's a big day in Hooperton." Max cracked a smile, and I saw the strain on his face, the strain and relief. "Mom and Dad are on their way there now."

"So we've got the house to ourselves for the rest of the night."

"I mean..." He looked up toward the third floor. "Grandma's apartment is pretty messed up, but the windows are all open now. It'll have to be professionally cleaned, but there was no actual fire, at least." He shook his head. "They said the smoke should clear out enough in the next few hours."

I nodded, shrugging off the blanket. The night seemed strangely warm anyway, probably the adrenaline kicking in. A sheriff's officer came looking for Max to get some kind of official statement, and they wandered off together, leaving Claire and Steve standing with me. Only Claire wasn't looking at us. She was looking up to where the third floor was now brightly lit, smoke still drifting away from it.

"Who's that?" she asked, squinting.

Standing at the window of Grandma Kate's apartment was Aunt Emily.

An unexpected bolt of rage surged through me. "I've had just about enough of that bitch," I muttered. I gestured curtly to Claire. "Come on. Steve, sorry, this is girls only."

He gave a low, amused snort. "No problem."

Claire, wide-eyed, looked again to where Max and John Bell were standing talking with the sheriff's officers, but she gamely walked with me. The blunderbuss was now in the hands of one of the deputies, and John was gesturing wildly, clearly trying to explain that the ancient weapon had been fired multiple times, but nobody seemed to know by whom. It *hadn't* been him, though. Apparently, guns didn't usually spontaneously go off on their own.

They didn't even notice us heading for the house, and that was okay. There were a few last things I needed to understand about what was going on here, and only Claire could help me out with that.

We stopped in the kitchen so I could rewash my face, though the EMTs had cleaned me up pretty well. Claire looked uneasy. "Why is she up there in the grandma's rooms? That seems kind of rude, don't you think?"

"Rude is a particular skillset of Emily's. You'll get used to it." I glanced at her. "She's Emily Winslow, if you know the name."

She blinked at me. "From *The Family Five?*"

"Oh great, you know it. Let's go."

I'd half expected Emily to have fled the smoke-heavy third floor by the time we headed up, but her room was empty, the door left open. A quick peek inside was enough to convince us not to explore further.

"It looks like a lingerie bomb went off in there," Claire whispered, awed. "Does she have an extremely needy boyfriend or something?"

I thought about Joe in his paper-crowded lake cottage. "I think she likes to keep herself busy. Shopping's one of the ways she does that."

"I guess," Claire said. "This is all primo stuff, though. So either she's got a deal on shipping, or she spends a lot of time somewhere other than Hooperton."

I thought about that as we moved up the stairs to the third floor. The smoky stench hit us before we reached the first land-ing. When we got up to the Grandma's room, I could see why. The firefighters had sealed off her apartment with plastic, but Emily had ripped part of that down. After we stepped through, I tacked the plastic back up. Might as well keep the cleaning of the rest of the house to a minimum.

"Oh, look, Delia has a friend! Hello, there, friend."

Aunt Emily's voice was so loud it startled me, and her peal of laughter rang out through the room. The smoke had dissipated somewhat, leaving a veneer of grittiness in the room, but the air was surprisingly clear, almost cool, with all of the windows open. A steady breeze had kicked up at this level, and I was glad for my hoodie. I supposed it was a little more understandable for Grandma Kate to light a fire in the summer if she'd caught a chill from the breeze.

But the windows had been closed when I'd been up here before. I was sure of it.

"Emily, this is my friend Claire. Claire, this is Max's Aunt Emily."

"Well, aren't you pretty."

The edge to Emily's words caught me off guard, and I turned to look at Claire, who was giving every indication of being a rabbit caught in the spotlight. "Um, thank you," she managed.

I noticed the lit fireplace, and I scowled at Emily. "Is that safe?"

She shrugged. "The damper's open now. There was nothing wrong with the fireplace, just the witch who was living up here, keeping it all to herself." She refocused on Claire. "Do you model? I'm a model, or I was. Not so much anymore, though the acting continues."

"You're Emily *Winslow*," Claire gushed, as if she'd suddenly figured it out. "I'm such a fan, but—" she coughed on cue, and Emily straightened, clearly delighted.

"The smoke is terrible here—come on, we'll go downstairs," she announced. The two of them moved toward the door, and I let them go. I looked around the grandma's living room. I'd never been up here, but now I wondered why that was. It seemed almost, homey, and smaller than I expected. There was a little kitchenette with a mini fridge and microwave that I could see through the far door and then what looked like a couple of bedrooms off another hall. And of course, the door to the roof, which would have looked like any other door, except it was now barred with a thick plank of wood hammered into the doorframe. No one would be getting back onto the roof that way, at least not anytime soon.

My gaze drifted back over the walls and I frowned, peering a little closer. The smoke hung heavily there, like it had been stuck to the walls. I walked over and grimaced at the stench of it. Cleaning this place was going to be a bitch. But I realized that the smoke was adhering to the wall in actual patterns. Patterns that looked like letters. Almost despite myself, I reached out, but I felt the heat from the walls a few feet away. My fingers throbbed a little, and I remember the sting of my hands as I'd touched Grandma Kate. Her clothes had been soaked as well, I assumed with water, but that didn't make sense. And she'd smelled sweet. I stood back and studied the wall, and finally—finally I could read what she'd written there, in a thin, spidery scrawl. A chill skated over me, and something roiled in my stomach.

It read "Jesus."

I took several steps back, my gaze sweeping the space. Instead of the expected epithets and curse words, the walls were covered in prayers, scratched in the hand of someone who'd actually been taught penmanship. But how could that be?

"Delia?"

I turned at Claire's nervous voice and realized it was coming from the hallway. I ducked back out of Grandma Kate's bedroom. The two of them hadn't gotten far. They stood at the top of the stairs, and Aunt Emily had taken Claire's hand and was stroking it, over and over again.

"You really do have pretty hands, such pretty hands." Her actions grew harder as I approached, until I could tell her nails were scraping against Claire's fingers, digging into the back of her hand.

"Ouch!" Claire tried to pull away, but Emily was faster. She jerked Claire's hand toward the staircase, and the stairs seemed to surge up at the same time, although of course that was my own imagination.

"*Emily.*" I rushed forward, forcibly knocking the woman away from Claire. Emily looked at me, startled and something wild and rough flashed in her gaze. For a moment I thought she was going to fight back, and I squared up against her, ready to channel some of my spinning, chaotic energy into what I was meant to do. But just that quickly she stepped away, deeper into the hallway past the stairs, her eyes sprouting big, wet tears.

"Oh my God!" she cried. "Oh my God, I'm so sorry! I don't know—I don't know what happened. It's just this place—this miserable floor in this miserable place!"

Claire had yanked her hand back and was staring at Emily now, even as she started to rock a little on her feet, her fingers rhythmically rubbing the skin that Emily had stroked, as if Max's aunt had somehow managed to rub some of her crazy onto her.

"I don't know what's *happening* to me," Emily cried, lifting her hands to either side of her head. That rooted me to my place as well. My mind flashed to Mrs. Klein's sister, Iris, ripping the hair from either side of her head in clumps, leaving behind an ugly welt that oozed blood. I didn't want Claire to see that, but when I reached for her, Claire spun away from me, too, her eyes wide, too wide, and glazed.

"What is this place, Delia?" she asked, her gaze darting from Emily to the open staircase she'd nearly been thrown down. "What happened here?"

I knew what she was asking. It was what everyone wanted to know. Why them, why here, why now. *Why, why, why.* No answers spun up from the empty blank space inside me, the space where answers had come before. Had those answers always been the truth, though? Right now, I didn't care. They would have been better than the answers I came up with, the only option I could offer anyone, anymore.

"Nothing happened here, Claire, except some very unhappy people did some very unhappy things to each other. That wears on a place, on a house." On a soul, I thought grimly, thinking of Joe. "You know how you walk into your grandmother's room back home? Well, this isn't so different from that. It's just a room with a lot of memories built up."

"Memories!" Emily practically spat the word, drawing our attention back. "Don't talk to me about memories. Do you know the kinds of parties I was invited to, back when I was loved? None of you people could have gone to *any* of them."

Claire and I exchanged a startled look. "Aunt Emily?" I tried, though she sure as hell wasn't my aunt.

It seemed to work, though. She straightened tall in the corridor, her hands clasped to her heart. "I was the star. I was *beautiful.* I had my entire future in front of me and now—look at me." She flung her arms wide. "I'm stuck here, tied like a fly on a string. And it will never let me *go.*"

Her crying started up in earnest then, and it was a fearsome sound, wet and long and loud, the sound of a child hoping for someone to come along and pick her up and comfort her. Only it was just Claire and me, and we couldn't pick up anyone. Especially not a crazy anyone.

Claire finally seemed to gain some understanding of this, and her feet began to move. She shuffled a little closer to me, almost touching, as we watched Emily cry. Then we took a long, slow step toward the stairs.

Emily's crying turned to shrieks. "No! You can't leave me! You won't!"

That was enough for us. As Emily burst after us, we turned and scrambled down the stairs, half-running, half-stumbling. Emily pounded down right on our heels, and I imagined her reaching for us, straining for us, and then we were onto the second floor and running hard.

"*Max.*" I fairly screamed the word and then he was there, rushing past us, strong and confident. I stopped, and Claire came to a shaking halt beside me, gasping as we both turned—and saw Max with a crumpled Emily in his arms, Emily clinging to him like he was her savior, and Max awkwardly patting her, trying to disengage her but even more trying to give comfort as he half-turned to edge her back toward her own bedroom.

Over his shoulder, Emily lifted her head, her bleary eyes finding us almost drunkenly.

Then she smiled, triumphant.

THIRTY-FOUR

Breakfast the next morning was a quiet affair. Sam and his parents were still at the hospital. Emily hadn't stirred from her room. The Bells had brought another rescue horse to the back paddock—as sure a sign of spitting into the wind as I'd ever seen, but it seemed to be working.

Claire and Steve were down by the fence. She wore a hoodie over her T-shirt and shorts despite the warmth of the morning, while he remained in the same clothes he'd worn yesterday. They stood inside the paddock with the Bells, feeding the old mare.

"I think they're going to convince Dad to bring horses back this way, little by little. Rescue horses can be touchy. So we could split the paddock," Max said. We sat staring out at the homey scene, our untouched bowls of cereal on our laps. "Then, gradually, when those horses do okay, I think they'll push him to bring back quarter horses."

I nodded. Max had stayed in his aunt Emily's room for too long last night. Eventually, the rest of us had fallen asleep, waking up in three huddles to find a fourth huddle in the other chair. Max, sitting closer to Claire than to me. Steve, for his part, was closer to me, but it hadn't been weird. He'd just been... Steve.

I didn't know how I felt about him—or Max and Claire, for that matter. I didn't know how I felt about anyone who wasn't actively possessed right now.

"How long will Grandma Kate be in the hospital?" I asked Max.

"She's awake and pissed off, so probably not long. She is asking where her visitors are and seems affronted we're not already there, according to Dad."

I laughed. "They'll let her see people?"

"Oh yeah. I half-think Dad has bribed them to keep her there for a while so we can get her apartment cleaned out. Mrs. Bell said people are coming later this afternoon to start that process—move out the furniture, anyway, see what can be salvaged."

"Probably good for her to not come home yet."

He slanted me a look. "Can you do stuff remotely? Heal her, or whatever?"

I sighed. "I don't think Grandma Kate is a problem anymore. But I do think we need to go see her, after Claire and Steve finish out their pony fix."

His gaze wandered out toward Claire again almost eagerly, and I realized she was who he'd been watching, not the horse— and certainly not Steve. I could understand that. Claire was bright and sunny. Clean. Soft. Filled with hope and possibility.

Nothing like me.

I put my hand on my belly, feeling the emptiness behind it.

"She okay after last night?" he asked.

I nodded. "Well, as okay as you might expect. I don't think she's going to let anyone touch her hands again anytime soon.

You know, Emily seemed almost normal there, for a few minutes. Before she snapped again, anyway. It was like I was looking at someone else entirely."

"Yeah?" He shook his head. "I really don't know her all that well. She's always been a little strange."

"Well, your mom knew her, right? They're sisters, after all. And she knew her enough to be okay with her coming here. That has to mean she wasn't always a complete freakshow."

"I guess." Max shook his head. "I just don't know what happened to make it all turn so bad."

"Yeah, well." I set my bowl on the wicker coffee table, most of my food untouched. "I think I know who does. We should go visit your grandmother."

The silence inside my head was still unsettling, and it weighed on me more heavily as the morning went on. There was no snarky commentary when the horses nickered. No snide insights about the Bells or their history. Just...me. My own shallow thoughts echoing in the space Palemerious had occupied for fifteen years.

I kept reaching for him without meaning to. Turning inward to ask a question that would never be answered. It was like missing a tooth with your tongue—the absence more present than the thing itself had ever been.

By the time we got to the hospital with Claire and Steve, it was nearing eleven a.m. Grandma Kate had been moved to a private room, a luxury in the small hospital, but one naturally expected by her and supplied by Mr. Graham. Max's parents had left a half hour earlier to take Sam out for breakfast, and I breathed a sigh of relief. I wasn't up for them yet. *One Graham Cracker at a time* was my motto, for as long as I could manage it. We left Steve and Claire in the waiting room and went up to see her.

The old woman eyed us soberly when we walked in. She had a portable oxygen mask set up beside her on the bed, but she was breathing fine without it, lifting the apparatus every few minutes to suck on it like an addict getting a fix.

"What's going on with my room?" she croaked to Max, her voice still betraying the ravages of the night before. "Your mother is going to use this as an excuse to throw out half my things. You know she is."

He lifted his hands placatingly. "Half your things are probably not salvageable, Grandma. There was too much smoke damage." He paused. "Can you remember what happened?"

"I had the damned damper open," she snapped, fussily. She lifted the mask to her mouth and took a drag. "I wasn't born yesterday, and I'm not dying tomorrow. I know when a damper is open or closed."

"It's a pretty good likelihood it was closed when you hit the floor."

"Well, that's as may be." She sniffed. "I'm not going to deny falling asleep. That's what good people do at night."

She glowered at me. "You're going to do it tonight, aren't you?"

I lifted my brows, going for guileless. "Do what?"

She snorted. "I'm not an idiot. I know what Max here went looking for when he came back this spring and the horses were dead, and poor Frank was half out of his mind but trying to hold it together."

She turned to Max, training her marble-bright eyes on him. "Your mother may have thought she was slumming when she married into the Grahams, but she chose smarter than she thought. Sooner or later that family was going to fall to rack and ruin, her and her sister both. She's lucky to have Frank here to help pick up the pieces. And you, come to think of it. She had you."

Her gaze swept back to me. "But you've been taking too damned long. Father Neismeth stopped in and saw me, and he told me what you got in the church. He asked how it went, and it about broke my heart to tell him you hadn't done a damned thing yet. You haven't even said a novena for your old grandma, Max."

"Well, we had a few other things going on," Max put in, gently, like he was talking to a horse he was about to put down. "It'll be okay."

She turned back to me. "You went up there, didn't you? To my rooms. You saw what I did."

"Yeah." I shifted uneasily, self-consciously putting a hand on my stomach. "Why didn't it work?"

"Balance shifted," she shrugged. "I'm an old woman; I can only do so much."

"What are you talking about?" Max's words were tired. "Emily wasn't even in the house when this shit went down, and Claire's brand new to the place. If the balance shifted in any direction, you'd think it'd be in our favor."

"Mmph. You get the books?"

She was staring at me still, and I shook my head. "There are books?"

"Should be. Little smoke won't worry them anyhow. You should use 'em, if you can. If it doesn't hurt."

I thought about my hands, the sweet smell of her clothing even through the smoke. Holy oil, I was willing to bet now. Props.

But props served a purpose. "Do you know anything from back when everything first happened that could help? Anything at all?"

She twitched a hand on her coverlet, the spotted, gnarled fingers looking newly frail beneath the snaking tubes and harsh white tape. "It was a long time ago."

"Grandma," Max pushed.

"Give me a minute." She smoothed the coverlet out, her gaze shifting to the window but not really seeing out of it. "A long time ago, like I said. Longer'n what it even seemed, since we were out in the country. The pace of the city didn't hit us so hard, not really. It was a place to kind of store up rest so you could go out and work some more."

Max had drifted back to me during her ramble, and I was glad I was sitting down. Grandma Kate smiled softly, but there was no joy in it. "Emily, when she came down from the city that summer, she was so tired. Such a pretty thing, but you could tell in her skin, her hair, that she was running herself too thin. Those first few days, she slept round the clock, then she was like a flower opening up in front of us. She was a sweet girl."

I tried to reconcile that image of Emily with what I'd seen over the past few weeks. Laughing and bold, brazen and cunning. Hard. That was the picture I mostly had of her. Emily was a tight and bitter woman, not a girl at all. Certainly not a sweet one.

"Were you in the house when Carol Ann cursed her?"

"What?" Beside me, Max shifted so far back in his chair that he knocked against the wall, while Claire gasped from her perch by the door. "What the hell does that mean?"

But Grandma Kate merely sighed and fixed her gaze on me. "I was there. We all were there, really, which was part of the problem. Carol Ann was more gifted than she knew. More troubled too. But I couldn't see that back then."

"She didn't like Emily."

"Oh, she didn't mind the Emily that came to us at the start of the summer. The broken bird Emily, who'd just come off a bad run of auditions in L.A. and was too ashamed to go back up to the city and face her friends. She liked that Emily. She was quiet and a little sad. Pretty, but in a beaten-down way." She waved a thin-boned hand. "But that Emily didn't last."

"Why the occult, though?" I pressed. "Why did she choose that way to find an answer?"

"Why do kids do anything? She read about it, heard about it. Occult was in the movies. Joe might have even said something, I don't know."

I nodded. "And that night? What do you remember?"

"I remember that when she started playing her little game with that nasty board, there were five of us in the house. But by the time she stopped, there were easily a dozen more." Grandma Kate fixed her gaze on me. "And they never left."

WE EXPECTED to return to find a quiet house, but we were wrong. Sam and Max's parents had returned, and the Bells were there as well, along with a horse trailer large enough to contain the entire Kentucky Derby.

"More horses!" Claire practically bounced in her seat, laughing self-consciously when I glanced back at her. Max smiled beside me. A nice smile, open and hopeful. Something in my face made Claire's joy ebb off a bit. "What? I think they're good luck." She turned to Steve. "Don't you think so?"

He nodded in agreement, even gave her a smile, and I turned back forward, feeling happier than I trusted myself to feel. Was I happy that Steve was making a new friend? Or just glad that he wasn't focused on me...and shouldn't that make me sad? Or angry? Or...something? I batted away these pointless thoughts, impatient and irritated with myself. I needed to focus.

We left Steve and Claire at the barn and walked toward the house, Max watching the paddock the whole way. Now there were a half-dozen horses back there, and Mr. Graham stood against the fence, his hands gripping the top crossbar like he needed it for support. "This was your idea, wasn't it?"

Max shrugged. "I figured if they were already old and infirm, they would soothe him. Dad, I mean."

He left unspoken the end of that thought. That if his father had taken another gun out to the paddock, at least the horses were at the end of their lives, unwanted by anyone else.

I patted his hand. "You're good people, Max. I don't care what they say about you."

He snorted, but as we came around the house, we noticed the trailer had hidden another car. A car that wouldn't have screamed cop to me, necessarily, except that the license plate read 411—DUI.

I squinted at the porch. Officer Hernandez sat on one of the rocking chairs, watching us figure out she was here.

"That's a Chicago police pool car," Max observed, in an offhanded lawyer-like way. "Friend of yours?"

I grimaced. "Something like that."

She stood as we popped open the doors and trotted down the steps. "Hello, Delia. Beautiful day. And you must be Max Graham?"

"I am," he said, extending his hand for her to shake.

"Pleasure to meet you, Max. Delia and I met after Rabbi Mordechai passed. She mentioned you several times, so when I couldn't find her, I figured I'd take a drive." She gestured to the damaged house. "Looks like you've had some excitement."

"But you're not here, officially?" I asked, because Officer Hernandez didn't look at all like her usual self. Her hair was brushed down around her shoulders, and she was in a loose T-shirt and jeans, and tennis shoes, definitely not in uniform.

"Not officially, no." She shook her head, squinting down

toward Claire and Steve at the paddock. "I kind of thought they might be here."

"Any of Delia's friends are welcome here, always," Max said firmly.

Officer Hernandez's eyes darted to Max, then back to me. I had to hand it to her; she sure didn't miss much. "Friends are good," she agreed.

I peered at her. "So...you were looking for me?"

She smiled at me, shrugged. "I've been a cop for ten years. Which isn't a long time by some standards, but it's still taught me a few things. Sometimes, you just have to go where your gut tells you to go and figure out why once you get there." She nodded at Max. "The rescue horses were unexpected."

"We like to shake things up."

She nodded. "It'll be dark soon."

"Soon enough. I hope you'll join us for dinner?" A midwestern offer, easily and authentically made. Max might have a house full of demons, but he also had good manners.

"Oh, I think so." She looked at me. "I had a long conversation with Rabbi Ethan."

A chill slipped through me. "Another one?"

"Yep. He told me to tell you that you have no business doing what you're trying to do. That he's read some sort of file that Mordechai kept, and he feels terrible about everything you've been forced to see in your life."

Curiously, her words made me feel better. My stomach quieted, the emptiness filling up a little. "He said that? He's not coming after me?"

"Oh, no." Hernandez shook her head. "All he said was that his uncle was a good man, but he'd gotten a bit turned around when you came into his life. Apparently, Mordechai always thought he could help everyone, but sometimes people weren't his to help."

I frowned at her, newly confused. "And you decided to come out here after that? Why?"

She smiled, smelling of candy bars and coffee, and a sprawling family in the suburbs who couldn't understand why she'd ever left. "Because I feel the same way, but sort of in reverse. Sometimes people *are* mine to help. And today, Delia Thompson, you're my people."

CHAPTER

THIRTY-FIVE

It was a packed house at the Graham mansion that night, both inside and out. The Bells came up and joined us for dinner on the porch, which was picnic food brought in by the ladies at the local church. Joe had died, after all. Food was to be expected.

Mr. Graham stared out at the paddock a lot, commenting on the horses, and telling Claire about each breed. Steve had found a bottle of bourbon and was carefully nursing a glass. Emily was chain-smoking, which made me curiously happy, and drinking a little too much, which surprised me not at all. She sat on the opposite side of the porch from Officer Hernandez, who we introduced as a police investigator that Grandma Kate had hired to make sure no one was stealing her stuff.

It was a testament to Grandma Kate that everyone believed this.

I let them drink and eat, and I watched them, wondering when to begin. I didn't want to wait until nightfall, but I also didn't want to ruin this moment. No matter what happened, after tonight, things would be different. I would be different.

Different good or different bad, I wasn't so sure. And since I didn't have anyone to ask anymore, I stayed quiet.

The excitement built inside me as the evening wore on through homemade ice cream and bourbon slushes. We'd moved into the living room, and it was almost homey. Mr. and Mrs. Graham were sitting in wingback chairs, Max and Claire were on the couch. Steve leaned against the wall with his refilled glass. The Bells were fussing with the curtains, and Sam sat cross-legged on the floor, playing with his gaming device next to Officer Hernandez when I realized it was time.

I opened my mouth—and the doorbell rang.

"Oh! That'll be the Fairmounts," Mrs. Bell said brightly. "You remember the Fairmounts, don't you, Sam? Max thought they would enjoy coming over to see the horses."

I blinked at Max, and he gave me a reassuring smile. "Not exactly ten chanting holy men, but they're good guys. And they're big."

I smiled back at him. I didn't think big would matter so much, but if it made the family feel safer, then perhaps it might.

"We have guests?" Mrs. Graham's voice was frail-sounding, though, and she didn't move from her chair. None of them did. They were all waiting, breathing a little shallowly, their hands gripping the armrests of their chairs. Even Emily held onto her glass of wine a little too tightly, her gaze shifting from person to person.

"Keep them in another room unless—unless someone tries to leave," I murmured to Max. He hesitated, then nodded to the Bells. They left the room, but Max stayed where he was, watching me. Claire looked at me too, her eyes wide. Steve studied his glass. He knew more than anyone in this room what was coming, but he still didn't know it all.

"Go stay with the Bells," I said to Claire, and there must have been something different in my voice, something sure, because she scrambled to the door and through it, like a crab scuttling to safety. I couldn't really see her anymore, though. I couldn't see anything except the people in front of me, and not even them so much. They were almost transparent, that which was within leaking out of them.

I shifted my gaze to Officer Hernandez, and her smile was wintry.

"Not a chance, Delia," she informed me. "I'm staying right here."

A low, chittering laugh sounded somewhere in the house, but no one seemed to hear it but me. Max stood and pulled out a thin vial, then walked to the doorway. Awkwardly, as the others stared at him, he poured the holy water out onto the threshold of the room. He shuffled his feet when he did it, knocking into things, and nobody spoke.

Looking around the room, I smiled. I felt strong, empowered. I felt right.

"You all disgust me," I announced.

That drew their heads around, but in a flash, I wasn't seeing the Grahams anymore. There was no more Frank and Judith, Emily or Sam. Now that we were right up on it, their eyes flashed into something other than midwestern saucers of confusion or denial, mirrors of the world around them. They were peeled back, wide and rolling, and I could see what was within them. Who was within them. I could always see.

It was what I did best.

Distantly, I knew that Mordechai would sigh and shake his head, that Rabbi Ethan would be staring at me in horror. That Father Neismeth would recoil and all ten chanting men would flee the room. But I didn't have them on my side anymore. I didn't have anyone but friends who believed in me, and a cop with a hidden gun in her belt. So this was how it was going to have to go.

"Look at you," I whispered, feeling the excitement roll in my stomach—welcoming it. Reveling in it—ready to act. The voice I used was familiar and not familiar, right and wrong at once. But it was mine, this time. All mine, and only mine.

And it was still strong and fierce. A voice that demanded to be heard.

Suddenly, unexpectedly, names popped up in my psyche. Names and histories that I didn't put there.

"Agramon, Balban," I murmured. "You think I don't recognize you? That I didn't see you the first day? And little Abyzou, the least of you all and they gave you the choicest spirit to plunder."

I glanced back at Emily who had gone stiff and a little indignant. "That's right, Naamah. You they gave the least. The fading rose, the pointless woman who had already passed her prime if only you could see it. But I'll give you credit. You have done more with her than I would have expected."

"No," Emily murmured. I could feel the gazes of Max and Officer Hernandez on me, distantly, imagined the horror in their faces, the fear. I could sense the tension winding through Steve, the panic. But I wasn't here to do this in the way Rabbi Mordechai had taught me. I was long past that.

I sneered into Emily's face. "Don't think I'm going to gently coax you assholes into the night. You *revolt* me. I don't need to know *why* you trouble these children of Abraham. I know. Sonillion is a vengeful bitch, and you relegated her to that sad little lake house with its poor, corrupted soul. The moment I evicted her, she had all sorts of things to share with me. Mistake, dickheads. Big mistake."

I looked at Mrs. Graham. Her eyes were watery, transfixed. "You knew your sister would not be welcome here, that she would break everything, and you would have purpose again, purpose in putting it back together. But the cost—the *cost*, Judith. You didn't count on that. You let her come, in your weakness and pride. You led her into the sphere of your broken and rootless daughter. You had no control over your sister or your child."

Mrs. Graham tried to work up her voice. "We tried—"

"You didn't try shit. You hoped. You prayed. But you did nothing. And *you*." I shifted my gaze to the father, buried so deep beneath Agramon's hold that I was surprised he could see at all. "You were so easily led. Your money and your status blanketing you so well, it's a wonder you held onto any shred of your soul. Do you still hear the horses, Frank? You still hear them screaming? Agramon always did hate animals." I flicked a gaze at the mother again.

Sam started to cry. "Oh, no you don't, Abyzou. You scheming little fuck." I walked over to Sam and grabbed him up, lifting him high like he was a husk of bones. "I'm sick of you inside this boy. He is good and strong, and you don't deserve him. Begone and do not trouble him further, or I will make you *pay*."

"Howwwww?" howled the creature inside Sam in Sam's voice, with Sam's tongue, and then a faint and gurgling rasp erupted, panicked now. Knowing that mine were not idle threats. "I cannot—"

I looked inside Sam's outstretched mouth. The child was screaming now, his breath gusting back my hair, his face red with anguish, snot and tears running down it. Nobody moved, and it was curiously quiet, except for me and Abyzou. Only the two of us here in this moment, the beast down Sam's vibrating throat. "His tooth," I decided. "The loose one. Disturb any others, and you will regret it."

"Sam!" Mrs. Graham seemed to convulse in her chair, a twitch of her humanity, her maternal instinct struggling past

Balban's hold on her. I shrugged and felt the wave of evil stretch from me to her throat, caressing, holding. Tightening.

She stopped moving.

Sam's mouth stretched impossibly wide, and the screams grew louder, finally penetrating my haze. Loud, agonizing sobs of pain as the tissue around his teeth swelled to twice its normal size and burst through, bleeding as the tooth wrenched free and a cold wind went whistling out into the space. It screamed and raced around the room, unable to break free, unable—

And then it saw the chimney.

"Go." I smiled.

The parents were on their feet, and I turned to them. Frank held his wife, shaking her as her head lolled back. "Balban and Agramon, you have failed in your work here. You are no servants of Sonillion, you betrayed her. You have failed and now you will go."

"You cannot command us." The croaking voice erupted from Frank's mouth, loud enough that there was a squeak beside me, shuffling feet. Max and Officer Hernandez were now at the door, looking surprised they'd ended up there. They hadn't fled the room yet—not yet. But they would soon.

"I can do whatever the fuck I want," I retorted. "I can command whoever I want."

"You lie!" The force of the horde before me nearly overwhelmed me, and I took a step back, staggering. In a split second, I realized my mistake. With hasty words I had decoupled myself from divine power, putting myself out there without backup, without patronage. I wasn't strong enough to do this on my own—not solely on my own. I did require something to stand with me and for me to punch these demons out of the humans they so obsessively held. I was bold and I was prideful, and it was too much, too much! I was empty and alone, and I would *pay*.

But I couldn't fail. That panic overrode all other. That certainty was true and sure. Mordechai had warned me, over and over again, of the danger of letting a job go unfinished. I could not fail, or these demons would never lose their hold on the Grahams, their disease would only strengthen, Sam eventually falling beneath it, the house, the Bells, the town. Evil, once seeded, once challenged but not defeated, would ripple out like an infection, and it would never, *ever* be cured.

"*Please!*" I cried out across the vast emptiness that still filled me—knowing I deserved no help from Mordechai's spirit or his cabal of chanting men, that I'd be granted no sanction from God or priest. I was doing this all wrong, but it still had to be done! "*Please help me!*"

A cold wash blew through me then, a howling wind, and I stiffened as I stepped closer to the shrinking humans and the screaming horde, unfamiliar words in a tongue I didn't know, couldn't speak but somehow understood, surging up my throat with a tone that was low and snide and...

Achingly familiar.

"She lies?" I challenged silkily, and the screaming stopped, never mind the goggling eyes of the Grahams, their working throats, the straining of their bodies. Perhaps others could hear their howls of pain and horror, but I could not. For me, there was only silence except my own fell words. "She binds *me*, doesn't she? And I have walked this earth since darkness fell. You all have failed. You held domain here for what, seven years? A kingdom could be gained in seven years. A generation destroyed, yet you simply slept after you had bundled Sonillion away. You didn't break your humans' minds, you lazy fucks. They broke you. Begone."

They didn't ask how, like Sam's beast had. They also didn't

wait for psalms or smoke or chanting exhortations. Because, with this lie so carefully woven with an inspiration from God only knew where, I was done with props, I was done with them. I lifted my hands and cold wind flowed through the house, blasting into the Grahams, pressing them back against their chairs—their hair lifting, their eyes rolling—

The creatures left through the least damaging way possible.

But of course, there was still damage.

The mother's hand slapped against her ear, blood spurting forth. I flinched back, but there was no stopping the blackness that poured out from Mrs. Graham. Emily scrambled away, the fog of her inebriation the only thing that was keeping her in the room, I knew. Not just inebriation, though. It had been a busy afternoon. Max had done more than summon the holy family next door to ground this house, more than cover the chimney. He'd visited his grandma and her morphine drip.

Emily wouldn't be going anywhere.

Frank's demon, Agramon, had more of a hold on him than his wife's did. He thrust Judith away, as she bled and smoked, and whirled on me like a bear.

"You!" he roared.

I roared right back, and this time, it was my voice—only my voice. "You *shot* all your horses, Frank. You loved those horses, and you shot them. Their screams, their terrified screams when they saw what was in you, what you'd become. Do you still hear them now? Crying out in the night?"

"Stop it!"

"You stop it. Agramon isn't that powerful a demon. You should be ashamed of yourself."

I saw something skitter behind his eyes, and I grinned. "That's right, foul one. Come out, come out, wherever you are."

"Nooo," Frank moaned, but I could feel the demon now inside him, twisting and chittering. Wanting to escape, even though Frank's body was strong, his reach wide. It had been a good run, but it was time for it to end.

"Yes. Through the hand, I think. The nail."

"Too small," the beast whimpered, the sound like ripping claws through plaster.

"Cause as much pain as you like," I shrugged. I heard a gasp behind me and shook my head, remembering I wasn't alone here. "But if you do, you'll pay for it. I'll make sure you pay."

Frank's arm jerked as if it was going to come off, bending at an impossible angle. "Don't incapacitate him," I barked, and it straightened then, even as it swelled, expanding beneath the sleeve of his shirt, the threads going tight at the seams. Frank's lips pulled back from his teeth, his eyes going wide, terrified, but the swollen mass kept moving down his arm, toward his wrist. When it reached his hand, he spasmed, fingers flailing wide.

"Out, out, out," I urged. I could feel Emily behind me, struggling back toward awareness. I'd need more time with her, I knew. More time. "Come *on*."

I waved my hand and only then took note of it. My fingers were blistered, I realized. The lining of my palms had gone red and torn. I frowned at the skin, the edges turning black even as Frank's scream pulled my attention back to him. Why was I still harmed by holy icons? What evil worked in me still?

"No!" He wailed as his finger split in front of me, the skin tearing away from the nail as a cold wash of sickness poured out onto the carpet, once again like smoke. It spat and sizzled, and Frank shook his hand feebly, trying to get it all out, but only able to hold it out from his body, lank and broken.

"That was messily done," I sneered, and the coldness rushed through me again, but there was nowhere for it to go but up the flue, nowhere to go but past the holy water-soaked cloth that Max had carefully laid over the chimney. These possessor demons could not escape without the taint of blessed protection upon them. The ritual was an ancient one, the rites mostly magic themselves. But they would do the job. These dark spirits would be crippled for a few lifetimes, if they'd ever recover at all. Good.

Then I turned and looked at Emily, who scowled back at me.

"I know you," she hissed. "I know what you did."

"You think so?" But something within me twisted, just a hint—a shiver. Then the lightest touch on my soul withdrew like a whisper and was gone.

Emily didn't get the memo, though. "Why do you come to torment your own?" She undulated toward me, not quite contained by her own skin. "You have no quarrel with any of us. So why?"

I felt my arms go loose, like a fighter's might. I sensed the age of the thing inside of her, remembering its name. I didn't know much about Naamah, the seducer. There were so many demons of lust and avarice that it had been only a shot in the dark that had led me to that name. But she'd responded to it. So, good enough.

Officer Hernandez still stood at the door, gun drawn and pointed away from her at the floor, but Claire was back, I realized dimly. She'd come into the room to take the wailing Sam up in her arms. Steve held his glass up like a weapon, as if he could blind any demon that came his way—and maybe he could. He'd been treated poorly by those assholes in the club, but he hadn't been possessed. What if that meant something? What if there was a whole lot left for me to learn about Steve— about everyone?

Max, for his part, had moved along the sides of the room until he'd reached his parents. They were blubbering, in tears, and I felt their weary moistness all the way across the room. I flicked an irritated glance his way and opened my mouth to speak.

Everyone but Emily shut up at whatever I said, as if fire had come out of my mouth, but I couldn't really bother with that. Emily was circling closer, and she seemed too strong, despite the booze. Happy. Too happy? Doubt sliced through me, quick and cold.

But I didn't have the luxury of doubt anymore.

Emily laughed, only it was a strange laugh, a double laugh, a triple. I looked at her harder and realized the problem. Not just Naamah was here. Not just Naamah. The things swirling around inside Emily were more than one creature, more even than two. "What have you done, Emily?" I whispered.

"*She* opened me up, you know," Emily spat back. "I had no idea. The strength, the possibility."

"The damage." I was still reeling from Frank and Judith, but deep inside myself I sensed the wrongness of what was happening inside Emily. Another something skittered in her eyes, and I sharpened my gaze. *Another one?* "Ashtaroth."

"We can do this all night." Her voice now sounded like an unholy choir. "You cannot defeat me, even if you *have* bound Palemerious. Not and have her live. Which isn't exactly winning, is it? Killing this broken creature to get us out? Poorly done. Poorly done." A roll of voices added to the first—how many demons were in her? Just what had Carol Ann Graham done to her aunt who made her so jealous, all those long-ago years?

I smiled into their faces, reveling in their rage, their joy, and decided to lean into their misbegotten belief. It was the demons who believed, after all. So much more than humans. "It's not only Palemerious working here. Remember that."

It was the first time I'd said the demon's name aloud, and I shivered with another roll of forbidden power. My voice was strong, epically strong, and somewhere deep inside her own mind, lost behind a keening wall of darkness, Emily heard it too. Heard it and cried out for help from me. And I would give her that help.

Because there was power in props.

I walked over to the table between the two wingback chairs. The chairs where Mr. and Mrs. Graham had sat like sentinels, not feeling what was between them—or perhaps they had. Maybe that was the reason behind their docility. They wouldn't remember this terrifying night. They probably wouldn't remember a lot of things from these last seven years.

I opened the ornate box on the table and lifted out a crucifix. Then a rosary. Gifts from Father Neismeth. My fingers smoked a little, but they'd already been blistered black—I'd long since stopped feeling them. That was worrisome, but I wasn't about to stop. If I still had demon goo clinging to my soul somehow, causing me to react to holy icons, so be it. It might take a while to shake off fifteen years of possession.

Behind me, the things within Emily croaked a collective laugh. "You think that is going to bind me? You think I care about trinkets and beads?"

"You don't." I smiled, realizing that Rabbi Mordechai never had me hold these tools during an exorcism. Only he held them, he and the people he was helping. The people who looked at him with fear and terror and doubt and desperation. Only it wasn't the desperation of man that was emanating out of them. It was the desperation of the creatures who sought refuge in man. "But I don't care about you."

My fingers slick with my own blood now, cracked and smoking, I placed the crucifix on Emily's forehead, and she flinched back, hard, but I followed her even as she stumbled over the table and collapsed onto the couch. She screamed with abject terror, her mouth hanging open, elongating into a rictus of pain. I could feel the arrival of other people at the door. Some of them coming in? I couldn't tell. I draped the heavy rosary over Emily's shoulders, and she growled, feral, scrabbling back on the couch. I was reminded of the lesser demon that had plagued Iris. That had not required so much effort.

This did.

"Naamah and your servants, leave this woman, never to return." The words sounded gnarled and ancient, and my mouth felt like dust. Suddenly, there was a second person at my side, and another cross was pressed into Emily's arm. Her eyes were wild as she tried to jerk away, but Claire didn't budge. And it wasn't just any cross she was using. It was her own delicate cross from her necklace.

"Leave her alone!" Claire shouted. Max was beside me on the other side, his face resolute as he lifted a thermos of holy water. As Emily screamed, he poured the whole thing's contents on her head.

"No!" Emily clapped her hands to her forehead, and I got down to whisper in her ear.

I don't know what I said, then. I was in pain, terrible pain, a touch once more on my soul—one I both welcomed and reviled. And I whispered things to her that my mind didn't want to fully comprehend. I told her of what was waiting for her, when she and her fellow creatures came out of Emily. The long life ahead of her, the pain and the tears and the waiting, always the waiting.

I told her of the emptiness too. Because when I was done with them, if they didn't leave her right then, and in the manner of my choosing, they would not be able to enter another soul for a *millennium*. And what lay in wait for them before that millennium struck was anyone's guess. The world was an uncertain place. God was an uncertain master. And I had learned so much in my long life—

"No!" The creatures came then, finally, bursting up Emily's throat. She coughed them up with blood and bile, the spew flowing over her like dirt down a trough. I knew this wasn't an illusion, however, like Mrs. Klein's sister. I knew this was real, and the remains of Emily's esophagus would not be right for months after losing spirits this way. If ever. The mouth was a *terrible* choice.

Then again, Emily fell back, away from the creatures she emitted, and it was as if her face had been set free from shackles. Her body was loose, light. The body of a late-thirties actress and model, beautiful and carefree, her blonde hair spilling around her. She was out cold, and God only knew when she would wake up again, but she was free.

She was free.

They were still vowing violence and retribution when they rushed up the chimney, even though I was the only one who heard their sickening threats.

But when they reached the top of the chimney and encountered the holy water-soaked shroud I'd had Max hang over it, I wasn't the only one who heard them scream.

Laughter rolled just on the edge of my consciousness, rich, full...and achingly familiar.

THIRTY-SIX

I was at the paddock when Max found me, wrapped in a blanket as if it were the only thing keeping me tethered to the earth. My shoulder still ached where the duck carving had punched through.

My hands were worse—blistered black where the crucifix had burned deepest. I'd wrapped them before coming out here, but the bandages were already spotted with seepage.

It was morning, early. The sun rose over the far woods like a benediction, mists chasing away after the late-night thunderstorm. Officer Hernandez had told us not to call ambulances— off duty, out of jurisdiction, defending an exorcism. Not what she'd told her people.

We'd bundled the Grahams into cars and sent them to the hospital with the Bells. Then watched them all go.

The living room was trashed. Soot streaked across the hearth, demon ichor staining the carpet. It would need cleaning.

But it was finished. The horses nickered softly around me, nosing for treats. I'd already gone through my hoodie full of apples.

"Claire's still asleep," Max said, not because I'd asked but because he had to say something. "Steve's with her. He looks like he may never sleep again."

I grimaced. I could sympathize. "Any news from the hospital?"

He shrugged. "Mom and Dad under observation. Sam remembers nothing. Emily's still out." He paused. "Grandma woke up screaming right when everything went down. She hasn't stopped talking since."

"What'd she say?"

"She wants to go visit Carol Ann. Says she's ready now."

I doubted that. "Probably should hold off on that for a minute."

We walked in silence toward the house. Max slipped his hand into mine, squeezed, let go. Like he hadn't seen me at my worst last night. My worst and my best.

When we rounded the corner, Officer Hernandez's car was back in the drive. And Rabbi Ethan stood on the porch.

Max kept walking—but I stopped short.

"Hello, Delia," Rabbi Ethan said, coming out to meet me. "Let's walk for a while."

Max turned to watch us go, but didn't follow.

We walked in silence to the paddock. Ethan unhooked the gate with practiced ease, gesturing me into the grassy field. The horses kept their distance. I was still staring at the horizon, feeling like there was something there that I'd lost, when he finally spoke.

"Tell me about the first day you met my uncle."

The memory rose unbidden: Mrs. Rachtman's dogs, a child crying inside a stranger's house, my mother's rules forgotten. "I heard a *yalda*. A little girl, crying. I went inside and saw Mordechai standing over her. Her parents were there, terrified and hopeful at the same time. She hadn't been sick long, but they knew this was no ordinary illness. They'd known."

"And what did you see in the child?"

The name rose like bile. "*Kasadya*."

Ethan stopped walking. "You were ten years old, Delia. How did you know that demon's name?"

I blinked. "The same way I always know."

"Always *knew*, though, correct? Even before that day?"

"I didn't know I could do it before that day."

"Well...I think my uncle did."

The slight judgment sliced deep. I bristled. "Mordechai believed in what he was doing," I said stiffly. "The people believed in him. If he saw something in me, then good. He was my friend from that day forward."

"But why did he use you for such dark work?"

"I don't know. Maybe he thought I was strong enough, even all the way back then." We had stopped at a break in the grassy field; over a rise I'd never really noticed before. We were almost to the tree line, and here there was a shallow, rocky stream that poked out from the woods and into the paddock grasses, running for about thirty feet before it went through the fence line again. Fresh water for the horses. Had they diverted the stream or diverted the fence line to include it?

The rabbi said something again, his words poking at me, and I frowned at him. "It's done, Rabbi Ethan. I don't need Mordechai's help anymore. Or yours."

Rabbi Ethan spread his hands. The stream was at my back, and he was before me. He seemed bigger than he should be. "You are no longer plagued by Palemerious."

"I'm not, no. And I'm weaker because of it. We were one— and now we're not."

Ethan's face hardened, but it was an act, I could see. His

words were too, deliberately harsh and provocative. "So you really believe you're to blame for my uncle's death?"

"No. I mean..." I took a faltering step to the side, my stomach cramping, and I grabbed at my waist. Around my fingers, I could see the heat rising off me, the sun seeming to bake into me, causing everything around me to shimmer. "I don't know," I finally said. "I didn't mean to hurt him. I'd never have hurt him deliberately."

"And yet—*you* were hurt," Ethan said, gesturing to my hands. "The burns will heal, but not entirely. You carried an incredible weight for a long time, Delia. These marks will be permanent proof of what you survived."

"Oh." I glanced down at them. "Will they, um, fade?"

He hesitated. "Eventually. Your possession was...certainly unusual. Mordechai tried, in the end, to free you. But now you have freed yourself."

He drew in a deep, shuddering breath, lifted his hands. I bowed beneath the words he spoke, feeling them run over me and into the water, taking some of the pain away. Some of it— but not all of it. Never all of it, I suspected.

At last, he dropped his hands to my shoulders, anchoring me back to the earth. He squeezed, then stood back. "My uncle left some items for you, in his will."

I gaped at him. "He did? His shawl?"

That made Ethan smile. "If you want his shawl, we can defi-nitely make that happen. But I'm the executor of his will, and I need to review everything he's designated, make sure we can honor his wishes. You understand?"

I didn't, but I shrugged, my mind still on my image of Mordechai in his frozen-air office, wrapped in a shawl of moss green and cinnamon. "Sure—I mean, whatever's appropriate."

"It will take some time to make sure everything is in order. When I can, I'll send them to you."

He spoke some more, then, meaningless words meant to soothe and simplify a life that no longer made any sense. I didn't mind so much, though. I didn't mind much of anything, anymore. He left me after a while, and I drifted.

When the day swam back into focus, I was sitting at the edge of the small stream, a blanket around me, Max by my side. It felt—strange, to have him here. To have all of them, him and Claire on one side, Steve on the other. I felt like if I spoke, my mouth would still have smoke and steam puffing out at the sides, like I was some kind of teakettle dragon.

I didn't want to leave the water's edge, though. I'd lost something in the water, and I wouldn't leave it.

Rabbi Ethan stood talking to Officer Hernandez, who also hadn't left. I didn't really remember so much when she'd come, but I thought it was a bad thing, her still being here. I looked out over the paddock, the trees. I remembered all of it. So I hadn't really been possessed. Not in the way that most people were, where they couldn't be held accountable for their actions, not all of them. Not the worst of them. I remembered everything. Most everything, anyway.

I didn't quite know what to do with that.

I looked back at the stream. There'd been something of mine there.

Something I lost in the flow of the rabbi's words. I missed it.

"Hey." Steve finally spoke. "How, um—how do you feel?"

"Weird." There, I could speak. I had a voice. I was still a functioning human, somehow. "How much of that—what did you see?"

"What, with you and the rabbi? Or last night?" He eyed me. "You do remember last night, don't you?"

"You know, most of the time when people are asked that, it's because somebody had sex."

He barked a laugh—Claire did too. Sunny and free, her

laugh. Different. "Never let it be said you did anything the easy way," Steve said. Even Max grinned.

I reveled for a moment in the fact that I had a sense of humor. Had I always? But Steve was clearly waiting for me to say something else, so I thought hard, for his sake. "I think I remember most of it, last night I mean. I remember being in the front room. I remember thinking we had everything we needed. I remember Claire leaving and you and Officer Hernandez at the door." I stiffened, peering at her. "You came back."

She nodded quickly, her eyes oddly bright. "I came back."

Max nudged me. "What about the rest? You were kind of impressive."

"Was I?" I considered that and felt the ache inside my belly again. I had been turned inside out, and while I was back to being whoever I really was, I didn't know what that meant. Not really. And I wasn't sure I even liked that girl, the bits and pieces of Delia who was left behind. There was no Rabbi Mordechai, not anymore. There would be no more Rabbi Ethan, I was pretty sure. He'd go back to his life and his people and his family, and I would go back to my duplex, with the Soos on the other side of the wall and Steve splitting his time between the work and the booze and the surviving.

"Yeah, you were." Max pulled me out of the hole I was staring down. "You talked right to those—to whatever it was inside of Mom and Dad. You pulled them out just with your voice and hands."

"And the holy water and sanctified objects." I shook my head. "I didn't have that much to do with it."

"That's not true. I couldn't have held up those things and spoken that way, even if I had all the words."

"You did, though. You, Steve, and Claire. Officer Hernandez too. You stood for all of them."

"Only because of you. It was something you had, something you are."

"Something you should still be," Claire put in, a little forcefully. "Seriously and for real."

I chuckled. "I think Rabbi Ethan would have a problem with that."

"I don't know." Max shrugged. "He said you had been doing this too long, that you had watched Mordechai one too many times. That you'd learned how to do all of what he did and you believed, fiercely, in it."

"That's why you were successful," Claire put in.

It was everything I could do not to stare at them. "He told you that?" I asked carefully. "Is that what he told Officer Hernandez, too?"

"That's what he said." Max leaned closer to me, so did Claire. Then Steve leaned in, too, smelling of orange juice and bourbon and something else—something hopeful. None of us looking at the other person. "But what I know is this. I know that I needed you. I needed you more than I needed anyone, anything, in my whole life. I needed you to believe in what I was saying and to actually take action. I'd gone to shrinks, Delia. A dozen of them. I'd gone to priests. Mordechai was the first rabbi I'd gone to, and by the time I reached him, he was gone too."

I winced. "Well, that wasn't really his fault," I said quietly. Clearly, Rabbi Ethan hadn't told these guys everything.

Max didn't slow down, though. "Bottom line, coming out here was a risk. You knew it was a risk, that you might not be able to help, but you came out anyway. And you saved our lives."

"And can do it again," Claire said, never one to miss making her point.

"Claire..."

"I think she's right," Steve said abruptly, startling me.

"Claire told me about your skin, the day you came to see her. That was the day you came to the club for me too."

I grimaced. "Claire's got a big mouth."

She giggled. "I *also* told both of them about Brad. About what you did, warning me."

I blinked at her. "I wasn't doing that to be nice, let me assure you."

"But you still did it," Max said. "It would have been crueler for you to let her relationship go on, knowing he was cheating on her, right?"

I hadn't thought about that. "I guess." I squinted at him. "Wait, she told you about that?"

"I told him *everything*," Claire said, with emphasis. "He's an *investor*."

"He's coming back," Steve said, jolting me all over again. "The rabbi guy."

Claire's nonsense slipped away from my mind, like a breeze over the water. We stood, and I folded up the blanket, suddenly self-conscious. Officer Hernandez waved from the paddock fence, but she didn't come any closer. I felt kind of bad about that. How much did she know?

"Max, thank you for inviting me into your home," Rabbi Ethan said as he stopped in front of us. "I appreciate you trusting me. I suspect your sister will as well."

Sonillion. The name snaked through me, cold as ice, so harsh and horrible, I sighed.

Rabbi Ethan frowned at me. "That's not a good name to know, Delia," he said, as Max looked at him in confusion.

"Yeah, well. It's one you should know. She's not done yet."

He tilted his head. "Did you know my uncle had a file on you?"

I grimaced. "I saw it, but I didn't read it. I didn't get a chance to."

"I didn't think so." His smile was gentle. "Would you like me to send it to you?"

I hesitated. Rabbi Mordechai had known what I was the moment he'd laid eyes on me. He'd never tried to stop me, though. Never tried to help me, not until the end. He'd wanted me for what I could bring to him. He'd wanted to protect me from myself, maybe. He'd tried to keep me safe enough, close enough, so that I couldn't do harm to myself or anyone else. There was no telling what all, exactly, his reasons were. Because he'd guessed wrong, in the end. About his own strength, about mine. About the creature that was inside me, crouched and waiting to spring. I didn't know.

"I'm...I'm sorry. Truly." It wasn't an answer to his question, I knew. But I wanted to say it anyway, and I felt the tears surge up inside me, tears so hot and fierce I realized I'd been waiting to cry them for days. Weeks.

"I understand." Rabbi Ethan's sigh was heartfelt. "There's a reason why we call the leader of darkness the Hinderer, Delia. Do you know what that reason is?"

Another question to answer, as if I'd memorized it.

Because I had.

"He keeps people from God. He—it—whatever, hinders people in their relationship with God."

"That's exactly so. And when Rabbi Mordechai finally reached for you that last day, after he had made all his prayers and given you all the advice he felt you most needed to hear, what do you think happened to him?"

"I think I might have killed him." I squeezed my eyes shut, and the tears did fall then. Max made a choked noise beside me, but not of revulsion, not of disgust or fear. Just grief. He reached for me, held me, and my shoulders shook as the rabbi stood in judgment before me.

But the rabbi wasn't done. "My uncle didn't only have

blocked arteries, Delia. He had acute rheumatoid arthritis. There was a reason why his office was always freezing cold. There was a reason why he had started moving more slowly. He was in pain, sometimes constant pain, and still he went out and served his people, still he went out and touched their lives. Even though he had retired, he went. He went because of you, I think. He went because he wanted to show you that he could. He went because it was still the Creator's plan for him to do so."

"I know." My words were a broken sob. "I'm so sorry."

"And that last day, he didn't want to be kept anymore from meeting God. And you helped him with that, Delia. You helped him in his greatest moment of need."

"I—what?" I looked up at the rabbi, his face swimming as my eyes still filled with tears.

"Your whole life you knew that something had been wrong inside of you, something you wanted to fix, something you wanted to heal. It's why you worked as a dog walker at ten years old, when your mother was too drunk to keep tabs on you. It's why you painted your walls and stayed apart, and why you chose to fight."

"I didn't choose that."

"You're wrong," the rabbi said simply. "And in the end, the undoing of your shadow creature was that you let yourself be drawn into Mordechai's embrace. It would have been smarter, by far, to step away from the grasping arms of a rabbi who knew your strength, who knew that the heat of your darkness would be his final test."

"A test he failed."

"A test he passed." The rabbi reached out a hand and placed it on my shoulder. He didn't flinch. He should have flinched, but he didn't. "We should all die doing that which we most feel provides good. He wished to make this sacrifice to show you what you were capable of, to open your eyes to see not only what you didn't want to see, but what you needed to see. That you were strong, Delia. That you let him hold you, Delia, even as he commanded that which was inside you to go, to flee, to begone."

"It didn't go."

"It didn't, not that day. But it was nevertheless unmasked. You left that night a changed person, and only you knew it. You, and my uncle. Because you gave up his name, at least part of it. You saw the demon within you for what he truly was. *You* were the one who knew the other demons' names, Delia. Always you. And you finally named your own as well. And that was the moment that everything changed."

"But why did Mordechai have to die?" The question was too soft, too plaintive. But I couldn't help asking it.

"Because his work was done." Rabbi Ethan shrugged. "Yours isn't."

WE TURNED, then, to the house, and Max slipped one arm over my shoulder, his other hand into Claire's. Steve took my other arm, linking me, anchoring me. Connecting me still to this world of sky and earth and people. I didn't know what my work was. I didn't know what life would hold for me. I mostly didn't want to know.

"Goodbye," I whispered into the stillness of the morning.

Hello, something whispered back.

Or maybe I imagined that.

THIRTY-SEVEN

"I'm telling you, this is the place!" Claire said excitedly, her blonde hair swinging in a perfect ponytail as she twirled in a tight circle. "I've been eyeing it for weeks now, and it's absolutely perfect."

"It's not perfect. It's way too high-end." A month had passed since the Graham estate, and most of my wounds had healed. The shoulder still pulled when I lifted my arms overhead, and my hands—well. My hands were worse. Thick, shiny tissue that looked like I'd grabbed a hot skillet and held on.

Claire said they looked badass. I thought they looked like what they were: proof I'd touched something I shouldn't have been able to touch and survived it anyway. Despite what Rabbi Ethan thought, the scars looked like they may not ever fade.

I frowned as I took in the soft-toned desk, the neutral walls, the buttercream guest chairs and empty bookcase. Light filtered in through the tall window that looked out onto a dappled asphalt parking lot with crisp lines and well-tended cars. "Seriously, how much does this even cost a month?"

"Girl. You've got to meet the market where they are. If someone wants an exorcist and they don't want a priest or a rabbi, trust me, they have more than enough money to spend. They'll want to feel like you're worth it." Claire moved over to the window, clearly cataloguing the makes and models of the vehicles, like I had. "I told Max about this place, and he didn't even blink. He gave us the first six months' rent and said he wanted in as a silent partner as soon as you could draw up an agreement. And if you *didn't* want him to be a silent partner, you could consider it a pre-payment for whenever he's ready to have you see his sister."

She blushed. "He wanted to be here today, but he's visiting Carol Ann again. He's gone twice already." She smiled, a little shy. "We've been...talking some. It's new, but it's good."

I grinned at her. "That's great, Claire. Really. Keep me posted—I mean, as much as you want."

Her blush deepened. "Yeah, well, he may be contacting us officially anyway. He's pretty sure Rabbi Ethan's going to bail on him."

"Are you serious? He said that?" I made a face. "He has to know I'd help Carol Ann for free."

"Of course you would." She pointed at me. "He knew you would say that, and that's why he was comfortable with this advance. Isn't this place amazing? It's got totally the right vibe."

I shook my head as I looked around, but like with most things, Claire wasn't wrong. The office was on the second floor of a pocket neighborhood filled with 1920s-era mansions, about half of which had been converted into office space. This particular building was perched on a small hill, offering a short, steep incline for drivers that led to secluded parking in the back lot.

According to Claire, it was "absolutely perfect for anyone who didn't want people to know that they were, you know, going to see an exorcist." The rest of the building was given over to therapy practices and even a yoga studio on the first floor. The place positively vibrated with healthy feminine power.

"Well, it's definitely pretty," I agreed, staring at the woven white rug under the desk and guest chairs. With any luck, I wouldn't get any bleeders in here. I lifted my hand to hold the Hamsa hand amulet between my index finger and thumb. I was ready to wear it now—hell, I rarely took it off. "But how is anybody going to find me? It's not like I'm going to hang a shingle that says Exorcisms-R-Us."

She grinned, a little conspiratorially. "Well, I don't think you're going to have to do much, if any, advertising. You said Mordechai's clients came to him by word of mouth, right? So we do that. Steve, Max, and I *all* know people who know people, especially Steve."

I blinked at her. "He does?"

"Yes!" More bouncing. "You know he games, right? Well, gamers know lots of people in all the shadowy places. You'd be shocked at what kind of communities exist online, dedicated to paranormal stuff. And they *all* have members who live in Chicago. It's a big city!"

"I don't think that's the best—"

"And I don't think you need to worry about it," Claire said firmly. "You need to worry about setting up your computer, putting together a business plan, and getting really big, old books in here that look creepy, but not too creepy, you know what I mean?"

That made me smile a bit as I thought about Mordechai's office. I wondered if Rabbi Ethan would be sending me any of Mordechai's old books. If he was starting to waffle on helping Max with his sister, I kind of doubted it.

"I do know what you mean," I told Claire, and she burbled on, practically dancing on her toes as we came out of the back office and into the well-appointed sitting room.

"So, your office is yours to decorate however you'd like, but the building's owners requested that your receiving room conforms to a particular aesthetic—*this* aesthetic, in other words." She pointed around to the existing furniture out here, which included a comfortable-looking, cream-colored sofa, another white rug, taupe-painted walls, more hardwood floors, and serene-looking electric sconces that glowed with a soft light. "They think it keeps the entire building grounded, and it's pretty, right?"

I waved that off. "It's fine. No one who comes here is going to want to hang out on this couch for very long, so I shouldn't mess it up."

"Exactly!" She beamed. "Okay. I'll let you stay here and soak up the vibe while I go grab us some coffee and bring up the electronics."

I stared at her as she swung out of the open door and clicked down the hallway. "What electronics?" I demanded.

"You'll love them!" She called back down the hallway, but I let the words slide past the carved doorway and down to the somatic healing practitioner in office 216. I should probably look into who my new neighbors were. Someone would probably be up for therapy appointments with the new exorcist in 212.

I turned around slowly, soaking in the vibe, as Claire had directed. It was a good space, I decided, and if Max had prepaid for six months, it was, at least a place for me to hang out between shifts at the deli, if nothing else. I found I didn't much feel like sleeping in the house anymore, at least not in my own bedroom. In the weeks since I'd returned from Max's house, I'd painted the walls a soft rose, bought new comforters and sheets, and abandoned the room entirely for the first floor, taking over the couch. Steve had taken one look at my new bedding situation and hit the computer, and the next day a futon had arrived, which miraculously had fit alongside the far wall of the living room. It wasn't a long-term solution, but it worked for right now.

Right now was about as far ahead as I could think.

I was about to venture back into my office to try out the chair when a voice from the hallway startled me.

"Delia Thompson?" The words slid in and over my shoulders, practically tugging me around, and I whirled half expecting to see a mass of shadows ripping toward me, pain and darkness and rage—

Instead, I looked up and up higher still, as a tall, well-dressed man stepped through the doorway, his dark eyes sweeping the room with the same curious assessment I had given the place. For a half second, I thought it was the man from Descent, whose name I had forgotten but whose long, lean, incredibly hot body still showed up in my dreams on occasion, haunting my memories. This guy could've been his twin: dark eyes, dark hair, Eastern European cheekbones, all coiled strength beneath a suit straight out of Chicago's high-rises. He was money and he was power, and he had no business in my office, I was pretty sure.

"Um, yes?" I managed.

"Your associate, Claire Bickwell, said I could find you here. We spoke downstairs." His voice was smooth, dark, and smelled like whiskey-steeped chocolate. It also continued to tug at me, urging me to step closer.

I stepped back. Firmly. "I hope she also told you that we've just moved in today. I'm not going to be able to help anyone for a while."

"Oh, you misunderstand." He tilted his head, his smile deepening into a satisfied smirk. "I'm not here for your help, I'm here to help you."

"Well, thank you, but we're still getting started here." I

gestured to the room with its standard-issue furniture. "I'm nowhere near ready to hire."

He smiled. "Then how fortunate that I am already bound to you."

I jolted back, channeling a visceral survival instinct, but the man moved swiftly, reaching me practically without taking a stride and grabbing my wrist before I could clutch the amulet around my neck. His fingers were cool and firm, his grip precise but not bruising—a command wrapped in velvet. And I knew him—*knew him*! Even as he stared at me, his own dark brown eyes flared red for the barest a second to prove his point. Though of course, that was impossible.

"Hello again, Delia," he murmured, each syllable a dark and deliberate claim.

I stiffened in his grasp, swallowing hard. "Bullshit," I finally managed. "Palemerious is gone. I evicted you."

"You did. And that name is gone, certainly." His thumb stroked once along the inside of my wrist, a slow, deliberate drag that sent a shiver racing up my arm. "But when you released me in a house full of shedim, you gave me the power to absorb their skills. And when you summoned me, I returned. Summons are very powerful, you know. Especially from someone like you."

"I didn't summon you."

"You cried out for aid during your final strike against the Grahams. Anyone who would help, you said. Anyone who would come." His smile twisted, as sharp as his words. "The Almighty had other concerns that night. I didn't."

Heat crawled up my neck, part shame, part something darker. I *had* called out. In that moment of desperation, when the demons threatened to overwhelm me, I'd thrown my plea into the void—

"That wasn't for you."

"And yet." He lowered his head just enough for his breath to ghost over my knuckles. "Now, I am Lucian Gray..." The words were spoken like a hard-won confession, dangerous and intimate. Without breaking my gaze, he turned my captured hand palm-up and brushed his lips across it—a whisper-soft kiss, cool at first and then warm, like a brand of smoke and heat sinking into my skin.

Desire curled low in my stomach, traitorous and sharp.

I wrenched my hand free, stumbling back until my shoulders hit the doorframe. My fingers flew to the amulet at my throat, clutching it hard enough that the edges bit into my palm. The iron heated against my skin, and Lucian took one smooth step backward, his expression unreadable.

"That won't work forever," he said mildly, though his eyes tracked the movement of my hand like a predator.

"Yeah, well. It'll work until we establish some boundaries." My voice came out steadier than I felt. "Big ones. Very definite ones."

"Noted." He inclined his head, but the smirk never left his face. "Though you should know, that little charm of yours won't protect you at all from what's coming."

I narrowed my eyes. "Coming from where?"

His expression shifted, humor bleeding into something colder. "Your performance in the Descent establishment and at the Graham estate was...noticed. Your ability to name your enemies, and the violence with which you've dispatched them, have already reached the ears of the powerfully corrupt and the tongues of those who curry their favor. You've made enemies who don't forgive easily."

"Then I've been making enemies since I was ten years old."

"Not like these." He moved to the window, hands sliding into his pockets with effortless grace. "You humiliated Sonillion's servants. Crippled them. These are demons with scores to settle and an eternity to nurse their grudges. They'll come for you, Delia. And when they do, that amulet and your righteous fury won't be enough."

My stomach clenched. "Then I'll find another rabbi. Or a priest. Someone who actually knows—"

"No one knows what I know." He turned back to face me, leaning with one shoulder against the doorframe, and for the first time, something almost honest flickered across his features. "I've walked among them for centuries. I know their hierarchies, their feuds, their weaknesses. I know which ones can be bargained with and which ones will burn your world to ash just to watch you suffer." He paused. "And I know how to kill them. Truly kill them. Not merely banish them for a few decades."

I wanted to laugh. To tell this once and always demon to go to hell—literally. But the weight of his words settled in my chest like stones. "Why would you help me?"

"Because I have debts of my own to collect," he said, lifting a winged brow. "Scores that need settling. And you, Delia Thompson, are my best chance at doing that."

"So, you need me."

"As much as you need me." His smirk returned, sharp and knowing. "Convenient, isn't it? We'll form an excellent partnership."

I tightened my grip on the amulet, feeling its reassuring heat. Every instinct I had screamed that this was a mistake. That inviting a demon—even a reformed one, even one wearing a magnificent suit and a gorgeous face—into my life was signing my own death warrant.

But I'd learned something these past few weeks. Instincts could be wrong. And sometimes the most dangerous choice was also the only one that made sense.

"Fine," I bit out. "But you're not my partner, *Lucian*. You're my assistant. You do what I say, when I say it. And the second you step out of line…"

"You'll banish me again." He didn't sound particularly worried. "I understand."

"Good." I forced myself to release the amulet, though my hand trembled slightly. "So if you're going to work for me, start by explaining how the hell you went from smoke and shadow to—" I gestured at him. "—whatever this is. And please be succinct. I don't need your bullshit misdirection right now."

He tilted his head, considering. Then he moved closer to me; not quite within arm's reach, but near enough that I could see the unnatural stillness in him, the way he didn't quite breathe like a human should.

"Funny thing about the shedim," he began, his voice light, almost casual, though his gaze remained hard. "They're weak, half-formed creatures. Neither angel nor beast, but human enough to wear a man's face when it suits them. When you cast me into that nest of them at the lake house, desperate and dying, they thought I was prey." His smile turned cold. "They were wrong."

My brows shot up. "You attacked them?"

"I took what I needed. Their tricks, their masks, their shapes." He spread his hands, a mockery of innocence. "That's how I can stand here now, Delia. Not smoke, not shadow. Flesh." He tapped his chest once, the sound oddly solid. "Would you like me to prove it?"

"No!" I snapped, though a different answer coiled within me, sly and sinister. "No."

He shrugged. "As you wish. But know this: I can walk in daylight now. Eat, if I choose. Bleed, even. So I can stand with you to fight whatever comes."

"But you said the shedim are weak," I countered. "Presumably, that means you were higher on the totem pole than they were."

"I still am, for the most part." He held his hands up, examining them. "I've yet to experience any limitations."

"But why would you trade down?"

His smile turned almost fond. "Because shedim can wear human faces, Delia. And I wanted—" He stopped himself, jaw tightening. "I needed a form that could stand beside you, not inside you."

The admission hung between us, raw and dangerous.

I winced, dropping my amulet to rub my hand over my brow. "Jesus Christ."

"He won't help you, I'm afraid." Lucian's expression hardened. "But I will. That's the bargain, Delia. Your emerging skillsets and my knowledge of the dark. Together, we might actually survive what's coming."

The sound of heels clicking in the hallway made us both turn. Claire's voice carried down the corridor, bright and oblivious. "Delia? I've got the laptop and—oh!"

She appeared in the doorway, arms full of electronics, her eyes going wide as she took in Lucian. "Oh, Hi! Um, have we met? I feel like we've met, but I—"

"Claire Bickwell." Lucian's voice shifted into something warmer, something definitely more human. He offered her a smile that could have melted all the circuits in the tech she was carrying. "We did meet, but very briefly. I'm Lucian Gray. I'll be working with Delia."

"You—I'm sorry?" Claire's gaze ping-ponged between us. "Since when? Delia, you didn't say—"

"It just happened," I said flatly. "Lucian is leaving now."

"I am?" He raised an eyebrow.

"You are." It was my turn to smile at him. Coolly. Definitively. "We'll talk later. When I've had time to think."

For a moment, I thought he might argue. Then he inclined his head again, that infuriating smirk still playing at his lips. "Of course. But Delia?" He paused at the threshold, his dark eyes finding mine. "Don't take too long. The clock's already ticking."

Then he was gone, his footsteps fading far down the hallway with unnatural quiet before I fully registered him moving through the door.

Claire set down her armload of tech with a thud, staring from the doorway and back to me. "Okay. What the hell was that?"

I sighed, sinking onto the cream-colored couch.

"That," I said, "was a terrible decision."

"Mm…" she responded, scooting to the door to peek out. "Well, please tell me we'll be making more of those."

I snorted, my hand drifting to the amulet, now cool and steady in my grasp. "Oh, I'm pretty sure you can count on it."

AUTHOR'S NOTE

This is a work of fiction featuring demons, possession, and exorcism practices pulled from multiple faith traditions—then thoroughly mixed, bent, and occasionally broken to serve the story.

I've taken creative liberties with theology. Many of them. On purpose.

The narrators are unreliable. Delia is figuring things out as she goes, her demon is a liar, and even the rabbis don't tell her everything. Nothing in this book should be taken as a fully accurate representation of any genuine faith tradition, religious practice, or theological belief system.

All characters, events, and circumstances are fictional. Any resemblance to actual persons, living or dead, or real events is coincidental. Any errors are mine—whether from research gaps or deliberate creative choice, I'll let you guess which.

AUTHOR'S NOTE

If you're looking for canonically accurate demonology, please consult a theologian. If you're here for a dark demon romance, welcome aboard.

ACKNOWLEDGMENTS

Books don't exorcise themselves into existence. I had help.

To my publisher, Tanya Anne Crosby of Oliver Heber Books: Thanks for not running when I pitched "possession romance with body horror—no, really, it'll be fun." Your faith in this weird, dark story means everything.

To my editor, Sally O'Keef: You saw what this book could be and pushed me until it got there. Thank you for helping me walk a little deeper into the shadows.

To my cover designer, Kim Killion: You made a book about demons look this good? Witchcraft. (The good kind.) Thank you.

To Judi Soderberg and Sabra Harp: Thank you both for your invaluable feedback, and Judi in particular for your tireless effort to teach me how to use commas and match verb tenses correctly. If the devil's in the details, he'll have his hands full with you. I'm incredibly grateful for you both.

To my proofreader, Kesha Young: You caught things I read past a hundred times. Any typos that remain are first-level demons I accidentally summoned after you cleaned house. Sorry about that.

To my readers: Thank you for taking this journey with me, and for being the kind of people who aren't afraid of the dark. Mostly.

And to Geoffrey: You made this a better story, as you always do.

Also by Jennifer Chance

The Accidental Exorcist

Wicked As Sin

Sexy As Sin

Guilty As Sin

Fang & Fire

Court of Talons

Crown of Wings

Gatekeepers of the Gods

Courted

Captured

Claimed

Crowned

Boston Magic Academies

Touch of the Mage

Blood of the Mage

Heart of the Mage

Soul of the Mage

The Hunter's Call

The Hunter's Curse

The Hunter's Snare

The Hunter's Vow

Witchling Academy

Teaching the King

Tempting the King

Taming the King

About the Author

Jennifer Chance is an award-winning author of magical modern romance and romantic fantasy. She is also the urban fantasy and paranormal romance author Jenn Stark. For free reads, news, and a magical escape from the ordinary, connect with her at jenniferchance.com (linked).

link: https://www.jenniferchance.com

fb: https://www.facebook.com/authorJenniferChance/

A small press bound by the belief that every voice matters.

Sign up for our newsletter to learn about new releases and more.
https://oliver-heberbooks.com/subscribe/

Follow us on social media:

facebook.com/oliverheberbooks

instagram.com/oliverheberbooks

amazon.com/oliverheberbooks

youtube.com/@OliverHeberBooksPublisher

www.ingramcontent.com/pod-product-compliance
Lightning Source LLC
Chambersburg PA
CBHW021018310726
48969CB00006B/1451